SUN
IN THE AMBER SKY

CLIFF STAMMERS

CRANTHORPE
—MILLNER—
PUBLISHERS

Copyright © Cliff Stammers (2025)

The right of Cliff Stammers to be identified as author of this work has been asserted by them in accordance with section 77 and 78 of the Copyright, Designs and Patents Act 1988.

All rights reserved. No part of this publication may be reproduced, stored in a retrieval system, or transmitted in any form or by any means, electronic, mechanical, photocopying, recording, or otherwise, without the prior permission of the publishers.

Any person who commits any unauthorised act in relation to this publication may be liable to criminal prosecution and civil claims for damages.

This book is a work of fiction. Names, characters, places and incidents are either products of the author's imagination or are used fictitiously. Any resemblance to actual events or locales or persons, living or dead, is entirely coincidental.

First published by Cranthorpe Millner Publishers (2025)

Printed and bound in the UK through Xpedient Book Print

ISBN 978-1-80378-261-4 (Paperback)

www.cranthorpemillner.com

Cranthorpe Millner Publishers

PROLOGUE

At nine years of age, Fabián Gonzalez tightly gripped the strings of the kite as he tried his hardest to stop it from hitting the ground. He squealed with delight when, from high above, the red-eyed dragon plunged to meet the scalding sands of the beach at Playa Urdiales, northwest of Bilbao.

As it dipped and flew, the kite almost entwined itself in the nylon mesh of a nearby abandoned volleyball net. A net that had been fashioned from some threadbare sky-blue fishing twine, stolen almost a couple of months before from under the noses of the two fishermen who owned the oldest of the boats, which were moored close to the point of the northernmost reach of the bay.

On the day he was learning to fly his first kite, the sands had been hotter than usual, and the water seemed cooler because of that. Fabián's older brother had swum a long way out and was now holding on to the side of one of the boats, so that he could regain enough strength to swim back again. Beneath him, the water was very blue, almost purple in places, and perhaps crimson in others, like a huge liquid bruise.

Looking down, Fabián's brother could see his feet, and

beneath them he could see small silverfish darting through the shadows cast by the ripples of the water on the surface of the sea. He could see his mother pacing along the edge of the beach, a beach that was emptying out now that the sun was beginning to descend. She was looking out toward him and waving her arms. He waved back at her with the hand that wasn't holding on to the side of the boat.

He called to her that he was safe.

"*Estoy bien, Mama!*" he shrilled. "I'm okay, Mama!"

She called something back to him, but he couldn't make out her words. The breeze that was blowing out from the shore carried them over his head.

Fabián remained oblivious to all of this. He was struggling to keep the kite in the sky, and it was proving to be tricky even for his father. His arms were poised at all times to take the reins from his son in case they began to twist uncontrollably, making it difficult for him to handle. His father was careful not to take the task on completely by himself. He wanted Fabián to believe that he could perform this trick alone, and so he remained crouched behind the laughing boy, and together they roared with pleasure each time the kite undulated and wrestled with the winds high above them. Dipping and dancing like the fish that dip and dart across the ocean floor.

As the evening settled in across the beach, most holidaymakers were beginning to think about scurrying back to their hotels. It was at about this time of day, close to four-thirty, that clusters of local people woke from their siestas and took a swim in the water. They did this habitually before getting ready to set up their stalls for the night. Stalls that ran all along the beachfront. Fabián's parents were the same as every other. On evenings, his mother sold the small brass trinkets that his father made during the day.

But there was trouble coming.

It was around that time that the *diputación provincial* had begun to recognise that they could take a considerable share of the money that these tradespeople were making by levying a charge based upon the location of the stall. Naturally, those stalls in the best locations paid the highest charge. And, of course, the local municipality had deemed that *all* of the stalls were in the very best locations. They *all* had to pay the highest charge.

When the policy had been introduced a few years before it had caused uproar among the community. The head of the authority that introduced it had his house daubed with paint, and his windows smashed in the night by having smooth flint rocks slung through them. He eventually had to move his family away after his daughter began to be bullied at her school.

This was not because she was the daughter of the head of the local authority, a man who had introduced a charge that was hitting the incomes of the parents of most of the other children in the school, but because she had an acute psoriatic condition that a small group of school bullies teased her about. She wept constantly in her bedroom. The tears stinging the marks on her cheeks. Making them smart and turn red. Her despair making everything worse.

Now, the stall charge had recently been increased, and Fabián's parents were beginning to feel its painful bite harder than usual. His father had spoken of leaving the stall to his boys, but he was lately beginning to worry that if he did, it would just be a millstone around their necks when the taxes went too high.

The old ways were always under constant threat and, without interest from the younger generation, they could not survive. And so the wheel turned.

But that day on the beach, flying the kite with his son, he cared very little for anything else in his world. Certainly, he didn't care at that moment for such things as the stall charge or the trinkets he made, or his eldest boy hanging limply from the side of a boat out to sea and out of his depth.

Or even how the country was going to change now that Franco was dead. He was at that moment a contented man. A man who valued simplicity. Earnest simplicity.

His wife was calling to him and he was just looking at the kite, not hearing her. But still she was calling him. He could hardly make out her voice above the sound of his own focus and the squealing of his youngest son. Not to mention, above the sound of his own laughter. But still she called to him and still he looked only at the kite. The sound of her voice began to rise in volume, and he recognised that his focus on the kite was about to be interrupted. Still looking at it he yelled back to her, and he just about heard her tell him that their other boy was too far out, and that she was fearful for his safety.

The realisation of potential danger suddenly dawned on him, and he abruptly gave the reins of the kite to Fabián and turned to face his wife who was standing ankle deep in the surf. He looked out behind her and saw Fabián's brother swimming strongly back to the shore. Behind him Fabián wailed as the kite fell softly to earth and puttered along the surface of the sand. His wife walked back to sit down on the straw mat and began to start gathering their things together. Her husband was left standing on the damp sand proudly watching the strength with which his eldest son was swimming back to them.

It's a scene that Fabián has carried with him through most of his years. Often, he thought about the kite and wondered what had happened to it. If ever he was keen to feel sympathy or kindness towards anyone, he would think about the kite and the afternoons on the beach down at Punta de los Cuervos. He would think about his brother and his father and about his mother before she died from the pancreatic condition that claimed her too soon. Fabián never really understood what took her from him. He understood much less why.

At fifteen, he fell in love. He told his first girlfriend all about that afternoon and she loved him all the more for his tenderness and his gentle spirit, and Fabi, as he now liked to call himself, spoke often to her of birds and wildlife. He would walk with her and be able to identify different shrubs and flowers and mosses and fungi. He told her that he wanted to become a marine biologist or an agricultural chemist when he left university. He would marry her, he would say. She would blush when he said it and smile at him when he wasn't looking.

At seventeen, Fabi dropped out of school and promptly began his own descent. And from a significant height. He fell straight into the lap of a group of friends with whom he had started to get drunk far too often, until one day his interest in flora and fauna gave him an opening into a different kind of herbal market. He moved east with two of the group and settled in a bedsit in Barcelona where they would take it in turns to sleep on the floor. When it was his turn, he would lie awake all night with an ache inside. He'd be thinking about flying kites with his father on the beaches nestled around the Ensenada de Urdiales. He'd be thinking about his mother who had left him on his own.

At nineteen, he changed his name to Iker because he was getting deeper into his business and was starting to make some real money. He needed to be anonymous. He needed to change his name mostly to protect the people closest to him. He had already heard threats made about his brother's business back home selling meats and cheeses, and he wanted no trouble for his brother who was a kind and honest and genuine man. A man who worked hard in his shop, and whose purpose now was to care for their ailing father who had been left perpetually shattered by the death of his wife, and who spent most of his days sleeping off hangovers in a room darkened by thin curtains woven from sadness.

Eventually Iker met Gomez who promised him all the protection he wanted if only he would be loyal. Which is what he chose to be. Loyal. Before long Gomez was feeding everything Iker ever needed to get to understand how to fly high like the kite, and in time Gomez became the very embodiment of the dragon face that little Fabián had stared at so intently with his father on those afternoons so many years before.

Iker realised then that for all of his life he had been trying to be in the sky, flying and undulating, dipping, and twisting in the salted winds blowing in from across the Bay of Biscay. There was a freedom up there. A freedom that he envied. And soon he became jealous of Fabián, the person he longed to be again, and he became jealous of the kite that he so fondly remembered dancing across the beautiful days he had spent with his family down on the sands at Punta de los Cuervos.

Days now gone forever.

PART ONE

ONE

Water had spilled over the edge of the pool and, as it evaporated in the high sun, I could see some tiny bugs that hadn't escaped the deluge. This was how I was feeling: struggling to be free of a world that was disappearing all around me. A world without which I couldn't survive, but within which I might drown.

The bugs had tried, but were failing to get away from the puddle that was evaporating rapidly, leaving them floundering and fighting to live. Their struggle tinted red. Orange-red and crimson. Running from something. Running from mortality, fighting against the heat, and trying to be free.

I rested my head on my forearms, folded against the edge of the pool. I closed my eyes and listened to the voices that were calling and laughing all around me. Although so near, the open sky stifled their reverberance and carried them far away. It was as if they were divorced from the same place as me. As if they were voices without source. Voices on the breeze. Pointless laughter. Base laughter. In many ways, a disagreeable sound.

I sensed Edie's nearness, and I opened one eye, squinting directly into the sunlight that framed the hotel walls, like a golden starburst. I watched her then, carrying two orange and red cocktails towards where we had our towels. She had developed a new walk since we'd arrived in Portugal. A carefree way of moving that suited her. She moved with ease among all people and was never without words whenever they were needed.

I knew her well now, and I could read her moods and I could sometimes see when she bristled with impatience, and whenever she did, which wasn't often, she would close her book and refuse to open herself. And it was then that she could quickly become the same Edie that I had met back in Amsterdam the year before. Inward and sullen. Ponderous. Contemplative. Consumed by introspection.

On that day, I watched her as she swayed among the crowd, me in the pool. I breathed deeply as she pushed her lounger with her shin and moved it closer alongside mine. She raised one of the glasses in my direction and signalled that it was fresh and cold, and I knew it would taste like the day's first dip in the ocean. I swam the short few metres across the pool and climbed out to be at her side. I lay in the sun looking at Edie and I felt the heat pull the water from my skin as if it were unpeeling a layer from off me.

In the months since we had made our crazy move and stolen a small consignment of drugs from the guys in Amsterdam, Edie and I had been living a wonderful life together. Perfect almost. Perfect, that is, in the fleeting moments that we were able to forget that some significant muscle must surely be looking for us. And even though they hadn't yet found us, in my mind it would only be a matter of time. If we kept moving, we might be able to dodge them until a point when they might give up looking for us, and only then might we be able to keep up this pretence.

Always, in the back of my thoughts, there was Boaz. And, of course, there was Dieter.

Edie, if she felt this too, was good at not showing it.

Back in those halcyon days, shortly after we had arrived in Portugal, we lived solely in the here-and-now. We lived only for the moment. We were existing to keep the other content, and on that day, we had surrounded ourselves with a crowd of people, lying in the sun at a holiday resort in the south of the country. I was taking no notice of anyone, and neither was Edie.

"How's the water?" she asked me, her voice pronounced and deliberate and warm. Suspended in confidence.

My friend.

"Nice," I replied and smiled at her. "I like the smell of the chlorine."

I could taste it on my skin. The cleanliness.

The water seemed so fresh in the pool. So giving of life. It was iridescent from the light of the sun, hot and alive above us in the volcanic Portuguese sky. Laying there that day, I felt that I was close to something.

I remember the water well. The shock of the cold as I plunged my shoulders beneath it and the coolness on my face as I swam through it. The chill in my eyes that made them sting a little but not too much. My body alive. My senses awake. Vibrating.

The pool wasn't busy, but seeing Edie with the cocktails was enough to lure me out.

Then there she was. Edie. A woman for whom I'd been developing too much fondness. Too much by far. But she had captured my heart. I watched her often, and every move she made kind of hypnotised me. Every silent moment and every laugh drew me closer to her.

I remember once, in those early days, we'd had a small quarrel and she had said, "Please be kind to me," and I left the room and began to cry.

What she meant to me is hard to describe. What we were beginning to mean to one another was something vibrant, something visceral and real. I reflected on the possibility that there is nothing like a big secret to keep people close, and our secret was pretty big. We didn't talk about it a lot, but when we did, we found it hard to stop. Both of us were surprised that we'd not heard more from Amsterdam. Were we even being hunted? We asked ourselves this on more than one occasion. Sometimes we considered that we were free. That maybe they had called it off, and that maybe no one was looking for us. But the relentless doubt, the constant reality of not knowing was so hard to live with. Maddening. Debilitating.

That day in the beautiful Mediterranean sunshine made it easy for us to completely forget about Amsterdam at the bitter end of the year before. We simply didn't know if Boaz was looking for us. Maybe he hadn't parted with his money when we did what we did. Maybe the ownership of our actions belonged with Timo. Maybe Timo was the one we had cheated. I was beginning to not care so much. Not yet. I took a sip of the cold, peach flavoured cocktail. It wasn't good. It was far too sweet. It had ice in it. Too much ice and too little alcohol. I closed my eyes and faced the sun. My whole body raised itself up and I floated upwards and upwards more. The sense of well-being that came through those rays was magical. A gift from nature to us all.

We were in Albufeira then. We'd come south just for a short while, always moving. That was the plan. We had money, and we were living well. But soon we'd need to earn again. Edie was adamant that she was not going to work in any shady places again. That's her phrase, not mine. *Shady places*. Edie was determined to find something 'out in the light'.

Her contact in Portugal was a man who we are going to call Rogerio, and like a lot of people in this story, that is not his real name. Edie had fully expected him to be grateful when we delivered him his stolen consignment, and she expected him to offer us both some work in his organisation. But the very opposite happened. To her surprise, when she asked him about any work, he told her there was no way he could trust anyone that might do to him what she and I had just done to 'that fool in Amsterdam'.

Of course, he was right.

We just didn't see it. Any chance then that we might find some kind of safety net with him in Lisbon was completely out of the question.

So, not knowing what to do next, we had stuck around a few days and waited until we had our cut, which he was true to his word about. Honour among thieves, I guess.

Then we got out of there. Edie was sure that her contact, Rogerio, didn't know Boaz well enough to be making any calls to him, but she still didn't feel safe with him knowing where we were. We naturally, and probably rightly, assumed that he wouldn't want to call a man he'd just robbed. But he might want to anonymously sell the information of our whereabouts back to Amsterdam to make a little bit more money. Edie was sure that it wouldn't be difficult for Rogerio to make some calls, find out about Boaz and anonymously let him know where we were. She was certain that would be information that Boaz, or Dieter, would be willing to pay good money for. So, all in all, disappearing under the radar was perhaps the best option for Edie and I. Probably it was the only option, and in many ways, it suited us. We liked the mystery of it. We liked the feeling of ambiguity. We became ephemeral, like we could transform ourselves at any moment. We felt like faeries. Like shapeshifters.

So we went north to Oporto. We don't know why there. It didn't matter. It was far enough away, but not too far, and it was north and not south. We figured that south would have been an obvious direction, so we did the opposite, and ended up hiring a smart, tidy apartment in the centre of Oporto, a lively place with a lot of late-night bars and clubs. It kept us entertained and we easily made some casual friends. It was a young kind of place, gregarious and happy.

The streets were quiet up until about midnight and then suddenly they filled with people. I can remember being in a gallery that doubled up as a bar at about three in the morning. The guy I was with, Antonio, told me it was quiet because 'nobody is out yet', and sure enough, by seven a.m. the place was packed. This was a crazy town.

Antonio played in an electronic music band, and he was pretty popular in Portugal. He showed me a video of one of his gigs. It was in a cave and the camera was restless, moving from person to person. I felt dizzy as it swung between the stage and the crowd and then to outside where it was brilliant sunshine.

I said to Antonio, "It's broad daylight! I thought you were playing in the night," and his reply was that he was the headline act and so didn't go on until the end. He said that it was ten o'clock in the morning before his set began.

We fell in with this mad crowd. They were like the Amsterdam people we had known with similar characters and personalities, except that they were a whole lot more eccentric, a lot more extrovert, and they seemed a whole lot less concerned with themselves. But of course, with people like that, the opposite is most often always true, and their latent narcissism often eventually breaks through.

Antonio was a king of this sort of thing.

He ran a small music studio where he recorded not just his own stuff but also the music of dozens of other acts. He had recently started his own label and was also playing his own sets on an underground radio station to promote it. He was well known. A clever guy. He had it roughly worked out. He ran live sets at events as well and was, on the whole, pretty popular.

On more than one occasion, people would be introduced to us who had just arrived from Amsterdam. Surprisingly, this happened quite a lot. We didn't tell our new friends that we were from there. I told them that we had recently flown down from the UK. We'd been on holiday in the Algarve and had decided to stick around and see more of the country. That was our story. Nothing exciting and, of course, we didn't use our real names. And we especially didn't use the false ones that Boaz had christened us with.

In those days I really had begun to lose myself. Not having a consistent name made this feeling even more pronounced. Psychologically, looking back, I can see now what a large part this plays in our story.

There was one time when Antonio was playing at an event out of town in a very quiet village where an outdoor nightclub had recently been set up. I travelled alone that night, I can't remember why Edie wasn't with me. But I got a lift down with Antonio's friend, Roberto. He was Brazilian and he spoke no English at all. I spoke no Portuguese, so we just played a lot of high energy electronic music in his car as we drove the ninety minutes to the club. It was fun. We laughed a lot and language was not a problem to us. When we arrived, it was late like it was always late in Portugal. On this day it was about two o'clock in the morning, something like that. You needed a lot of stamina to get the most out of that country.

We drove down a series of very dark, completely silent lanes. Roberto turned the music off and stopped the car for a moment and we could hear the distant thump of a bass drum coming from our left. We drove on and soon saw lights glowing in the night sky just behind the trees. We made our way slowly to the gig, but as we got closer another car was travelling towards us coming in the opposite direction. The lane was very narrow, room for one car only, but Roberto was not having any of it when the guy facing us refused to back up.

Roberto refused too and a stand-off ensued. Each car was now parked facing the other and Roberto's good humour was long gone as he sat crazily hitting his horn time and again, waving his hands at the man in front of us.

Something unbelievable happened then.

The facing car drove up the side of the embankment, but it was too weak and too steep to hold it. I was convinced that this other car was going to topple onto ours. As our car pulled alongside this other one, both Roberto and this man had wound their windows down and were shouting, waving their fists aggressively, threatening one another.

And then my heart stopped.

The guy in the other car leaned across the lap of his passenger and, opening the glove compartment in one fluid movement, took out a gun. He pointed it right at me. I tasted real fear. He pointed it then at Roberto.

There was a brief moment of high tension, filled only by

silence and the vacuum it brings. That silence was suddenly very loud.

And then they both laughed and slapped their hands together in the air above us. From the conversation that followed, I understood then that they were friends and that this was a game they were playing. I didn't find it funny. I just wanted to be with Edie. It gave me an insight into just what could happen if Boaz ever caught up with us. It made me understand how I probably wouldn't see it coming, and I was sure that if it did happen, it wouldn't be as quick as a bullet either. Boaz would be certain to want to make sure that we suffered, of that I had no doubt. I thought then of Edie back in Oporto and wondered why on earth I was in a stranger's car in the middle of a forest having a gun pointed at me. I wanted to go home.

I can remember, one sun-soaked afternoon, looking at Edie and trying to imagine a countryside without colour. It was impossible. I tried to imagine a sky without stars, and then a field without life. Not possible. A sea without fish, or a river without stones and rocks and pebbles. I tried to imagine a beach without sand and a mirror without a reflection. The poles without snow, or a desert without heat. The sun without fire. None of these things were possible.

I tried then to imagine my life without Edie. Also not possible.

The depth of my feelings was becoming wider. We had grown so close since what we had begun to call 'the event'. In Oporto our lives felt as if they were without boundaries. We were free to make choices. It was a good time. Good and real. We had built a nice life there and we liked it.

But how long could it last? I thought about going back to the UK and taking Edie with me. She wasn't keen, so I didn't push it.

Edie spoke about returning to her family near Cologne. But she thought it was risky and said that she'd only do it if I were to join her. It was my turn not to be keen.

So we didn't act on any of these ideas. But out of all of this, one fact soon came to be obvious to both of us: that neither of us could consider a future without the other. We had become dependent on one another. Perhaps it was the weight of our secret – of 'the event' – that was binding us together. Comrades, if you like.

Whatever it was, I found it intoxicating. I found our mutual dependence on one another to be exhilarating, something intuitive. Primaeval almost. We were animal, and we were exultant in the presence of one another. If we were apart, I didn't like it. I thought I could easily remain solitary. I could easily be an independent person, comfortable and happy in my own company, but I was wrong. I had begun to change. Aren't we always changing? Visiting Amsterdam had shown that to me. Already I was winning in that respect. The trip had been worthwhile after all.

But what about my dream? It had always come and gone in waves. I couldn't predict any trigger and I could go weeks without it occurring. At other times I could spend nights on end being continually haunted by its relentless presence. I'm sure that there's an obvious psychological explanation why this happened. But psychology didn't interest me. I've never been one to try to find plausible explanations for such things. I'm firmly of the opinion that things just happen. External things, that is. Internal thoughts and processes attached to them could be influenced, that I believed was true. For example, eat healthily and your mind will be healthy too. And what I mean by that, is that with a well-balanced vitamin intake, a mind can be strong. It can order thoughts and priorities correctly. Get the balance wrong and the mind can become random and chaotic, and a random and chaotic mind can, and probably will, lead to confusion and lack of focus.

Vitamins, fresh air, green trees. These are all good solid blocks upon which to build a positive personality. Dark rooms, inward perspectives. These were bad things. External events could not be controlled.

Sure, I could choose not to place myself in among a group of criminals brandishing knives on a run-down project somewhere in a city suburb. But what actually happened if I was in that group is totally beyond my control.

Picture me, for example, standing in among ten, hostile, hooded men and girls. The shop outside of which we stand is not letting us in. There has been a fight in there a few moments before and now they're trying to close the shop. You would immediately expect this to be a situation you'd not want to be in. But I can't control how the others around me are going to treat me. I can influence, but I can't control. I might be seen as an interloper. Or I might be seen as an all-round solid guy. They might even like me. Or they might hate me and blame me for them not being allowed in the shop. This is all stuff I can't control. So, I don't try, and neither do I try to predict, or second guess. Not ever.

Things will happen. Pure and simple. Be aware. Keep your eyes open. Use judgement learned from past experience. But don't try to control.

One evening Edie took my hand. She held on to me like that for nearly half an hour. When I tried to free my fingers, she pulled them back again. We didn't speak in all that time. But we were still communicating. I put my arm around her, and she leaned into me on the sofa we had at our little flat above a shoe shop in Oporto town centre. It was a small, two-person sofa with a boldly flowered pattern. Red flowers on an orange cloth. Big red flowers. Poppies possibly. I don't remember now. We didn't need more than this. If friends came to us, they'd sit on the floor rolling joints and passing them among us. There was room for a CD player and two crappy little balsa wood speakers. And the sofa. And in the corner a plastic plant.

We had a small, portable colour TV but we never switched it on. Not once can I remember it being on. We played music all the time. It was our great love. I can still hear the songs she used to sing, and the songs I would sing back at her. We had favourites. A lot of old stuff.

Give me your hands, you're wonderful!

I had a guitar too. Steel strung. Recently serviced, it was in good order. I played it quite well and for a little while I took it and played it in the centre of town, with a box in front of me. I did okay like that. Made a little something, enough to get by on if we were careful about what we spent. It was a weird thing to do, to stand and sing in front of total strangers. I didn't do it for long. Pretty quickly other people that played in the square started to turn up and play alongside me. It was perceived as their pitch, I guess, and they were trying to warn me off. Who was I to be moving in on their territory unannounced? A foreigner too!

I could sense that this hostility would only grow, and then one day Antonio, the techno guy, walked past me and began laughing and throwing coins at me rather than into the small cardboard box at my feet. It upset me enough that I decided to stop doing it. Shortly after that I took a job in a petrol station. I was, at first, a forecourt attendant and then after a while I got promoted to be inside at the checkout. It didn't seem like a promotion. I preferred to be outside.

Edie took a job in the shoe shop beneath where we lived. She hated it. I can laugh now at the stories that she used to bring up to our flat. She would have me in hysterics as she recounted how 'playing' with the feet of strangers all day had left her without any desires whatsoever. Not for food, or music and certainly not for anything sexual.

We spent about two months living like this and the year, like an exotic flower in a botanical garden, slowly unfolded around us. Then one morning I realised how fast time was moving since 'the event' and I was beginning to dare to think that we had perhaps got away with it.

I was not working that day and I was in the flat with a cup of coffee. Sweetened. For once. I was playing my guitar and thinking to prepare a sandwich. It was about one o'clock when suddenly the door to the apartment slammed hard against the wall on to which it opened. I jumped up and instantly became agitated, my heart picking up pace hard and fast. My hands felt as if they had been electrocuted. I couldn't see the door, it was around a corner and in a small alcove, but I knew for certain it had been either forced open, or it had opened hard.

Edie ran into the room. She was in a state. Shaking and pale. Not at all like her.

"What's up?" I asked her loudly and urgently. "What's wrong?" I said again pushing past her and closing the door checking it was not broken. I looked at the wall against which she had opened it so forcefully, and I thought then of the damage and how much the landlord would be charging us to fix it. I could do it myself, I said internally.

"I've just seen him!" she said and began to hop between her feet, up and down on the spot. "He was outside the shop!" she said, almost crying now. Her voice rising in pitch.

It took a few moments for me grasp what she was telling me, and when it did, I felt a cold wave sweep over my skin as if I were back in that pool in the Algarve. I took no time at all to understand what she meant, but nevertheless, I needed it confirmed.

"Who?" I asked. Although I think I knew.

"Franck!" she said urgently. Almost screamed it.

I became silently afraid and felt a strong urge to throw up. Fight or flight? I told myself to be rational and I was aware that I should not let Edie get a foothold into how I felt.

She continued. I sat her down.

"I'm ninety-nine percent certain it was him," she said, "he looked into the shop. *Right* into the shop!" She paused.

"David, I think he saw me! Oh God what are we going to do? It was him. I know it was him. He won't be here on his own. Dieter might be nearby. And that animal, Joep! We have to get out. We have to get out now! Oh, God!"

She was becoming hysterical. I tried to calm her and began to roll a joint. I had to stop because my hands were shaking. If we were to run away, then the problem we'd have now was that we had no money left. It had all gone. Our options were limited. We both had jobs. Not great jobs but it meant that we could live okay in a nice little apartment with a TV that we never watched, and a music system that could fall apart at any moment if you played it too loudly. Leaving all of that meant that we'd have to find a new town, and immediately find work in that new town. There was going to be a challenge ahead for us. That much was clear. Real and clear.

Edie threw her clothes into a bag. I did the same. We weren't thinking. We were just reacting. I picked up the guitar and we snuck down the stairs. "Sorry, Mr Landlord," I remember saying under my breath as we crept down the hall. I'd left a little money and a note, but it barely covered a week's rent, let alone the two-month notice he'd want from us.

We went to a hotel on the edge of town. We stayed there that night. I remember that we didn't leave our room. I ordered two bottles of wine to be brought up and several beers. We drank the lot in among an endless stream of joints, all of which we smoked leaning out of the window.

"Are you sure it was Franck?" I kept asking Edie. She became irritated as she grew more and more tired.

"Yes, yes of course I'm sure," she snapped, but that soon began to soften as it changed to, "Yes, I'm pretty sure," and then to "I think it was him."

By the end of the evening this had become a full-blown reversal.

"Well, I'm not completely sure," she said eventually.

So I started thinking about obvious things.

And then I had an idea.

"OK. Deep breaths," I said, pulling hard on my joint to emphasise the comment. "Let's not run. Let's go back."

She looked at me incredulously. Uncomprehendingly.

"The landlord won't have been in the apartment," I continued, "It's too soon. Let's just lay low for a while and see what turns up. Let's not force events Edie. We can't force events. We can only try to influence them. We can't control what other people might do. And right now, Franck, or Joep or Dieter …

whoever, has not threatened us. You're not sure you've even seen them now."

She said nothing. But she was definitely listening, and she seemed to be considering what I had said, sitting on the bed, her whole body nodding backwards and forwards, her brown hair tucked behind her freckled ear. I carried on speaking.

"We might easily find another town. Other work. But equally, Franck, if it was him, or Joep, might find these things too and wherever we run, we will always be looking over our shoulder.

"Look at it this way: if it was Franck, he didn't see you, no? Or if he did, he didn't recognise you. If he's checked the town out and not found us, he'll continue looking but he won't continue looking in Oporto.

"In other words," I continued, "he'll have turned over our stone, but he won't have spotted us. He'll be on to new stones very soon."

I left Edie to think about the feasibility of this. I myself wasn't at all convinced that it was the correct approach, and I guess I needed her endorsement before we could move on with it.

And so I waited a few moments, and then added, "My biggest concern is how, if it was him, did he think to come to Oporto? Who the hell knows we are here?"

It didn't take too long, maybe ten minutes, until Edie agreed with me about returning to the apartment. More than anything else, it was the easiest thing for us to do and it was her who spotted that.

"But we don't have the key," she said. "You put it back through the door."

"I'll break it," I said. "That'll explain the damage to the wall. I'll say we were out all night and we'd got pissed up and we lost the key but then found it at home after all. Something like that. It'll work. It'll costs us, but it'll work."

"We'll have to fix it right away," she said. "I don't want to sleep in there with a busted door."

She was right, and I told her that I agreed and that I would fix it right away. Then she said, "And what about the shop? I left there suddenly and didn't go back."

"Easy," I said. "You were ill. Simple. Just apologise. Grovel a bit. Be sincerely sorry. They won't sack you after just one absent afternoon. We live above them for Christ's sake. They won't want to piss off their neighbours will they. They won't want you hanging out banners above their shop!" I said, and we both laughed for the first time in a few hours.

She held on to me all night that night, and in the morning we took the amber bus back into town. Once again, I had the vaguest sense of my dream as I sat watching the people outside, when the bus went through a housing estate and then a shopping mall very much like the one that we went through in Erkrath many months before, when this entire scenario began.

The rest of the day played out exactly like we arranged it. Even the element of control seemed to go as I had imagined. Edie walked right back into her job, and I apologised to a very pissed off landlord. He was on the verge of throwing us out, but I calmed him down and bought him a bottle of something. I can't remember what it was, but I think it was probably a cheap brandy. It doesn't matter. Whatever I bought him it pacified him, and we were able to remain in the apartment above the shoe shop in which Edie worked. He did put us on a warning though. One more thing like that and we would be out. He was fair.

My job at the petrol station was unaffected. I walked right

into my shift that weekend as if nothing at all had happened. Although, whenever I was out on the forecourt or when I was at the cash machine, I was eyeing everyone suspiciously.

This subsided after a week or so, but I was always looking for people who might resemble any of the characters we had known in Amsterdam, and for sure there were a few times when I thought that I had seen someone I knew. But, luckily, I was always able to stop myself from negatively responding. I could detach myself from the process of reacting in a panicky way.

This made me think then that Edie had indeed panicked. That she'd seen someone who looked like Franck. Not that it was him. And this justified our decision to go back.

Although I then began to understand that if it had not been Franck, and that Edie had just seen someone who looked like him, that meant we were most likely still in some significant danger, and that we should definitely be keeping up our guard.

But there was one more thing, one pivotal question that was starting to prey on my mind now: how did they think to look in Oporto? What had led them there? Was it Edie's contact Rogerio making educated guesses?

But if they'd looked in Oporto, and hadn't seen us then, like a virus, did this mean that we had an immunity from being seen again? Had we had Franck and Joep and Dieter and his boys in our world already? And if they hadn't seen us, did that mean that we were now free? It was a preposterous idea. Truly ridiculous. But we had to cling to something positive. Our minds were under too much strain from the constant anxiety that we were carrying around, and we were desperate then for normality. Neither of us said it, but we were both seriously regretting ever compromising Boaz in the way that we had.

We started to take a few more chances as each day passed, and this was how we had begun to exist in those days. We were worn down by the stress of what could be shadowing us, so we had begun to live in a kind of carefree way. For the sake of our own sanity, I guess.

But I was very clear about one thing: that this could be a big error. And so I voiced this to Edie later that evening, and she agreed with me. We concluded that there was still as great a risk as there was before and that we might easily be discovered if we let our guard down. We agreed that it was not a nice way to live. That we didn't like it at all. Suddenly then, the idyll of our new life had been compromised. The perfect picture had been blemished.

The frame was broken.

TWO

Portugal was, on the whole, very kind to us. We liked it there. Oporto especially. It was a disarming town, delicately chiselled from a network of cobbled streets with thin luminously coloured shopfronts set along either side. Yellow, red and orange buildings stretched down to rickety riverside walkways teeming over with cafes and tiny restaurants and tapas bars.

The buildings were tall, much like Amsterdam and much for the same reason, housing places to store grain and pulses high up away from scavenging rodents that used to stow away on the trading ships that once took their moorings all along the harbour front. Like Amsterdam, Oporto also was a city by the sea with a history of trading. Especially the well-known port wines that gave the country and indeed that city its name. Situated in the north alongside a river estuary, Oporto is a pretty and cosmopolitan place. A sophisticated city of creative people. Edie and I felt well at home there.

Everywhere appeared red, and if not red then a hue containing red, like rose or vermilion or crimson or violet, and as night broke across the waterfront where we sat, the sun glowed like a neon disc the colour of smoked fish. A salmon-flesh sun with its cherry-pink rays warming Oporto and the people around us as they stretched themselves out like cats, languidly bathing in the lengthening shadows of the day.

A cluster of wrought iron tables and chairs populated the grey-bricked courtyard. Every seat was taken. Underfoot there were these regular slabs of paving, uniform and rigid, divorced from the aesthetic. The air was warm and smelled sweetly of cardamom, jasmine, and cinnamon. A gentle clamour of cushioning voices rose and fell in gabbling ripples. People agreeing and disagreeing, discussing their worlds and their opinions of their worlds. My beers tasted good. Edie's wine, a rose, crisp and cold.

Over my shoulder a shop front was adorned with fussy linens, all flowery pillows with frilled edges. Lace framed doilies and embroidered antimacassars. A cream-orange curtain hung ornately alone in the central window, gathered at its waist, it reminded me of dancing.

Out of the corner of my eye I thought I saw a shadow. On the periphery of my vision, I thought I saw a shadow. But it soon was gone.

And my beer still tasted good, and it still tasted cold.

I contemplated my own pre-occupations. My mind filled with the adventures of last year in Amsterdam, and the surprise at how things had led me to that place shocked me into a deeper and still more unreal frame of mind. I tried to reconcile my singular mindset of that time with the conviction that it was all a part of the greater plan. The greater plan that would lead us to our own intellectual utopia.

I rested with that thought for a while as Edie drank her wine and I drank my beer, sipping at the bitterness I took to be yet another metaphor for the state I found myself in.

I ached without her. I wanted her with me always. This feeling was unnerving. It made me feel vulnerable.

A family at one of the tables stared vacantly around about the yard, not speaking but communicating in that special way of associative thought. Words are not always necessary to communicate effectively. The young boys' eyes met mine and darted away quickly to become fixed on the window behind me, the one over my shoulder. He looked at his father and then again at me, only to dart again towards his mother and then to me and then toward the window that sat behind my shoulder. My left shoulder.

On the table in front of them sat two, white polythene carrier bags that they were going to throw into our disposable society, and I reflected then on just how much rubbish each one of us generates during our lives, and I thought about how much good we created and decided that we each made more rubbish than good.

And then I wondered about the height of the pile of non-perishable litter that I had been responsible for up until then, and then I wondered about the height the pile would be by the time I'd finished building it, and if it would be partly responsible for my death in the end anyway? And would this have any bearing on my status in the afterlife? Does God give you credits for tidying up your flat and recycling your paper?

I decided it was a question of conscience. Like so many things it always came back to being a question of conscience. Drinking too much alcohol and being able to cope with the depression of waking up with a headache and eyes that have trouble focussing all day long was a question of conscience. Being rude and abusive to shop workers and being able to live with yourself after doing so was a question of conscience, even though it's very clear which side of that question of conscience that any decent person should favour. Trying to decide whether I should give up smoking again that year was a question of conscience. Running drugs across the border: drugs that young adults were undoubtedly going to be fed, was a question of conscience. But here, of course, it's unequivocally clear on which side of this question any responsible person should fall. So, although conscience is a guide, it should never be the definitive and deciding factor.

I felt that there was no rule to live a life by. No one certainly could tell me what to do. It wasn't anyone's business to do so. It was all down to what I considered to be ethical and morally sound. And after that, it was what society considered to be ethical and morally sound.

I didn't feel that I needed to be dictated to, but at the same time I did see the need for such shepherding for those that didn't have the capacity to search for any truths, nor indeed harbour the inclination to search for them.

Conscience was my new word, and I decided it needed a capital "C." Conscience, together with attitude could lead the way to Contentment, deserving also of a capital "C."

Peace is a combination of awareness and wellbeing, and of not trying too hard. That was what I concluded in those days. I think it still works fairly well now.

And more.

If my Conscience was strong and healthy – and it would only become strong and healthy over time, as it was a self-supporting, constantly evolving thing – then it would be a thing to be grateful for. It would be a thing to respect and to use as my very own in-built barometer. A thing that would eventually lead me to become an entirely separate entity within my group of peers and, indeed, outside of such a group. It really was an exciting concept that I had decided I should devote some time to exploring. I chose to become a little more considerate of others as a starting point. It made me happy, and I smiled at the boy the next time he furtively glanced in my direction.

He poked his tongue out at me.

In the dimming light of that stinking courtyard, I turned my attention to two streetlamps placed in the centre of it. They were in the style of Victorian London lamps, the kind that would notoriously explode without warning, often seriously injuring anyone that happened to be passing by.

They were of the type that Edison used to light up the Holborn Viaduct, or at least I imagined they were. In the dimming light of the courtyard I waited for them to be illuminated. And I thought about Edie.

And I thought about Mayo Maya, or Natalia, to give her real name back to her and I thought about the danger she would have been placed in. I thought about Boaz and about how he was almost certainly a man who would carry revenge in his heart for all the while it remained beating. And then I too had an innate sense of being threatened. Our lives, suspended and inanimate. But still we felt we had no need for plans. Well, not immediate ones at least.

Edie and I had slowly begun to learn to live with the recent sighting of Franck and I think we were both glad that we hadn't fled. But there was no ignoring it completely. That whole episode had left us on edge and Edie had started to change. It was clear that she was becoming less sure of herself. More skittish. Less confident. Not like her at all. Maybe it was all the drugs we were starting to consume.

A few weeks had passed when one night I was sitting in the flat waiting for Edie to come home. Earlier in the day, she and I had a disagreement and it had played on my mind all day. Our argument had kept ricocheting off the walls of the apartment for the whole time I was there. All day I'd been hearing my ugly comments echoing in my head, haunting me to distraction.

It had started simply because that morning she had been telling me that she wasn't feeling fulfilled, and I had been short tempered about it and had ridiculed her a little. I didn't mean to hurt her. In a way I think I was just expressing some kind of black humour in my usual heavy-handed way. But whatever it was she took exception to something I said. I don't blame her. I didn't blame her then. It was just how I felt. We were both very tense. Whether we could admit it or not, we felt hunted. It was hard to face.

"Why are you trying to destroy what we have?" I asked her sulkily. "Why are you being so destructive with our relationship?"

"It's not much of a relationship," she had said. "We don't go out. We're too afraid to go out!" She was right. We hardly ever went out anymore. Sitting in the courtyard by the estuary had been a rare event and, even then, both of us had been paranoid that we might be seen. It was not easy to relax.

"I'm not afraid Edie," I had said. "You're being ridiculous. I'm not the one who fell apart because I imagined I'd seen someone."

"Imagined!" she had shouted. "How dare you? I didn't *imagine* anything! I *definitely* saw someone and if it wasn't actually Franck, then it sure as hell looked like him. You agreed with me at the time!"

"Agreed?" I said, "How could I have agreed? I didn't see him! And neither did you!"

It was too much, and it made me unhappy to be speaking this way. Why was I being like this with her? I should have recognised then that she was vulnerable. I should have been sympathetic to the fact that Edie could be starting to unravel, but I just went at her hard. Dispassionately. Unsympathetically. Looking back on this now, my cold heart feels so hollow. She was there in front of me asking for my help and I was tough on her. Much too tough on her. Too acerbic. Too judgmental. Vicious, almost.

This troubled me all day. I was unhappy with the thought of it. I wanted just to hold her and to tell her I loved her. To tell her that I was *in* love with her. I wanted to tell her how much she meant to me and to apologise for being so brutal. I wanted to tell her that I had thought it over, that I had calmed down and had now realised that I was being hard and impenetrable.

She was downstairs in the shop at work. I knew she'd be up in the apartment just after six o'clock. Every day she always was. I had my words in line in my head. I had what I wanted to say perfectly well ordered.

But by six-thirty she had still not come home.

I was unnerved, anxious even. But I assumed that her boss, Rosa, had asked her to stay back and help with something.

By seven o'clock, when Edie still had not come upstairs, I was becoming unsettled. I walked down the stairwell to the front of the shop where I caught Rosa locking up.

"Ola, Rosie," I said to her, and then in English, "Is Edie not with you?"

Rosa looked at me and said, "No. She went a while ago. She left early, in fact. She said she was meeting someone. I just assumed she was meeting you."

When she saw the concern written on my face, she said, "So it wasn't you. No. I don't know where she is."

After an awkward moment that seemed to stretch like elastic, before snapping back again, she said, "Look, here's my number. Call me if you need to. Or if she doesn't come back until late and you're worried. It's not a problem. Call any time. I live alone so you won't be disturbing anyone."

Rosa scribbled her number on the back of a sales receipt she pulled from the bottom of her purse and then she left. I looked at the number but couldn't read a couple of the digits. I hoped I wouldn't need to call her.

Another hour passed and I then began to panic a little. I opened my third beer and rolled another joint. I thought that the smoke would keep me calm. But it probably didn't.

Where was she?

I thought of course about Franck. Had it been him after all? I began to think then about how often Edie was unreliable like this, and it wasn't often. This was way out of character. If she was meeting someone, why didn't she tell me? Maybe she did, and I had forgotten. I tried to remember if she'd told me she was meeting someone that day. My heart rate had picked up and I was pacing the room.

Two more beers, and another smoke.

Nine o'clock came and went and I started to wonder aloud what I should do. Where the hell was Edie? Panic was setting in. The hollow solitude of not having her around now building inside of me.

Was she punishing me for the quarrel we'd had earlier in the day? I doubted that. It wasn't her style. I felt ill and I imagined then that the flat would now remain empty forever. Here I was swinging between fatalism and occasional bouts of even-tempered rationality. No logic. No calm consideration. No authentic judgement.

I started to imagine how I could no longer live without her there. The air, so rich with serenity and so rich with familial moments would become stale, and cold and empty. No Edie. I couldn't bear it.

At ten I thought I heard a click in the door lock. I got up to look. I hadn't. I opened the door and looked down the stairs, nearly toppling down as I did so. Drunk now. And stoned. And empty.

I went back inside and reached for another beer. It was the last one I had, and this too made me anxious. I recognised my growing dependencies. It didn't feel good. I could sense the problems gathering on the edge of my life. Should I go out to look for her? I was too drunk. I was falling over as I moved.

It was now after ten o'clock and she was supposed to have been home four hours before. Something bad must have happened! But what? What had happened? Where was she? Maybe she was in a bar with a friend of Antonio's. Had she been taken? Maybe right now Franck was threatening to beat her again unless she told them where I was. I couldn't think like that! What horrible thoughts I had in my head! Logic and calmness were slipping languorously away from me, like a love slipping away across the surface of an ocean. I reached out for her hand, but she was drifting away. She was too far away already. Out of reach.

I spent the next two or three hours in that frame of mind. The lack of any more alcohol didn't help me. I thought about calling Rosa, but what would I say? And then it was quite suddenly almost one o'clock in the morning and Edie had still not come home.

I concluded she had left me. She had gone. And I felt the deepest, and most suffocating despair. What had I done? Why had I driven her away? She was something good. Someone good. And together we had cultivated a life that felt right. A life that was worthwhile. A life not to be lost.

What we had was over, as quickly and as devastatingly as it had begun. She had gone away. And I had to accept it.

I was tired, mentally. I had to rest. How could I go to bed without her? How could I *ever* do that? I lay then on the little two-person sofa and hung my legs over the end and sobbed quietly to myself. Always, from now on. To myself. By myself.

When the door opened at two o'clock in the morning, and Edie came falling through it, I ran to pick her up from the small table over which she had collapsed. She was very drunk. She was dishevelled and unkempt. But not hurt. Nothing beyond superficial.

"Edie! Where have you been?"

And again, "Where were you?"

The relief was enormous. I held her close. I kissed her eyes, and I buried my face in her hair.

Edie couldn't focus. She tried to speak but made no sense. I didn't care. She was with me. I felt a lightness in my chest. I could smell things again! I realised then that my sense of smell had disappeared in my state of anxiety. It was almost as if my mind and my body were channelling all my senses towards recovering what was quickly becoming my disintegrating sense of hope.

I didn't attempt to interrogate her now. Instead, I put her in our bed and returned to the sofa. She could sleep it off. We could talk about it in the morning. Which it nearly was.

I didn't want to think about where she'd been.

Nor why we hurt ourselves like this.

I looked at her and said out loud, "Close your eyes. Sleep now."

But she didn't hear me. I imagined her then in the arms of someone else, and it was like a punch to my chest. I sat up and leaned forward heavily, curled up into a desperate curve and breathing hard, in out in out, my ribcage dramatically expanding.

I thought about Edie packing her things into a bag and watching her walk down the stairs and away from me forever. Whoever it was, they would tell her how she was the most special thing in their life. They'd tell her that she meant everything to them. They would smile at her as they lay in bed together and they would whisper to her how much they wanted to look after her and protect her from people like me. She would be lonely, and they would be her friend. And I would be lost, and empty and hollow.

A fool in her eyes. A failure in love.

*

I'll give credit to her. She somehow managed to make herself available for work at nine o'clock the following morning. I don't know what conversation she must have had with Rosa in the shop, but she didn't come up for lunch at one, like she often did, and so we didn't speak about the night before until almost a full twenty-four hours had passed. Which for Edie was a clever move. Because by then I wasn't bristling with the indignation of having been taken for granted, which was how I felt about it.

But, of course, we did eventually speak about it. I couldn't let it go. I wanted to, but it would not have been healthy. I made myself strong for the conversation. One that I did not want to have. But one that I knew we must.

"Do you want to tell me?" I asked her. It was difficult place to start.

"No. Not really," was her quick reply, unhelpful and harsh. I would have to try again.

"Okay then," I said. "Can I demand that you tell me? Do I have that right?"

"No, you don't," she said with steel in her voice, and she fixed me with a look that told me to back away.

"OK," I tried once more. "So, were you teaching me a lesson? Were you punishing me for my stupid behaviour yesterday morning? Because I concede," I added in an attempt at reconciliation, "that I behaved badly with what I said."

She looked at me but said nothing, inviting me to continue with my apology. In her eyes she held the gaze of a woman insisting I should elaborate. I saw it and I obeyed.

"I'm sorry if I came across strongly. I just care about you

Ede," I said more plaintively now. Softly, and earnestly. "I just care about you very much. You must know it, surely."

She looked then at her lap and at the fingers intertwined there, resting on her dark orange, almost umber, knee-high skirt that she wore in the shop. Her waist was nipped and trim and her arms slender like her neck, classically long. Her waterfall-clear eyes, now sad, were set like emeralds in her bright and plaintive face. Her hazel-brown hair styled in ringlets. Ringlets that she'd recently begun to grow out a little.

Her apricot skin glistened then in the soft evening sunlight that spilled across our apartment. Edie. My Edie.

I had started to forget even that she'd been out until two in the morning without trying to get word to me where she was. I imagined her again, lying in bed with someone else and the pain hit me hard in the middle of my soul. The sadness of such a thought was so easily sparked into a small rage as if petrol had been thrown over the flames of my love for her. I became upset and angered in an instant, and so indignantly, like a fool, I went on the attack. I could never control my emotions. It was difficult to function.

"Where were you?" I demanded now, raising my voice a little and undoing the positive steps I had started to make.

"You can't just throw yourself through the door in the middle of the night, pissed and barely able to even breathe let alone speak!"

She said nothing but unfolded her hands now, her demeanour protective once more. I carried on the attack, as stupid as it was to do so.

"Where were you? Why didn't you tell me you were going

out?"

"It wasn't planned," she said.

This was better. Dialogue. At last!

"Where were you?" I said it again and again. "Who were you with?"

This was the wrong question. For me. The fear of someone charming her away. Why did I ask her that?

"A friend," was what she said. A friend. And the way she said it took all the noise out of the room. It was like a candle burning in a glass jar that goes out when the lid is replaced. Gone. In a short time. Not instant. But quick. Close enough.

I thought I understood what she was telling me and so I stopped speaking then. I looked at the floor. I stood up and walked to the kitchen and walked straight back again.

And I wished for all the world that I hadn't wanted to know. I wondered what difference it was going to make. Do we always need to know the truth? Even if we suspect it's going to hurt us. Why would we want to wilfully know about something that we are convinced is going to be so painful? Something hard. Something intolerable. Something that could yield nothing good. I sat down in a small table chair and leaned forward, and into her personal space a little.

And quietly I asked, "Is it over?"

And the words ... I could barely even say them in that order.

And I felt myself fighting to not cry. *Edie how can I exist without you?* That was what I wanted to say. To implore her not to go. *How can I live alone after all the beautiful moments that you have given to me? How can there be anyone you love more than you love me?* These were all the things that I was thinking, and I was thinking them all at the same time. But why couldn't I say them?

I noticed then that she was crying. There were tears. I wanted to hold the betrayer; if that was what she was. But I couldn't hold her. Through her sobs I heard her say, "It's not what you think. I can't explain now. But one day soon, I will."

It was enough.

I went to her then and held her tightly as she wept like I'd not seen her weep before. Her anguish was real, and it was hard. It burned. It flowed from her in a torrent of pure emotion, a torrent which we both were all too aware that the spring of which was 'the event'.

What the hell had we done? We'd put ourselves in an impossible situation on the day that we stole those drugs. We'd given ourselves the smallest chance of survival. Negative odds.

This was not acting. This was real.

I took solace in that I'd heard her say the words 'It's not what you think it is', and that was enough for me at that moment. I didn't pursue it anymore. She'd held out, and she'd got one past me. She'd gotten away with it. I knew that all too well. But right at that moment I simply did not care.

Later in the night, I felt her next to me. Just the very edge of her presence. An intransigent feeling. Spectral almost. I was filled with such gratitude that, right then, we were still side by side. Her breathing was shallow in the darkness and was punctuated by tiny, weightless sighs. My mind was turning circles and, when I closed my eyes, I could see Edie with someone else. This time, a man with strong arms. Stronger than mine. A man with bigger dreams than me. A smile wider than mine. I hated him. He terrified me and the vision I had of him burned me up from the inside out.

And Edie, so small as she curled up against his chest. This man: her new friend. She looked at him then, the way she once looked at me. She tells him that she's never going to let him go, her eyes wide and filled with desire. In my mind, he pulls her closer and kisses the top of her head as she murmurs and smiles back up at him. I hear him: *It'll all work out alright*, he says. *I'll protect you.* Edie gives up her heart in that moment. She inhales his scent, and I am forgotten before the next breath leaves her body.

I whispered it very quietly, but I'm not sure she was awake.

"I love you," I said.

And ever so gently, at the height of the darkness, as a new day promised to come and carry us away, to keep up safe, together for the rest of our lives, I felt her squeeze my hand.

*

In the morning it was clear she was being eaten up.

She told me straight. "We have to leave."

She had said it unequivocally. It was a strong statement of fact. Not a request. Was this the sudden realisation that we were still in real danger? Most likely.

I shuddered at what we had done. How could we have given ourselves this burden that it seemed we were destined to carry for the rest of our days together. The never knowing. The never understanding. We were handicapped by this. As a couple. And for what?

The money was now all gone. We'd bought ourselves what? Time to get to know one-another? We could have done that anyway. We could be living like we were living then, only much sooner and without any threat, if only we had taken the gear back to Boaz and then left to discover Portugal.

No hiding. No stress. No second glances at people we hardly knew. No suspicions about people we met. Every person I ever saw from that moment on, I saw as a potential threat to us. To me. To Edie. And now look at what was happening. I had Edie in pieces sobbing into my chest. In pieces! Falling into pieces. And I was now going to be consumed by jealousy and doubt.

The never knowing.

The never, *ever* knowing. The afraid-of-asking. The afraid-of-knowing. Forever.

I didn't pursue it then. She was always a good-natured girl, kind-hearted. She made mistakes, I made mistakes. None of this was unusual. It was sad, and it could be disappointing, but it wasn't malicious. I think that was the key to my forgiving her. She was not vindictive in any way.

I ran through a series of potential cases. Was she seeing someone else? Was she planning to leave me? Was she in touch with an old lover and not telling me? Difficult as these thoughts were, they were none of them compared to the real fear I had of Edie leaving me or being taken from me by Dieter and Boaz and thrown into a canal somewhere outside of Amsterdam. Out by the airport, as they used to say.

I can hear Boaz: "Take her out by the airport."

I had never admitted it before, but I knew what he meant, and I had heard it said maybe twice. Certainly once.

I didn't ask Edie why she was so insistent that we should leave. I was punch drunk from the impact of all the information that was coming my way. I didn't press her on it. Should I have? Yes, I think in hindsight that perhaps I should. I simply couldn't answer her. I knew she was right. We *had to* leave. But I couldn't process that kind of upheaval. Not right away.

So I descended into silence. I made decisions slowly. Deliberately. I couldn't hear Edie at all then. I knew she was speaking to me, but the words made no sense, and I became aware that I was shutting them down. Making them silent. Wilfully misunderstanding them. Not even recognising them as actual words.

My mind turned everything she said to me into an incomprehensible new language. A language I did not speak. I knew that I was doing this consciously. It was a peculiar thing. I was doing it on purpose. I retreated into myself for no more than two or three days while I struggled to find a path through the bewilderment.

"We must leave."

She kept saying it, without giving me any solid reasons. I struggled to piece together this most obvious picture. Edie was telling me plainly that she feared for our safety, but for a short while I simply couldn't think clearly.

Then, almost instantly, this wilful bafflement became something else. Something familiar. Something that I recognise now as being a depressive state. A miasmic state. Catatonic, almost. Wordless and lost. Warm and empty. Like sitting inside on a winter day and watching a soundless wind move the branches of a tree. Like a TV with the volume down.

I began to notice things that I perhaps would not have noticed if I could hear more clearly. With one sense denied, the others become heightened. In this unreal state I fixated on my dream then. I welcomed it for all of its familiarity. This, I assume, was my subconscious giving me something it already recognised. In fact, I'm quite sure of that. But again, it's not of any interest to me *why* things happen. Or even *how*. It's the fact that they happen at all that I find so fascinating.

Through such deafening silence I see a friend approaching.

I am on a train. Or maybe a tram. I am passing alongside, or possibly over, an expanse of water. I am seated. There is a cathedral. Or a church. It's a large city. There are too many people. They are all moving. They are carrying many bags. There are pigeons. Shopping? My vision blurs and the crowd shimmers, as if reflected on the surface of a lake. I hear bells. Large bells. Deeply sonorous. I hear children. Laughter. A school playground? Something blue. Tiny. Pale blue. Bald woman with dog. Hooped earrings. A lead. Heavy breasted. Duplicate. Tweed hats and jackets. Red stitching. Brown tweed.

I see myself in the window next to which I am sitting. I see myself endlessly. My image repeated. Infinite. Outside it grows dark. Then it's midday again. I see her, standing by the door. Waiting to get off. Waiting to get on? The train/tram slows. Signs on a platform. She looks towards me: beautiful, beautiful girl. Where are you? Who are you? Auburn-haired, green jacket. Army jacket? Soldiers? She is outside of the train/tram and looking at me. Intently. Through the glass in which I am reflected. Her hand to her face. Her hand to her head. Her fingers through her hair ...

... and slowly, I awake.

*

Something was coming. Painful and hot. I felt the blows of brutality gathering on the edge of my life, like mediaeval battalions gathering at both sides of a field, and I feared for Edie. For both of us. I had then an overwhelming sense that we were not safe, that we must leave Oporto right away. Edie had been warning me for two days and suddenly I understood her clearly. I could think straight again. I saw the danger then for what it was.

Time seemed to pass slowly, like honey dripping from a rotating spoon. The nights started taking over. They were dark and metallic. The early evening buttercup-coloured light that we had always adored, that moment when the sun brings the buildings to life, was appearing more and more like charcoal to us. Both of us. The air we breathed was becoming stringent and acerbic. The edges and outlines of the buildings that surrounded us were darkening then, carrying something sinister within their walls. The shadows of Boaz and Dieter were creeping close.

It was time to go.

And outside the sun was yellow. Hot and alive. The pavements were orange. The houses, too, were orange. Sepia. Porto wine was a dark, sticky, sweet red. Deep red. The countryside, parched. Gold, like hay. The soil underneath our feet was dry and hard and light brown, almost orange. Almost yellow. And like this, the colour wheel was about to turn again.

THREE

Imogen sits up in bed and swings her legs over the side. She leans forward and, with her elbows on her knees, she rests her bodyweight for a moment before lurching upright and rearranging her pale-cream night-shirt around her thighs.

She stands and stretches, reaching into the air above her head, twisting her back as she does so, and then walks to the toilet out in the hall, leaving her bedsit room door open on its latch. In the toilet she sits heavily and breathes deeply, again resting her bodyweight on her elbows. She raises her eyebrows a little as she registers the stronger odour of her urine that morning and she thinks about her meal the night before. Had she eaten asparagus? No. She had eaten boiled potatoes, string beans and a salted cod fillet with just a little sauce from a quick-to-fix packet. So why does her urine carry the unmistakable odour of asparagus? An odd thought. Soon forgotten.

Outside it's damp all over the Old Town of Nice. The air is filled with a warm mist, and she is waiting for it take the edge off the heat that has begun to slow the pace of life in town. Everyone has been waiting for a few days now for the thunder to gather overhead and wash away the stale air that they have been sharing, waiting for it to lift and to be replaced by the salted breezes from the sea. It is agreed that right now it's too hot on the Riviera, leaving many people gasping as they feed on one another's expelled air. Even down at the beach it is too hot. They are spending their days in the ocean and no work is being done. The city is beginning to melt a little. It does the same thing every year. Why should this year be any different?

Before leaving her room to go to the restaurant, Imogen checks herself in the little chipped mirror that her grandmother gave to her shortly before she died. Tacked to the top of the mirror is a photograph of the lady she had loved. To Imogen she was an invincible force, a woman of colossal fortitude. She remembers fondly how her grandmother would patiently explain the correct way to combat certain emotions, using words and phrases that her mother hadn't the understanding, or the confidence, to do. She would sit Imogen down and they would drink camomile or English tea as this magnanimous lady bestowed the gifts of wisdom and benevolent knowledge upon her granddaughter. Imogen had never forgotten what she said to her. Not a word of it. Not a single phrase.

Looking back at her in the mirror she sees her own self looking confident and secure. She puts a lot of this down to her *mamie*. Imogen sees herself now looking modern and she sees herself looking resolute. The tidy cut of her green jacket marks her out among most women of her age, and she knows that with a little more conviction she will be able to succeed sufficiently before she reaches twenty-five. After that she isn't so sure. But she has ideas.

Imogen checks her earrings and sweeps her light auburn hair away from her shoulders. She shakes her head and picks up the pale blue pillbox hat from beside the door. She feels that she will soon have to have her hair cut as it is starting to look too long and knotted, and it is sticking out from under her hat too much. She picks up a small clutch bag, also blue, as she passes through the door which she then closes firmly behind her. The bag isn't in keeping with the sobriety of her outfit but for now it is the only one she's got.

She walks quickly to reach the restaurant because the mist is beginning to thicken into drizzle. It soon becomes a warm rain and falls like a million needles tinselling down around her feet and ankles. It is surely now beginning to cool the houses and make the Old Town shine. She can smell the metallic odour of ozone drifting in on the damp air from the sea. She fills her lungs with it and smiles at the way it makes her feel. She is alive and free today, and she thinks to herself how odd it is that she knows that someday soon her life is going to change.

As she looks at the shops and approaches the railway station, a train is passing. And she thinks back to the night a couple of weeks ago when she was down on the Plage de l'Opera throwing stones into the sea. She thinks about the moped that had nearly run her down, and she thinks then in an abstract way about how she toyed with the concept of diving into the sea. About how she longed to swim with the moon that was reflected there. To swim all the way to England. She thinks about the cobblestones and how the mosses will be slimy on them this morning, and she looks at the windows of the train as it passes above her. And she thinks about being in love, about what it could mean and then about the gifts it could hold for her. She thinks about how she will be a good mother. The best. And she wants to be in love.

She wants to know how it will feel. Proper love. Real love. She's ready.

Imogen ponders the possibility of forcing herself to fall in love. She is a pretty girl and, when the moment comes, there will be no shortage of people to choose from. But she feels that she owes it to her grandmother and, of course, ultimately to herself to not be led anywhere she doesn't want to go. And she thinks about a lover on the edge of her subconscious. And the train disappears from view. The foreign lover. The English lover. The lover that she has often thought about. She builds him up in her mind's eye. Her model lover. She's doing it again. Thinking about this Englishman who doesn't even exist.

In the distance the Mediterranean sea appears on the horizon. And suddenly she is alert and back to her senses. But still in her subconscious she is thinking about love. She thinks about dropping pebbles off bridges in foreign countries and holding hands with someone she adores. She thinks about laughing over foreign words on menus in restaurants filled with flowers. She thinks about the padlocks that stretched across the vast pedestrian bridge she once visited in Salzburg; names of couples written on each one.

And she knows that she is supporting her dream by understanding that soon someone is going to come to her. That love itself was soon going to come for her. Imogen could feel the day approaching. But she is patient.

And she can wait a little longer yet.

*

The only decision Edie and I had to make now was about where we should go. She favoured distance, but I was less sure. She insisted that she wanted to go far. It didn't take much for me to agree. If we were going to go, we'd better do it properly. But which direction? I asked Antonio if he could put in a word with any of his studio friends to see if I could find a place somewhere to earn. Edie was furious with me for doing that.

"Why have you told Antonio that we're moving out?" she said. "I don't want anyone to be able to trace us!"

She was right, of course. Don't leave logistical things like that up to me. I was hopeless at it. I simply hadn't thought about the consequences of other people having any knowledge about us. We needed to leave no trail. I was surprised I couldn't see that, so when Antonio came back and said that he couldn't find anyone it was a relief. He asked me when we were leaving. He wanted to organise a send-off for us. I told him we were maybe already changing our minds. I told him that nothing was certain.

To me, this meant that we could simply slip away. He wouldn't be offended that we didn't stick around to say goodbye, and frankly, who cared if he was? None of it would matter once we'd moved on. I was sure that he was the kind of guy who would have forgotten us within twenty-four hours anyway.

Edie said that she wanted to go north, into France. We looked on a map. She wanted to go to Antibes, or somewhere near there on the Riviera. Nice. Or Cannes. She said she could find work in a bar. She said she'd have no problem because it was a busy area, with lots of places for people to eat and drink. I suggested Barcelona. We could hide more easily in a bigger crowd, and Barcelona was surely more densely packed than anywhere along the French Riviera. There would be more bars to find work in. If we didn't like it, or it wasn't what we needed, we could inch our way north. That would be my compromise. Edie agreed.

So that's how we came to find ourselves heading for Barcelona. Heading straight for the heart of bohemia. I smiled then at my old life on a crumbling housing estate at the edge of London, and for the first time I remember thinking how that was a ghost that was finally being laid to rest. Only then, at that moment, did I feel as if my life had finally changed for the better. I was excited. I was in love. And in spite of the danger we were in, we had some good days together at that time.

Turning our back on Oporto was a moment filled with exhaustion, and a little regret. For us both. But not for long. We had got to know one another in that place and because of that, surely it would forever hold memories dear to us. But we had no doubt that it was definitely the right time to move forwards. And so we did.

We left early one morning as the dawn was breaking through a late summer night, painting the clouds a light, opaque orange, the colour of peach skin. It was under these clouds that we said our silent goodbye to Oporto as we dragged our two bags over the cobbles behind us. The wheels clacking on the stones as we went.

The next few days were exactly what we needed. We found very quickly that to challenge ourselves like this was liberating and it reinforced my own belief that if ever you're in doubt about something, then the answer has always got to come down on the side of 'yes.'

And so as surely as it had arrived, Oporto was gone. It would remain a memory from now on. Our time there had forever moved from the present to the past, and now we were only concerned about the future, about our future, which for the time being was going to be in Spain.

When we got to Barcelona, we found a room in the Hotel des Beaux Artes near to a railway station on Allees Jean Jacques. I remember it very clearly. It was a red brick building with dark, iron balconies on every floor. At every window. Kind of like the Chelsea Hotel in New York. The entrance was a single, anonymous looking, heavy oak door with a fashion store on one side and a tiny bar on the other. As soon as we got there, we immediately set about trying to find something big enough for us to call a home. And, of course, we straight away began looking to find work as well.

In a place as vast as Barcelona the language was not going to be an issue for us. Portuguese was something we'd had to pick up as we went along, it was not a language that either of us spoke at all naturally. Spanish, however, was a little easier and really, within a matter of days we both knew enough to get by. Of course, having spent a couple of months in Portugal helped, but for Edie, educated in a German school, she knew enough in most European languages to make herself understood. But naturally, in any large city like Barcelona, English was always going to be widely spoken. Like it is all across the world. Like it seems to have always been.

We settled in easily, and quickly. Edie took work in another shoe shop. It made me laugh. I teased her about it, but she was less than pleased. I found work in a recording studio, which I was delighted about. It was a studio that was affiliated with a small, out of town radio station concerned mostly with local news and light entertainment. Mainly I was part of a two-person team looking after the cabling that ran under the mixing console in two of the vocal booths. Making sure there were no clicks or hums and buzzes. That was my new role in life. I liked it. It suited me.

Edie and I found that life in Barcelona came to us very naturally, and we began to get along well again, like we used to. Our recent upset had become a thing of the past and a kind of harmonious equilibrium returned, only now with a greater depth about it. An altogether more serious relationship was forming between us, and this renewal was something in which we both found warmth and comfort. The gravity of our respect for each other was important and so we built our new routines upon that.

These early days in Spain were good to us.

Until one morning.

It happened.

And things were about to change again.

I was on a train and in my nose, I smelled a kind of vanilla. I can still smell it now. A sickly, oversweet version of vanilla. And the light on the train was like vanilla, only more yellow, more like a kind of butter. A cream-coloured butter. The shadows were short. The sky was bright. The sun made me squint, even from behind dark glasses. I was coming back into Barcelona. The time was getting towards the middle of the day, short by a few minutes. I'd been out to the flea market at Calle dels Encants looking for anything. Looking for nothing. Passing time.

Edie was working and it was a weekend. I'd taken the overground train on the Rodalies. It was a beautiful day, bright and crisp and I didn't want to be underground. Subconsciously, I think, I always travelled this way, overground. And when I did, my dream was always in my mind. Perhaps it was destined to always only ever be in my mind. But on this morning, it seemed very real. It was one of those moments when the ephemeral nature of that which we cannot grasp comes into view. It languishes just out of reach, teasing me to take a hold of it. But it's too far to grasp. Too slippery to hold.

The train headed south, and then pulled into a station whose name I now forget but the image remains strongly planted. It was very like Amsterdam, that was the first thing I noticed. In fact, looking back, I now remember thinking that I was confusing myself that suddenly my train had pulled into a station just outside from the RAI centre in that city.

But then a chill ran along my forearms and crept up to the nape of my neck. I saw in the far distance the outline of La Sagrada Familia, in all its pomp. Still 'unfinished' even now. Cloaked in its perennial scaffolding the church sat silhouetted in the glare of the full noon sun and to the south, outside the window where I sat, a park filled with children. Laughter pierced the sealed tube in which I was travelling, and my ears seemed to filter out any other sound, amplifying the significance of the laughter that I could hear above all else. Could the Sagrada be the church in my dream?

There was a fountain in the centre of a park. With a cafe and some shops. A plaza. My nerves began to glisten. I felt excited. So, of course, I began to assess every person on the platform as the train on which I was travelling slowed to an inexorable stop. My hair bristled and began to rise on my arms.

It was now that I was expecting to see her. This felt more real than at any time before. If a girl in a green jacket, perhaps carrying a pale blue bag, had waved at me at that moment I would have thought it the most natural gesture from a stranger that could happen and as the train stopped, I began looking all along the platform as if looking for someone who I knew was waiting to meet me. I was fervently studying every face, looking into every eye that I could.

She must be there. Somewhere. After all these years I felt certain that I was about to meet her. To see her. My imagining of her was about to end and the dream would now be blown apart like a gas-filled glass bottle dropped from the top of a building.

I sat. Suspended.

Time. Suspended.

Breathing, thinking, feeling ... all suspended.

Suspended.

The train pulled away, inching at first, very slowly, and soon the park softly and silently slid beyond my view. The sound of laughter grew steadily quieter until I could no longer hear it, and the view of La Sagrada disappeared behind a backdrop of brutalist tenement blocks. Each one seeming to lean in on the other, fighting for dominance on the skyline like the people that lived there fought for their own existence.

For a few moments I sat thinking about all of this. My mind in a whirl. And then: the guilt. A kind of guilt. Not a real guilt. I thought of Edie and how in my mind I would have left her in a moment had the dream become a reality. This, I decided, was a devastating reflection of my relationship with her and from that very moment I began to doubt if I loved her as I thought I had.

And then I began to consider if she was not already ahead of me in this. My head was filled with doubt. A suffocating doubt. Edie was already falling out of love with me. I thought then about the night she didn't come home in Oporto, and of how I assumed she was with another man, and all my doubts and all the daemons that I thought I had laid to rest when we crossed the border two weeks before, suddenly resurfaced vengefully.

They seemed to creep like an ivy through the floor of the train. A train that up until a few moments ago was bathing me in a good light, in an optimistic glow of tranquil contentment but which had now turned viciously. And I was suddenly so afraid of myself and of everything around me.

This was how I began to think. This was the thought process that framed the next, illogical act in my story. Was this my madness? Or was it hers that made me feel this way?

I now know, of course, that it was the drugs that we had been taking. Too much by far, and moreover, far too often. But I didn't know that back then, when I thought that I was indestructible. When I thought that my mind was capable of a dramatic degree of shock and incredulity, excitement, and adventure. But it wasn't. Not forever.

And so it was at this moment that I tragically began to confuse affection with the carnality of raw sex in a way that only a non-thinking person could. I accepted my idiocy. I accepted this fate. I reflected then how things had been quiet between our sheets since we had arrived in Barcelona. I was unsettled. I took it far too personally and I beat myself up and put it down to the unusual hours I was working, and also to the incompatibility of our days that were anonymously rolling one into the other.

If I needed to get her attention, perhaps it would do to try to gain it in a sexual direction. I had my doubts, I will be honest. But it was then that I thought a good plan would be to ask Edie to play a role for me. For both of us. To become someone new. If she didn't like who she was, and she had recently been telling me this quite often, then perhaps it could be a positive thing to become someone new. A kind of empowerment even.

This, unbelievably, is a strand of logic that made perfect sense to me as I sat bathed again in buttercup sunlight on that train, on that bright and shiny day.

That I now had a plan calmed me again. I could feel an answer developing and I was convinced that this was a practical solution to a problem that, in reality, quite simply didn't exist.

I'll get Edie to become the girl in my dream!

That way my subconscious mind will have 'found' the girl I was looking for, and I would finally be able to settle and accept the person I was.

And so it was on that day, I decided that for Edie to wear a green army jacket, and to carry a blue plastic bag, and to wear an auburn or ginger coloured wig, cut short to the shoulder was a good idea. We could use it as a role-play thing. She'd not find it unusual in any way at all! She'd never think of me negatively or think that I was unstable in any way whatsoever!

And, yes of course she would fall in love with me all over again if I suggested this to her. What young woman wouldn't? She and I alone, lost inside of my dream. This had got to be a good situation! Surely, no?

Who on earth was I kidding now? Only myself. That's clear from a distance, but when you're locked inside your own great ideas, you simply don't see the irrational logic that so often surrounds them. When you're standing in a forest, you only see the trees. You don't see the actual thing you are standing in.

As a little girl growing up, Edie, like any little girl would, enjoyed dressing up and playing games, acting out roles. She had told me this many times, so I figured this would be similar. Certainly I considered that it would be similar enough to be able to, at the very least, approach the whole concept as a legitimate idea.

I wasn't quite expecting the response I got.

She looked at me with bewilderment at first and after a while, finally, she spoke.

"This is a joke, right?" she vacantly muttered. "You want me to dress up like a different person?"

Hearing her interpret my request in that way, threw onto it a light that I'd not decently considered, and I nodded sheepishly, looking at my feet, not daring to catch her bewildered gaze. I had nowhere else to rest my eyes. She continued with the most obvious question, one for which I was not prepared and one for which I had no coherent answer.

"Why?" she said.

Her voice was short and abrupt when she said it.

I shrugged my shoulders and I probably stuck out my lower lip as well, and said nothing, letting the silence between us act as a kind of buffer, a kind of no man's land. A dead zone. I gathered up my emotional baggage and dropped it at her feet. I needed to be out of that conversation quickly, so I tried to move things on.

"I'm sorry, Edie," I said in the way that any true coward would. "Let's forget it. It's a bad idea."

But to my great surprise she tried to keep us on the topic.

"I want to know why," was what she said, adding, "I'm not saying no to you. I just want to know why."

She had wrongfooted me. I looked at her then, demure, and undamaged. Edie, the confident girl. The one I had met the year before at a table outside the movie-themed café, adjacent to the Grasshopper in Amsterdam.

Maybe I'd called this right. Perhaps what was needed was a stab at an adventure like this. A little piece of the unknown. A bold, but reckless step into a kind of twilight: sexual or otherwise. But for all of this, I still couldn't answer her question truthfully. I was certain it would be unacceptable to her. But I had to say something, and I had to say it quickly.

"I just think it'd suit you," was what I said, and before she had time to digest this I added, "I think it'd be a good look for you. But before you do it permanently, maybe a test run is not such a bad idea?"

That was it. I could do no more. I could say no more.

It was now Edie's choice.

I waited three days for any definitive answer. But when it came it was positive. She had agreed. I was lost for a little while. Lost inside a small sexual piquancy. A little peccadillo of my very own making. I was lost inside of my own world, inside of my own dreams. Inside of my own forest, not seeing it. Only seeing the trees.

Edie, for now, was going to take on this most personal of roles for me, *with* me. I was ashamed. My own dream being brought to life. It was too much, and it was not enough. Both, at the same time. I owed her many things for this. I still do today.

I thought about asking her to wait on a train platform but quickly realised that would be taking things too far. She surely then would start to wonder what I was trying to achieve and once again I would have had no answer for her. I couldn't chance that scene again.

But the key thing I had to wrestle with now was that, yes, she had agreed to make herself like the girl in my dream, albeit in a sexual capacity, just not at all like the vision I carried around with me day after day, which was the vision that was starting to become more and more prolific as I began to grow less and less in love with Edie.

That night we went to a bar that was next door to a well-known nightclub. We scored a couple of grams of club-coke while we were there, badly cut with something unnatural and smelling of paint thinner. A waitress brought us a pitcher of pale beer and two large glasses of vodka. We toasted each other in one reckless swoop. I coughed. Edie laughed. I drank all of mine. Edie drank half of hers. I coughed again. She continued to laugh.

We began to bang our feet to the dance music bursting through the wall from the bar behind us and sank back into that fuzzy comfort of senselessness that coke would often bring to us. I was properly wired, and my teeth were aching with all the grinding they were doing. I looked at Edie as her hand vibrated exaggeratedly whilst she attempted to pour out some beer from the pitcher. The pale beer from the pitcher. The pale Kölsch beer. Crisp and clean.

I leaned forward and took it from her with both hands, and she laughed again and lit a cigarette and drank the rest of her vodka before I could get my hands on it. I was thinking of it. I was thinking of it. How did she know?

We stayed in the bar for about an hour and drank a lot more vodka. I went to the toilets and did another line and then stood at the bar to order more drinks. Edie took the wrap from me and went to the toilet too. I felt unconquerable. I leant against the bar, trying to get the barman's attention, and a short blonde girl started talking to me. I didn't care what I was doing. I grabbed at her and put my arms around her waist, noticing it was a little thicker than Edie's. It excited me and the girl nestled into me and raised her face to meet mine. We kissed a little, but I instantly backed away. I felt so guilty. Edie was only in the room next door.

What was I thinking? The girl looked mischievously at me. Like this was not a scene that was going to end easily. Not without her permission. Edie came back and I forgot the drinks and left the bar right away. I felt so guilty. Could Edie tell what I'd done? Or nearly done? Or what I was thinking of doing? Thankfully the girl didn't follow us outside.

We found ourselves then in a place called Café Orlando, which was comparatively quiet. We stayed there long enough to rub against each other and kiss hard. Deeply. Edie put her hand on my groin and squeezed me through my jeans. I bit the nape of her neck. She stuck her tongue in my ear, and we more or less *ran* back to our room. The intense thrill that we both felt sent bolts of energy through the very centre of our combined spirit. It caught us both in a snare, an animal trap built around tarnished cleanliness. It was so searing that we could have, at any time, fainted with pleasure.

The excitement shared by the two of us was immeasurable. Was this just a state of mind that we transmitted to one another? I reckon it must have been. The complexity of our life together was taken to new and surprising heights. We indulged one another with abandon. Every sniff that followed held a bitter taste of our darkest subconscious. Numb teeth, empty gums. We both knew it. We both needed it. Bodies that were restless became centred on one aim.

She wanted more than just me, but I couldn't compete with the drug we had induced, and I became a pilot for her ecstasy. This was justification enough. It was a madness that made us pass over what we regarded before as being wrong and being right. It made us want to push all the boundaries of what she could expect of me and what I could expect of her, and I wanted to break them all down, down into the bitter tasting mud in which we both yearned to wallow. But my God, it was beautiful for its entire tarnished doings. This was a ditch from which only sobriety could free us.

She burned me. Bled me. Beat me. Cut me. Fucked me! And if ever heaven and hell could meet on earth in the same place, it must surely have been there.

Day to day life from that point on became impossible.

Forever more.

I was addicted. Addicted to Edie.

The disintegration began to settle in at this time. This is where we began falling apart. It wasn't easy for either of us. But for her, I really felt that she was collapsing from the inside out. Properly collapsing. I'd brought this upon us, and I was ashamed of that. I had only wanted to regain her confidence. And her trust. Precious jewels. Put on a wig. Be someone else. It couldn't hurt, could it?

If there was just one thing that I had clearly understood about Edie, it was that she could not be pressured into anything. She had a very linear thought process. She was very much an A to B kind of person, no deviation. She was all straight lines. So if she was coming with me on this downward journey, she was doing it of her own free will. I couldn't be blamed, I told myself that. She obviously wanted to do this with me. She wanted the journey too. I told myself that if we were going to descend into a kind of hell, then I was determined we'd make the most of every step down.

Eventually we fell on to the mattress just as the sun rose, turning all in the room to a nondescript, mottled blue and grey. I simply lay on my stomach, too wired to fall asleep. Edie had no such trouble and slept right away. I knew that if I didn't move, then I would eventually pass out. I knew that I would eventually remain essentially the same, but without any senses to make me aware of my state. So, I summoned every strength I had left to me, and I struggled to lay perfectly still, and as I lay like that my world had the effect of pitching from bottom to top, from bottom to top, from bottom to top ... like a scrolling television. I felt ill.

With a passionate longing, the image of Edie and I having a quiet meal together formed clearly behind my eyes. Her skin seemed clear and bright and tumbled into a river below that carried her spirit for a hundred miles downstream and then far, far out into the sea. But even the sea would eventually overflow with her inexhaustible beauty as she dissolved into the water bone by bone.

And as she dropped down into that sea, then I too was falling as far, if not further, for Edie herself. As I tried to fall asleep, my shame at having been so intimate with a stranger that night drove it home to me. It made me believe that maybe in all this tarnished emotion, in all these rusted and ugly faces, I could find a diamond. And maybe I was right. And then finally I fell unconscious.

And then I had my dream.

And for the second time that night I felt as if I had betrayed her.

*

I am on a train. Or maybe a tram. I am passing alongside, or possibly over, an expanse of water. I am seated. There is a cathedral. Or a church. It's a large city. There are too many people. They are all moving. They are carrying many bags.

There are pigeons. Shopping? My vision blurs and the crowd shimmers, as if reflected on the surface of a lake. I hear bells. Large bells. Deeply sonorous. I hear children. Laughter. A school playground? Something blue. Tiny. Pale blue. Bald woman with dog. Hooped earrings. A lead. Heavy breasted. Duplicate. Tweed hats and jackets. Red stitching. Brown tweed.

I see myself in the window next to which I am sitting. I see myself endlessly. My image repeated. Infinite. Outside it grows dark. Then it's midday again. I see her, standing by the door. Waiting to get off. Waiting to get on? The train/tram slows. Signs on a platform. She looks towards me: beautiful, beautiful girl. Where are you? Who are you? Auburn-haired, green jacket. Army jacket? Soldiers? She is outside of the train/tram and looking at me. Intently. Through the glass in which I am reflected. Her hand to her face. Her hand to her head. Her fingers through her hair ...

... and slowly, I awake.

FOUR

I arrived late, but not too late. Even so, I thought I had missed Edie already. She and I had arranged to meet at the small cafe next door to the burger place at the top of Las Ramblas, barely a three-minute walk from the apartment that we were renting. All talk of Boaz and Franck and Dieter seemed so distant at that moment. It felt as if we had finally put a big part of it behind us and, for the meantime at least, it was as if we had our paranoia under control. I don't think that either of us was expecting to see any of these people in Barcelona. In fact, I'm not sure that the thought had even occurred to us up until that point.

The way I recall it now, we'd even started to dare to forget about what we'd done to them. OK, so two keys of coke added up to a lot of money, but it wasn't the crime of the century and so now we were starting to feel that maybe it wasn't worth the hassle to Boaz to keep his men out there, hunting for us. After all, it wasn't too far off a year that had passed at that point.

We should have known better, of course. A man like that was not ever going to give up on money. Not ever.

One evening I was working a late shift at the studio. I was in a bit of a hurry to get there, but Edie had said she wanted to see me. We saw the small gap between her work ending and mine beginning, as an opportunity to sit together for a while and so when she explicitly asked to catch up, then I was always going to be keen to be there for her. Besides, she said she had something she wanted to show me.

But when I arrived a little late, I didn't see her. Not at first.

And then I did. Only it wasn't the Edie I was expecting to see.

At the very first table that I approached a girl was sitting, a girl who I had looked at for a few moments before I had even registered that it was her. I laughed, sat down, and smiled broadly, feeling very pleased with my idea. She beamed as well, looking delighted with her new look. She possibly blushed a little. That's how I like to remember it.

"Well, well," I exclaimed. "Excuse me miss, is this seat taken?" and I pointed playfully at the empty chair beside her.

"Well?" she posited as I took my place alongside her and ordered a beer from the waiter that approached. I looked around. It was getting busy on the square. Evening people out to play.

"I like it," I said feeling a deep sense of satisfaction.

Edie seemed very happy then, and in truth, it did suit her. The wig. It was a flattering colour. Deep auburn. Almost red. Exactly like the girl in my dreams.

"Where did you find it?" I asked her.

"I went out to the market that you went to the other weekend. The one out on Calle dels Encants," she said. I smiled. "It's very good," she added.

"Yes," I agreed, "they've got all sorts out there."

"I'm going to go back," she said, "There's bound to be a green jacket there."

I agreed with her once more, and we laughed lightly. I, a little guiltily, I seem to remember now. I sat back and said little. I just looked at her. Smiling, and nodding. After a while, she became slightly nervous, but in a subtle way, and she leaned forward and laughed again, slapping me as she did. Tightly. On my leg. It was in moments such as these that I found the greatest comfort. The greatest affection.

"Oh, stop it!" she giggled.

I loved her very much. She was a revelation to me. How many times had I looked adoringly at her over the year we'd come to know one another, and how many more had I thought to myself that she was a strong and attractive force in my life and that I was so lucky to have her by my side.

We sat a little longer and made some small talk. Laughed at other people. I finished my beer and left her at the table. As I walked away from her, I looked back. Edie had put on a pair of dark glasses and if I hadn't known that it was her, then I'd have struggled to pick her out in that crowd.

Her mannerisms seemed also to have moulded themselves to fit the new look with which she was flirting, and as I made my way down Las Ramblas to catch a bus to the studio, it suddenly struck me that perhaps one inadvertent consequence of this little adventure was that I had, in some way, started a process of hiding Edie from those that were possibly looking for us. Boaz and his people. Perhaps one positive thing to come from this was a disguise that, if she developed it now, could become a completely natural cover for her. She might actually be safer from them if she manged to bond over time with this new identity.

Perhaps I should consider doing a similar thing? There could be no harm in it. None. Could there?

It's sometimes quite bizarre how we place so much emphasis on how we look. A part of it is, I guess, born from a consequence of a world that has, in the West at least, evolved so much around the endorphin hit of instant gratification. It's true that we almost always judge others within moments of first meeting them. First impressions last. Isn't that what I have always heard said? How true it is, and how wrong at the same time.

With a telephone it is so much simpler. A voice can be almost anything. How many times have you ever had a conversation with someone on a phone and wondered what they look like? Why should it even matter? Curiosity I suppose. And then you might ask yourself, would you even be speaking to that person if you could see them? What if that guy you're talking to on the telephone has a tattoo across his face? Or what if he looks unkempt, unwashed. Would you be speaking to them if you were in their physical presence?

On a telephone, anyone at all can sound attractive. And they can make such good sense. This is an illustration, if one were needed, that we should not judge people by how they look. But we do. We do it all the time and it's not right. It's not healthy. It's not at all positive or progressive. Or intelligent.

I mean, I might talk to Edie on the phone, and she might be taking her wig on and off. She wouldn't be sounding any different as she did it. The modulation of her voice, or the words she was speaking, they wouldn't be changing each time the wig was replaced or removed. Surely this is an indication that the emphasis we place on the physical is a fiction. Simply a cover. Like this book. Like any book. Take away that cover and the words remain the same. I guess we'd do well not to pay attention to such kinds of deceptive coating.

Later that evening I was working the studio with a guest who was sitting in the vocal booth whilst being interviewed. It was a local issue, something to do with homelessness on the outskirts of Barcelona. I couldn't catch a lot of it because my Spanish wasn't expansive enough, but the anguish that the guy was articulating came across plainly, and this too gave colour to my thoughts about how we judge people by how they look.

We tend to dismiss people sleeping under a motorway flyover, for example, as being a race apart from the rest of us. Like some kind of sub-species. But they're not. Maybe this is something to do with access to cash. I think we all work to accrue cash, and so those who have chosen, or have been forced to, forgo that struggle are seen as losing out in some way. Alien to us. Or maybe we envy them. Either way, they do not adhere to the same norms as everyone around them. As a consequence, whole other parts of their lives may be enriched in ways the rest of us don't understand. Camaraderie perhaps. Survival capacity. Independence.

After the guest had left, around ten o'clock, I had just to break the studio down and set it up for a live show in the morning. A musician was coming in, and she'd want to play her guitar live on air. There was a little bit of work to do because I'd rather set things up the night before than on the morning of the broadcast. So, before I started that, I thought I'd give Edie a quick call back at the apartment.

Lifting the plastic receiver of the pay phone that we had in the corridor by the toilet, I fumbled for a few pesetas to make my call. I was keen to hear Edie's voice. Even still this could thrill me.

I held the phone while it rang and rang and rang. No answer. I became a little unnerved. Not a lot, but I did wonder why she wasn't picking up. I checked the clock in the studio. It was 22:02. I dialled again in case I'd misdialled the first time. Still no answer. Maybe she was in the toilet or something. Maybe she was getting ready to turn in.

I walked back into the studio and began to disconnect the mics and un-cable them from behind their pop shields. After maybe ten minutes I hadn't settled, and I was again wondering all manner of outlandish, illogical, dark things. I remembered the day in Portugal when she had disappeared and had come home drunk in the small hours. I still hadn't been told who she was with that time. This continued to eat at me, and I was feeling a little bit hollow. A little betrayed. I was making it all up.

I thought I'd try her again. But the same thing. No answer. The call just rang and rang. Where could she be? Why was she not answering? Don't forget, this was in the time before mobile phones became commonplace. If the landline didn't connect, and often it didn't, then there was no other way to communicate, not like now where so many people have got so many ways to contact one another, but most of whom have got so little to say.

I called Edie two more times and there was no answer to any of my calls. I became concerned. Again, not overly so, but still the thought began to crystallise that she might be in trouble. It was almost midnight when I got out of the studio and almost thirty minutes past by the time I reached our apartment, which was in a small back alley behind the entrance to an underground car park at the northern part of the Las Ramblas, almost diagonally across from the hamburger place, next to where we often met.

The entrance to our apartment was behind an off-white, paint-chipped door that sat alongside a bakery. Unlock the door and there was a steep flight of stairs in front of you. Our place was up that steep climb and that night it was very dark as I began my ascent. As always, the smell of fried garlic greeted me when I opened the door and peered up the stairs. It was a gift to us from the bakery next door. There was no light at the top. Often, if one of us was awake, a crack of light would spill out from under our door. But this night it was completely dark. No light.

Slowly I continued my climb. The stairs made sounds under my feet. I placed my weight on each foot before lifting the other to continue, trying to move as quietly as I could. Closing the door behind me had plunged me into a thick, sticky darkness and I could barely see the steps beneath me. I waited a few moments for my eyes to adjust and my sense of hearing grew sharper. Despite having spent an evening in a studio, my ears were still in good shape, and I was now picking up on every single creak and crackle that I thought I could hear. I started to spook myself that Edie was in trouble. I climbed more quickly and opened the door to the apartment noisily. Instead of being in trouble. I found she was in bed. Asleep. Seemingly carefree. The carefree expression of those who sleep well.

I sat in the kitchen with a beer. I told myself that this kind of nervousness would have to stop if I were to stay sane. That is, if she and I were to build a solid foundation for our relationship. I wondered if she ever inflicted this kind of anguish on herself. I doubted it. I thought that Edie was far too pragmatic. I often thought that I was perfectly level-headed and rational and then I reminded myself that I was basing my entire life at that time on chasing a dream across the continent. Literally, using my own head to navigate my next physical and emotional direction. No, there was nothing pragmatic about that. I figured that I'd do well to allow Edie to dictate some, maybe all, of the rules from then on.

It was about a week later that she and I went back to Calle dels Encants together to look for an army jacket. Sure enough, we found one right away. It was an Italian one, with a silver-blue star patch stitched on to the collar. I liked it a lot and, like all clothes seemed to, it fitted Edie well. She smiled and fell into her role right away, winking at me as she tilted her newly auburn head to look in my direction.

"I like it," she smiled widely, standing feet apart in a flood of sunlight. These were the days. The fantastic days.

Looking back now, I have no real explanation for acting in the way that I did. Maybe it was anxiety. Maybe I felt guilt at being so happy, that I didn't deserve it in some perverse kind of way.

Maybe it was that. I remember being a kid and walking into town with my mother. It was my birthday and she had given me some money to choose whatever gift I wanted. I chose a plastic car track. For my toy cars at home. It was a fabulous thing. Red, white, and blue.

But on the way up the hill, walking back to our house on the estate I had this inexplicable and quite bizarre, overpowering sense of shame and deep guilt. Only I, of course, didn't know those emotions then. I was too young. But I felt them all the same.

I had an overwhelming and very deep sense of self-loathing. I simply should not have such a fantastic birthday gift. I never did open the box and play with that track. Not once. I hated it and I hated myself for wanting it.

I've no proper explanation for the way I treated Edie around this time. No explanation beyond it being immaturity. That same kind of inability to recognise my emotions, and the same kind of inability to articulate how I was feeling. I didn't really know to handle my own self. I definitely didn't know how to handle the emotions of others around me. It was a halcyon time, and I was so free with all my commitments. If one thing didn't work out, another would surely come along.

At that age I had an inexhaustible supply of good times ahead. But didn't we all at that point in our lives, where every event is an opportunity? Especially in the early nineteen-nineties.

I was part of that rag-tag generation of kids, with no ties, trying to find their way through life. Trying to find a way that was considerate of others, especially the wider community, but less so of my immediate peers. They could all look after themselves. I was profoundly concerned, often troubled, by political injustice and human atrocity. Globally. Nothing less than the entire planet was enough for me to occupy myself with.

Actual people I knew seemed far less important. Far more trivial. Again, that was most probably because almost all the people that I knew were comfortable and could bask in the luxury of choice.

If I'd known then that true love would only really appear once in my entire life, would I have been so profligate with it when it actually came along? And, in fact, would I even notice? How many people don't know when that solitary moment arrives? They think it is the real thing. Or, worse, they think it isn't, and so, they forsake the one who could really make them happy, the one who would evolve to be their long-standing soul mate on this journey we all take through our lives.

That person may have come and gone in a single conversation in a bar in some back street of my youth. Of your youth. Of her youth. Of his youth. I may have been on a bus riding past them as they stood outside a shop waiting for a friend. We may never have even met.

I tried to articulate these thoughts by developing a story about a guy who had recently passed his driving test and was out and about exploring southeast London. He took his car through the Danson Interchange, and on to Kidbrooke, where immediately before that there is a row of houses by the side of a very busy, three-lane A road. This guy was alone. Quite free, no ties. Some interests, but nothing substantial. At that moment he was exploring his newfound freedom, embodied by the car that surrounded him.

And so, as he drives past the row of houses, he sees from the road, one where a party is taking place, and the light in the front of the house grabs his attention. He drives right past. He's doing fifty miles per hour and it's a flash in his eye. He sees this light for just one second, but he has an overwhelming feeling that he should be in that house. The feeling passes within a moment, but the sense that he should stop his car, turn back, and go and find the party is extraordinary and very profound.

But he doesn't, of course. Who would? Instead, he carries on. He slows at the next set of traffic lights as they blink from red, to green and on he travels. Lights in his favour. No need to stop.

Now consider the same scene from a different perspective.

There is a girl who is at a party in a house by a busy road that leads from the Danson Interchange to Kidbrooke, and she has stepped outside for a cigarette and some air. The light in the window is strong and the condensation on the inside of the window is making it opaque and act like a diffuser. As she is looking at the window, she is reflecting on how alone she feels.

She is feeling that the people at the party are not her people and that she would rather be out exploring the wider world. She takes a drag of her cigarette and looks across the busy road as a blue car flashes by. She looks at the car then, and although she doesn't know why, she suddenly feels a strong yearning to be in it. She thinks it looks like a warm space. A nice space. Moving forwards. Not staying still.

Not stagnating at a stationary party in a house she doesn't know, filled with people she doesn't too much care for.

Her friend then calls her from inside the house and she turns and throws the cigarette down and crushes it beneath her shoe.

That's it. That's their chance. Gone in a flash.

Neither of them ever meets the love of their life. Each had that person pass in an instant and they both grow, meet other people. Have kids. Build families. But never do they ever feel that their true chance had ever been fully realised.

Is that how it is? Is that how it works, do you think?

The intransigence of belonging. That's what this short tale could have been called. Maybe I will write it one day. If I do, that's what I'll call it.

Beautiful. Light and alive. There's an energy in the 'not knowing', in the uncertainty of what may have been. The impossibility of it all. Turn left and you fall in love. Turn right and you don't. Not today.

This, I figured, was why I was chasing my dream. I knew that therein I had found the love of my life. But how can that be? Was I actually in love with myself? Is that what it was? Was the image of the girl just a female interpretation of me? The thought repelled me, disgusted me almost. Maybe that's why I tried to avoid facing it when I was conscious. When I was awake. Wilfully facing it, that is.

And like I said at the beginning of this entire story, would it be right to change the circumstances to fit the location in my dream? And wasn't that exactly what I was now trying to do with Edie. Sure, for now she was happy. We both were. But I knew that it was a dangerous game that I had started.

The box was open, and I wouldn't be able to force the curse of my private Pandora back in again.

I had begun the process of changing the circumstances to match my dream. Something I swore I'd never do. To falsely fabricate a series of events. If I asked Edie to stand on a platform, to wait with a blue bag or something, to pretend to see me for the first time, then it would be a fallacy. I would be truly insane. Legitimately so. I would be play-acting on a grand scale. No. It had to be spontaneous and with Edie it couldn't be.

Why? Because I had already met her!

If I knew one thing, I knew that the girl of my dreams couldn't be Edie. Of course not. We'd already started that journey of togetherness. Outside of the parameters of my imagined ideal. My actual ideal?

And because of this, it meant that she and I couldn't have a future. It wasn't possible, not if I was going to stay true to my own self. All of this would mean that she and I should be apart from now on. I would have to manipulate a situation where she hated me and would want to leave me. Because I was a coward. I wouldn't be able to make that call myself. I would have to make her make that decision.

And so, this is how I set about trying to make the woman I was in love with come to despise me. This is a bloody-mindedness that today I find almost impossible to confess. Forgive me, Edie.

Where did you go? What did I do to you?

What did we do to each other?

FIVE

One evening Edie and I were sitting in high-up chairs against a high-up counter in a tapas bar in town, our backs rigidly straight. Everything around us was calm, and we sat wordlessly staring out at a small, high-walled square in the Barri Gotic district. The stillness of this place was tranquil. It was everything I liked, hypnotic and serene. Bucolic, almost.

I filled my lungs with the stench of over-watered bougainvillaea blossoms that lay rotting in the baskets hanging from apartment windows all along the length of the cobbled passageways. Around me, the reality seemed a little unstable. Just a little unstable, as if it were gently tremoring. Like a pan of water one degree below the boil.

Across the square, two men dressed in brightly coloured clothes stood looking at a wall adjacent to the Església del Pi. I realised later that they must have been looking at some of the last bullet holes that remained in Barcelona, the surviving vestige of a civil war that had torn the city apart some sixty years before.

Barcelona gutters running red with the blood of the Republic – the red of the Catalonian flag. The intensity of the bombing by Fascist aircraft serving as a model for greater atrocities to befall

Europe in the ten years after Guernica.

The intensity of the bombing, sponsored by Mussolini and by Hitler, was an obvious blueprint for worse to come. A dress rehearsal. Pockmarked Barcelona. Pockmarks that Franco couldn't plaster over with his rhetoric. Pockmarks that in the modern age lay only two walkways from the Palau de la Generalitiat and the Ajuntament, home of the restored Catalan Government. Pockmarks themselves scarred by irony. Scarred by melancholy. Scarred by bitterness and by memory.

And as we sat pondering our lives in the square, I thought of a young Picasso who I know had rented some studio space overlooking this place. I sat then looking through his eyes, gazing down on the shadows that were forged from this sharp and pointy Mediterranean light. Picasso's eyes looking down at me now. Painting me. Painting the girl chasing pigeons. Painting the couple embracing. Painting the image of Edie and of me and my musings of the struggle for Catalunya.

And there he was painting Boaz, and Timo, and Franck and Joep.

Painting us all.

An image returned to me of Boaz. He was always going to be a part of my world after what had happened, there would be no escaping him and because of that I was constantly looking for him, always subconsciously. I was always expecting him to appear at any time. Anywhere. Anywhere I happened to be. Boaz was beginning to haunt me almost as much as the girl of whom I dreamed every night. All the time. And again, last night and again tonight, and now, in my waking hours, dreams of trains and rivers. Churches and ...

All of the cocaine that we had been consuming came flooding in and destroyed my balance. I wanted more and I wasn't prepared to wait because I wanted, wanted, wanted! It was a terrible drug. It appealed so directly to my ego that I found it difficult to resist. It was an expressway. Direct. Penetrating. My craving for it would always override my logic. To an alarming and debilitating degree.

For instance, I could imagine that I had ingested a half gram and then begin to grind my teeth and snort unpleasantly, but all the while I'd be throwing my own private, internal tantrum. I would complain to myself that I wasn't high and that it was only a pretence. A fakery. That life wasn't fair! And all the time I was aware of just how childish the concept was.

Over time I gradually learned to control it enough to breathe more easily and to rest at least a little bit. I learned to be kinder to myself. I learned to control it. But at the same time, I never wanted to let it go completely. Just less often would please me. Again, conscience taught me that.

So I drank a lot of vodka. It was the closest, legal, approximation that I could find. Almost a placebo. But never a replacement.

In Spain, the coke we scored was of a much better quality than anything we'd had in Amsterdam. It was less crystalline and softer, spongier than Boaz' wraps. I could cut it and it would multiply under the blade, puffing up into fatter lines that grew longer and longer the more I went on. It was less bitter and took away sensations in the back of my throat and across the bridge of my nose more intensely. In fact, it often felt as if my neck had been taken away, as if it did not exist and my head was simply suspended in air above my shoulders.

My heart would beat frighteningly faster, and more

immediately whenever I took it, which was often. It was cheaper too. A gram in Holland was costing me anywhere from a hundred to a hundred and fifty guilders – that's about thirty to fifty pounds sterling. In Spain I would pay about five thousand pesetas, roughly twenty-five pounds. and for a better cut too.

The counter at which Edie and I sat that evening was a wine-deep, dark mahogany colour. Well, a mahogany veneer. Tubular-framed.

Across from us a second counter was teeming with all kinds of tapas, and small glasses of sherry were dotted about here and there. There was no background music, just a soft wall of cushioned voices. Of conversation. All of it conducted in Spanish, languidly rapid, intense, and opaque, like so many words carved from ivory, or mother-of-pearl. In a few corners, people sat alone with glasses of wine and maybe a book. I thought that in London you'd rarely ever see that. It did happen of course, but not at all often. I mean, yes, I used to read alone in pubs, but it wasn't something that was commonplace.

Edie and I were chatting about something or other when I became aware of a guy standing to my right, trying to get my attention. I turned to him, and he politely asked if he could use my cigarette lighter as he'd left his in his apartment. I would have probably shrugged, and said something like "Sure," or "Yeah," and so he took the lighter from the counter in front of me and helped himself.

"You're English," he said as he placed it back again.

I nodded but said nothing.

"Thanks for the light," he said and turned to his friend who was exiting the toilet. The two of them left the bar and walked out into the darkening evening, an evening that held the light from the stars in suspension as the daylight slowly dissolved around us.

I turned back to Edie then, and we continued our conversation. We had barely even registered this guy's existence, although we had noticed that he looked like he might be Eastern Mediterranean, and that his friend was a black guy, maybe west-coast African. Ghanaian. Nigerian. Somewhere like that.

We continued to talk, looking intently at one another, and then out at the courtyard. We did that a lot back then. I remember waking one morning to find her propped up on her elbow, just looking at me. Simply looking at me. I turned to face her, and she moved my head back to where it had been pointed towards the ceiling above us.

"Stay there," she had said. "I love your profile. Your lips are shaped like love."

We saw these two guys again about an hour later. Edie and I must have walked the same route as them because we went to a different bar, this time on the Calle des Pau Claris, or rather, a small alley just off it. We found a pretty lively little place and I had to push my way to the bar. I left Edie by the door and forced my way through. When I got there, this guy and his friend moved aside for me to call for our drinks. He welcomed me right away. I turned and was oddly pleased to see him.

"Hey!" he exclaimed. "English guy. You let me use your lighter." He smiled.

"Hey, no problem," I said, shaking his hand. I told him my name. My real name. It was the first time I'd used it in many weeks, probably in many months, at least that is, in a social situation.

Subconsciously I must have been coming to an understanding

that perhaps Edie and I could now allow ourselves to start thinking of our lives as having been then in a post-Amsterdam phase. I must have been preparing myself for the reality that she and I were now able to think about putting time and distance between ourselves and 'the event'.

"Yannis," he said. "And this is Marco."

He glanced to his friend who raised his glass and nodded his head. Marco had a solid smile planted on his face, his lips tight and almost grimacing. He was smiling and I understood this to be assertiveness. Purposefulness. I respect that in a person.

Placing my hand lightly on Yannis' forearm, I turned to the girl who was now waiting to take my order from behind the bar. I called up for two beers and turned back to Yannis. I had to speak loudly so I moved in close to him.

"Nice to meet you," I said loudly into his ear. "Where are you from?"

"Greece," was his reply. "Yannis Kyriou. It's about as Greek as you can get, huh!" he laughed.

"I guess," I said. And then, "Are you living here? Or just on holiday?"

"A bit of both. Marco lives here," and he faced his friend who couldn't hear us, but who knew he was being included. "And I'm here visiting him to see if maybe I want to hang around for a while. I must admit, I have been here for three weeks now and I'm not so sure I'll be leaving any time soon."

I smiled, "Yes, it's nice here," I said. "I like it too," and I took the beer from the girl behind the counter.

I handed her my money and shook my head at her as she went to give me small change from the notes. She thanked me silently.

Holding the beers at shoulder height, I manoeuvred my way past Yannis, but not before saying to him, "Come and join us. We're just outside."

I got to Edie and handed her the small beer.

"That guy is in there. The one who borrowed the lighter just now. He's coming over."

She seemed fine as she took her beer from me. We were standing out in the street now. I lit a cigarette. It was a lovely, warm night in Barcelona and the streets were humming with like-minded people, all enjoying the evening, just drinking lightly, and chatting. I recall a lot of laughter. It was all around us. We felt among friends. There was no sense of arrogance, or of people trying to show off, and the ambience around us at this time of day was dry and welcoming. It all added to the friendly atmosphere that Barcelona can generate so subtly and so distinctly at the same time.

I can still picture Yannis and Marco as they came and stood with Edie and me. Without hesitation I said, "This is Edie," and I felt her bristle beside me.

It was one thing that I'd given them my name. We didn't know who these people were, but it was quite another that I'd now given them Edie's without first checking with her. This was wrong of me. I was doing this all the time. Forgetting myself. I was hoping I wouldn't come to regret it.

"Hi," she said, shaking their hands without dropping a beat. "Nice to meet you."

"Holland?" said Yannis, guessing at her homeland.

Edie barely nodded, sipping her beer, and looking darkly at me over the top of the glass. She said nothing.

"I thought so," said Yannis. "I can tell accents well."

Giving out innocent information to strangers was not something Edie was keen on doing and she was still protecting us in spite of the fact that it had been nearly a year since we had done what we had done. We thought that a year was long enough for it all to melt away. But we were wrong.

This concept, this misunderstanding of time is, in hindsight, another one of those unusual misinterpretations brought about by youth. Like looking at time through some kind of plastic prism, it warps and seems to pass, often in a non-linear way. Time tends not to run like a straight road. We've all known this phenomenon at some point or other. How often do we consider that something has passed very quickly? Or that time has moved very slowly? If time were truly linear, we'd never feel that would we?

"And you?" asked Edie, keen now to take the attention away from her before she innocently gave away too much.

"Greece," I said smiling at him and Marco. "I know all about Yannis already, he's from Greece."

We all four chuckled, and it was a nice exchange. It meant nothing. I started in on my fifth beer of the evening. It was a weekend, I think. Maybe a Friday. Neither of us were busy the following day and we ended up back at Yannis and Marco's place around two o'clock in the morning, listening to electronic music and smoking a string of endless joints. It was harmless stuff and we had made two friends that night, so we arranged to meet them again the following weekend in the same place.

A few nights later we were out again, in the same area. Only this time Edie was wearing the wig and jacket. She was my Edie, but not my Edie in these moments. I was enraptured by the role play. It was fun, but more than that I was aroused by her willingness to adapt to it so easily. To accommodate this peculiarity. I think we both were aroused by it, to be honest. This electric frisson, like a spark that creates life, was bringing something new to our relationship and we were both enjoying the exploration of this.

As we sat in a bar neighbouring the one where we met Yannis and Marco, I half expected to see them again. That would be funny, I thought. Would they recognise Edie right away? Would I then appear dishonest to them? Would I have to reveal that no, this really was Edie, and if that happened, what on earth would they think of us then? It might come across as odd to say the least.

She and I spoke about this. We thought it was funny. And we would have laughed at it. In some respect I think she was quietly hoping for something like that to happen. I'm pretty sure I was too. It could lead us anywhere. But it didn't.

Instead, we spent some quiet time nursing a couple of beers before we meandered our way back down towards La Rambla and then west of there to our apartment with its entrance behind the car park. The evening streets were bathed in a sodium light as we went, and the top of La Rambla was crammed with newsstands selling cigarettes and magazines and with Flower Stalls offering lilies and roses and gardenias of all colours and sizes.

Behind us the cars sounded their horns as people ran across the crossings when the lights were green. The whole soundscape was occasionally punctuated by the shrill beeping of the same crossings as they indicated that now was a good time to cross. The roads were wide, and I remember in some cases barely having enough time to get to the other side before the beeping stopped and you were deposited in a no man's land between two pavements.

I can remember one of the crossings at Placa de Catalunya, and I can remember how wide it was. You had to run to make the other side before the lights changed. Edie and I did this often. We made a bit of a game of it by counting to five before we even set foot upon the road. We'd always arrive just in time, falling over ourselves as we bounced up on the kerb at the other side. I can see her now grabbing at her wig which had started to slip as we laughed and fell into one another before taking the final few minutes' walk, arm in arm, to our apartment. We were very much in love then. Or so I thought.

Around us, shop front lighting was illuminating the air and seemed to be pulsing orange and yellow neon into our bodies. Could the light be so bright that it was penetrating our thoughts? Was it illuminating our ideas and our feelings? Was it throwing light over our senses? It certainly felt that way. It reminded me very much of Amsterdam, especially in some of the more, down-at-heel parts of the city. Something, we said to one another, must be combining to make us feel this good. To make us feel so alive. Everything then for us was an adventure.

We met with Yannis and Marco again the following week, and our evening took pretty much the same trajectory as the one before. We had a little food, and we went back to the lively bar and then on to their place for smokes. Marco pulled out a wrap of coke and offered a line to each of us.

At around one o'clock in the morning there was an urgent knock on the door. It opened and a thin little dealer came crashing into Yannis and Marco's apartment, along with two heavies that he had in tow. He was a nasty looking guy, all gristle and sweat and sinew, and he sniffed and giggled his way through the visit. His pockmarked face was covered in red blotches, and I found myself thinking of the wall in the square in the Barri Gotic where the soldiers executed their prisoners. He looked immediately at Edie. I knew she could handle him.

"Hello," he said to her, raising the intonation of his voice a little towards the end of the word. "I'm Iker," he said and then laughed without reason.

Edie simply looked at him. She didn't do anything more. I understood that he was wasted. Edie understood it too. I doubt that Iker even knew where he was when he turned to Yannis and took two small wraps from his pocket.

"Ten thousand," Iker said to him. "It's good shit, isn't it?"

Yannis nodded and gave him the money he had already prepared. He instantly began to usher him out of the place.

I found myself shuddering after he had left the apartment. A cool dampness somehow hung in the air where he had stood. That someone like Iker could ever have had a former life was hard to imagine. For him to have ever been a child seemed impossible somehow. To have run along the beach and played with a kite, to have hugged his parents and been fiercely proud of his big brother was completely incongruous with the person that I met there that evening. Where was he from? What was his story, I wondered? He was deathly pale. His eyes like translucent, watery pools. Stagnant. Infected with bugs. Buzzing with flies.

We spoke about him on our walk back to the apartment about an hour or two later. It was cold and it was early in the morning. There were a surprising number of people milling around, most of whom were seemingly pretty drunk. We had to be a bit wary of who was near to us.

After Iker, we spoke about our new friends Marco and Yannis.

"That Yannis is a very handsome man," Edie said to me. "I don't want to lose touch with those guys. I like them."

"Do you think he's handsome?" I said feigning surprise. "Really? I suppose he is. He's Mediterranean isn't he. You can't really go wrong with that."

Again, a few days later, she said coyly, "Shall we see if we can track down Yannis this evening?"

I had no problem with this. I liked them too and yes it was nice to have other company. Edie and I worked well in the company of others.

We went out to meet them. They weren't difficult to track down. We simply found them back at the tapas bar in which we had first met. 'Barro Cañete', I think it was called.

Yannis waved when he saw us. He was genuinely delighted to see us and beckoned us to their table. A third person was there, a girl who was introduced to us as Elena. She sat with her hands folded, palms up, in her lap. She was wearing a leather, short, bolero cut jacket with brown tassels like the one Maartje wore in Amsterdam and back in a world which seemed so very long ago now. And so very far away.

I thought she was attractive, and I made a mental note to tell Edie a little later in the evening. Elena waited for conversation to drop into her lap before she spoke. She and Edie got along right away. I think maybe she reminded Edie of Maartje. They had, after all, been friends back then.

She and Elena began chatting within moments of being

introduced to one another. Yannis and I walked to the counter to look at the tapas.

"David," he said, "Can I ask you something?"

"Of course you can," I replied. "What's up?"

And he started to tell me about his brother back in Greece, who was at a university there. In Athens, I think. Yannis was concerned that the brother was not focussing on his work and was about to drop out. None of this meant a thing to me. I don't know what I was supposed to advise him. What was I supposed to say?

But the point of the matter was that Yannis was considering me as someone whose opinion might count for something. In short, he was becoming a friend and in truth, I did like him a lot. I had warmed to him, and to Marco for that matter. As had Edie. I looked back at her and saw how she was now deep in conversation with this Elena girl.

It really did look to me like they had known one another for far more than just five minutes. I distinctly remember thinking that at the time.

*

A few days later, Yannis asked me to go with him to his dealer. He'd run low on hash and needed to top up. I wasn't busy at that time so said I would.

We walked to a bar that was about ten minutes from El Monument A Colom along the Avigunda del Parallel. This was close to the junction with the Marques de Campo Sagrado and was in a pretty anonymous looking part of town hidden below a pile of flats and apartments which were festooned with bulbous black iron-railed balconies. Many of them had iron hoardings across the windows. I forget the name of the bar now. It was something like 'Pazzaz'.

Yannis went off to one of the flats in the block, and I waited for him in the bar. It felt safer in there. I reminded myself of the gang outside the food shop in Erkrath when Edie and I left there last year.

The barman bent to pick up a polythene bag full of ice. He emptied it into the bucket that he'd been cleaning. He looked at me quickly out of the corner of his eye.

"How is it? Good?" he asked me haltingly. "You are English, yes?"

"Yep," I replied and gestured towards the glass as I drained it completely. It was easy to drink in such a hot place. It always is. He poured me another. We tried a couple more times to talk about something, but we both gave up quite quickly. I had a feeling Yannis wouldn't be too long, and I was right. I could see him crossing towards me and gesturing to leave, just as I was ordering another beer.

The barman – I now knew his name was Luis – opened me another bottle and gave me a fresh glass.

"It's okay," I said. "I'm going to walk with this one. I'll see you later."

"Okay," he said cheerfully. And then, "Two Fifty." I gave him a couple two-hundred coins. "Gracias," he said as I slipped off my stool and left the bar.

Just a few days later we were all back in our now familiar bar near La Rambla, sitting at the same table. All of us except Marco, who was late to arrive. Edie and Elena fell into step and began chatting like before. The speed at which they had bonded was remarkable.

I spoke to Yannis.

"How's your brother?" I can remember asking him. But he seemed distracted. He was looking out of the window to the street outside. Fidgeting. He was not his usual self, and something seemed off with him.

"He's okay, I think." And then he added, "where's Marco?"

As if I knew.

I tried again to engage him in conversation. But it wasn't amounting to anything. Yannis seemed preoccupied and I naturally assumed that it was to do with the absent Marco, or maybe he was a little wired that evening, I don't know. I ordered a couple of dishes of small chorizo sausages, some Padron peppers and some Cucaracha del Diablo, dates wrapped in bacon.

How can I remember that so accurately? Easy. If you've eaten that stuff, it can often be pretty memorable. We drank beers and we ate well, and the conversation began to flow. It was a Friday evening, and the street was filling up. So too was the bar. Yannis stood and said he was going to find Marco and that he'd be back shortly. He placed some money on the table, for the food, and swinging his jacket across his shoulder, he left us sitting there.

For a few moments, I sat waiting for Edie and Elena to involve me in their conversation, but when that didn't happen I was happy to lean back in my chair and light a cigarette. I was more than content with watching the world pass me by and I smiled as I glanced over the crowd outside and surveyed the stalls in the road.

The people buzzing about them. Picking up leather bracelets and brooches made from seashells. Putting them back again when the vendor told them the price. The warm evening air drifted into the bar and carried with it the scent of the perfumes and patchouli oils that were being sold from the stalls directly outside.

I watched a mass of people gathering, framed by the window behind Edie and Elena who were silhouetted by the light from the shops beyond. I closed my eyes and smiled. I opened them again and it seemed that even more people had arrived. Outside it was getting to be very busy indeed and I was surprised at the difference the warmer evening and the undoubted influx of tourists was making to the city that we had newly discovered. Edie looked beautiful to me then. More beautiful than I'd ever come to realise.

Her hair was backlit from the streetlamps outside and a vibrantly illuminated pale corona framed her stentorian face. Beauty was not a word one might readily associate with her when first seeing her. But it was there. Make no mistake. I looked at her chin as she chatted enthusiastically to Elena, who turned and looked at me and then looked back at Edie, who was barely registering my presence.

And then I saw him. At the window.

It was Franck.

I sat straight up. My skin bristled. My hair rose. It was him.

I'm sure it was him. A coldness crept across my shoulders and up my neck and just as quickly, he ducked out of the way. For a few moments, I said nothing. I did nothing. A vacuum waited to be filled.

I leaned forward and grabbed Edie by the arm. Without thinking I stood her up and led her to the toilet at the back of the bar. She looked at me. Confused, but knowing.

"Franck," I said, his name catching in my throat.

Her expression drained. Her face white.

"What? Where?" she cried and then, immediately, "Oh, no! Shit. No, no, no! Just when I thought we were getting this fucking shit together ..."

And she started to shake. I sat her down.

I was shaking too.

Elena was watching us. She didn't seem confused. Or even concerned. She lit a cigarette.

Edie began to cry. "Oh, fuck. What have we done? This is awful?"

She held herself together and looked nervously at the window.

"What have we done?" she asked again of no-one in particular.

But it was, of course, far too late to be thinking that way. Maybe it wasn't him, I instantly thought, and I said that out loud. By accident.

"Maybe it wasn't him."

Edie looked at me. "Please don't play fucking games with me, David." she pleaded. "Don't fuck with me! Was it him or wasn't it?!"

But the truth was that I couldn't be one hundred percent sure. It absolutely definitely looked like him. He was looking in the window with purpose. Whoever it was, was peering through the glass in a way that you might expect from someone who was deliberately looking for someone else.

We stayed in the back of the bar a short while longer, but

Elena seemed to be waiting for an explanation, which of course we couldn't give her. Quite soon Marco arrived, and then Yannis right behind him. Edie and I left at that point, dropping some money on the table for the beer and food.

"Sorry guys," I said. "We have to go. Let's catch up next week."

The walk back was a nervous one for Edie and me. We took all the little alleys and back routes on our way and, of course, we spoke of nothing else.

"How the hell could they have found us here?" she asked me.

And I was thinking the same thing precisely.

"It doesn't make sense," I said. "It can't have been Franck. How would any of them know we are here? It can't have been him. Just a horrible co-incidence."

I was wracking my brain trying to put a link in place, but there wasn't one. When we left Oporto, we'd bought a ticket at the station first to Madrid, then from there to Bilbao, and only then east to Barca. We didn't take any direct route. We took slow trains that called at several stations. I figured this might indicate that we were not going directly to the main cities in each instance.

And then another thing occurred to me. Maybe the Franck that was following us, if indeed he was, was not the Franck that Boaz kept on a lead. Maybe the guy we saw in Timo's place, the guy who *looked like* Franck, was the one we thought we had seen both here and in Oporto. Perhaps it was Timo who was on our case? Not Boaz at all. After all, who owned the debt that we had created. Who had been hit the hardest? We didn't know for sure that Timo had received money from Boaz. Perhaps we were looking in the wrong direction? I said this to Edie, and she agreed that it was possible. But also that it didn't really matter to us one way or the other. We definitely had burned bridges in both camps. We couldn't ever cross either of these guys. It didn't make things safer in either direction.

Not that I even thought that anyone was actually following us anyway. I simply couldn't be sure. I didn't really think that Edie had seen Franck, *either* Franck, in Oporto that day at the shoe shop. So, I honestly did not believe we were being followed. Even then, at that time in Barcelona, I had automatically started to tell myself that I was mistaken. It couldn't have been Franck. Tracing us there from Oporto was not possible. If it was him, then he's really poor at his job. I mean, he lost Edie in Oporto, and now he had lost both of us here in Barcelona. He wouldn't be telling Boaz, or Dieter about that would he! So, no harm done. That was the way I chose to view it all.

When I said all of this to Edie, she seemed to calm down a little. Quite soon we reached our apartment, and I made sure we walked right past until I was confident that we were not being followed. Three times we circled that block until finally I was convinced that we were clear to climb the stairs behind the door.

Inside, we sat and waited for the adrenaline to subside. No drugs for us that night. Only when we were calm, did we speak.

"Okay." I said as plainly as I could, and with as little excitement in my voice as possible. "What do we do?"

I think the answer was, nothing. I think we both recognised that we couldn't continue running, not for ever. Our nerves would be shredded in no time at all, even worse than they already were.

We both liked our life in Barcelona. We were both very happy in that place and we both figured that we perhaps ought to accept what was coming, if ever it arrived. We didn't want to live on our toes like this. To my surprise it was Edie who was the more emphatic about this. She, for certain, did not want to run again. Maybe one day. If absolutely necessary. But not yet. Not so soon.

She surprised me by telling me, rather knowingly, as she looked me directly in my eye, that there was, "no way they were after us!"

She seemed very, very certain about this. She told me several times that I had only imagined that it was Franck.

Finally, she told me unequivocally that it was, "one hundred percent not possible that we were being hunted still."

Her certainty about this is something I should have picked up on. But I didn't. I was only too happy for her to convince me and to put my mind at rest.

It was like she knew something that I didn't know.

Or, more likely, something that I didn't want to know.

SIX

Before you even touch the ground, you are breathing the odour of damp moss, trying to get some sleep. On your knees. You have fallen to the ground, and you are struggling to climb to your feet. Every slug that stuns you, defeats you and forces you back down onto the floor. Again you try to stand, and you find, to your great surprise that it doesn't hurt anymore. It's happened too many times for it to hurt. But instead it frustrates you because all you want to do now is to stand up.

Okay, so you'll accept it. You've been beaten. Your attacker has won and so you tell him that, simply because you only want to stand up now. After so long on your knees you want to stand up.

He agrees and says: "Okay you can stand now."

But as you clamber up, he hits you again.

And then again.

And so it goes until you can no longer even tell him he's won.

The next thing you know, you're lying on your back under a motorway flyover trying to keep warm.

*

Edie and I always made sure that the light was on when we had sex. It gave us a sense of freedom. I understood light to be a liberator. She did too and we spoke about this. We agreed that light can be a redeemer of many different situations. Throwing light on something, either as a metaphor or as a physical act, tends to add clarity. It tends to illuminate new facets, other angles. It can alter perspective and meaning, both physical and psychological. We understood also that not all the facets that she and I were discovering at that time were wholesome or healthy, or even kind.

We understood that we were at the top of a slide. Playing, and fooling around. Risking things.

Sure, sex was important, of course it was important, but it was not the main motivational force that propelled our lives along the tracks that we were still in the process of laying down. It did happen sometimes that the depth of emphasis we placed on sex could easily evaporate without any given warning, and again, although it was seldom that this happened, once one of us had initiated it, we each were bound by the mutual understanding that we would enjoy ourselves on an equal basis.

So let's focus now on the by-product of the by-product, namely, that is, the physical facets that we had uncovered, metaphorically, by turning on the light.

Well, of course there's the wig.

Hard to ignore.

Did we blend this into our sex lives? Actually we didn't, much to my surprise. I'll admit now that the idea of it had been a significant reason behind my motivation to ask Edie to play that role. I won't deny it. I can't. Sure, it generated an element of the forbidden, a small flirtation with a superficial danger.

However, I just couldn't bring myself to generate enough confidence to ever broach the subject with Edie. I think if I had, she would have complied. Whether she would do it willingly or not, I couldn't guess now, but she was a very encompassing girl, always keen to please. And to please not just me, but most predominantly to please herself. Like all of us. Perhaps this made her ironically selfish. If it did, it's not something that was a problem between us. Our relationship never suffered for anything like that.

I had noticed though that we were starting to be less subtle with one another. I took this to be a strength, although I think that Edie probably took it to be a fault. I thought that our newfound ability to criticise one another was a sign that we were maturing.

But I took it too far. As I'm about to confess.

What could often start as a gentle attempt to push this boundary a little further, and then a little further still, could so easily become a full-blown argument within moments and, dangerously, this was starting to happen more and more often.

I'm sure that the pressure of living like fugitives was becoming a major part of our problem. That, and our frightening capacity for alcohol and for drugs, which was becoming hard to satisfy.

It is true, I was far worse than her, there's no doubt about that. But we were both taking so many substances then that our lives were very definitely beginning to lose their framework. The exoskeleton of 'us' was in an aggressive state of decay.

We were not in control of the degrees of our consumption.

One evening, at a bar in town, we sat deep inside, towards the back protected by a small wooden cubicle. We leant across the knee-high table that sat between us as each of us looked intently at the other.

In Edie's pocket she had a couple of grams. She looked into my eyes and said, "Come on. Let's pick ourselves up a bit, eh?"

I laughed into my lap, my grin sliding down the front of my checked shirt, orange, turquoise and red.

I thought briefly about Franz Kafka and his burrow and about where I might sit if he allowed me in. Somewhere near the entrance? I doubted it. Near the exit? Well, where was the exit? How was I supposed to get out?

I looked blearily at the pictures that adorned the walls around us. Some photographs of Barcelona a hundred years before, more, or less. A picture of the inside of El Quatro Gats, an infamous drinking den and haunt of the city's bohemian community between the wars. We ate there once. It was not expensive. It was okay, but not as great as I imagined it ought to have been, and it had looked at that time similar to how it did in the little sepia daguerreotype at which I was staring.

"Some of the first photographs ever taken," a toothless old gentleman leant across and said to Edie in English.

His shirt was fastened tightly around his neck. He wore no tie, and the top button of his shirt was pressed into his throat. It seemed to me that this was restricting his speech. His voice was gruff. Serrated and old.

"Really?" was my reply, "is that so?"

I said it with more than a hint of sarcasm in my voice, something I unfortunately found easy to do. I cut him short. I don't know why. I even probably offended him a little. But I didn't care because I was so pre-occupied with more immediate events.

Edie had already left her seat and was headed toward the toilets yet again. She called a double vodka at me and so I stood and walked to the bar, looking all the while around and out on to the Carrer D'Arago.

I tried to catch the barman's attention. He missed me two times over and I became irritated. To pass the time I looked at another selection of black and white photographs stuck on to mirrors behind the bar and in the mirrors, I caught the reflection of myself. Then to my side, appeared Edie.

"Got my drink yet?" she asked. "That old boy's getting on my fucking nerves."

Edie was becoming coarse these days. It wasn't nice. I didn't like it so much.

"I'm working on it," I said. And then, "Feel better now?"

She rolled her shoulders away from me and through her smile, filled with glitter she said, "Yeah. You bet!"

She ambled back to her seat and started talking to the old man who was still intent on telling her his stories about the old photographs, only now Edie was smiling. She wasn't even listening to him, that was my guess. I knew she was smiling purely because she felt naughty and happy.

Alive, basically.

Bodies pushed me from left to right and I had to jostle to be seen. A woman to my left blew smoke across my line of vision and it made me smart a little. I felt quite alone standing there at the bar, all the while continuing to look out on to the Carrer D'Arago.

And then she blew smoke again. I smiled at her and leaned into the barman as he plucked cubes of ice from his bucket. He threw them into tumblers to which he was about to add some whisky. Behind me I could hear Edie laugh at the old man's comments and I instinctively looked towards her, and she caught my eye.

She left him and walked back to me. Clearly restless.

"Let me get them then. What do you want?" she said and slipped the wrap into my pocket, patting my backside as she did so.

"Whisky and orange, I think. A triple one. A *huge* one." And she nodded.

"Jesus!" I added as I walked back to our table. I'm still not sure why.

The old man seemed less inclined to talk to me when I sat down again, and sure enough, within moments he had moved to a different part of the bar. Edie returned with our drinks in no time, and I laughed saying something along the lines of 'women will always be noticed before men'.

I stood to go to the toilet and cut myself a line.

Like a kind of gothic romance, I viewed cocaine as having seen me through some difficult times. Times that I choose now not to recount, in case even the sensibilities of my closest friends might be offended. Times as anonymous as the birth of Christ. Times as anonymous as the end of a war, if ever it would come. Times as vacuous as an empty conversation. Times as resonant as a man at his typewriter so cold in the night. Times.

Then as I crouched over the cistern, chopping and slicing, I thought of Edie. The path that I had trodden seemed so relentlessly futile when I pictured her in my mind's eye.

A realisation then dawned.

And a commitment was born.

There is so much more to life than a perpetual need to escape, I thought to myself. *There is so much more to life than this relentless chain of empty genuflections. The falsehood of praying before this shadowy deity.* I looked at the coke. *There is so much more to life than the piling high of these poisonous tropes. These tarnished moments of debauchery. Nothing good is going to come of this.*

Sure enough, nothing ever did.

I looked again at the line before me, and I weighed it up in my mind as it wriggled like a thick white caterpillar, or like a mescal worm.

If things were equally balanced in my mind, I could be okay, I thought. *Just the right amount of cynicism would be a good place to start. This Conscience thing could work quite well.*

"Don't forget you made that discovery," I told myself out loud.

"Discovery!" I mocked myself then, and then in my mind again. *If my life is so fucking marvellous then how come I'm always trying to escape from it?*

I winced at the cliché. Ouch.

Okay, so it's not original, but I'm not always trying to be original. I'm just looking to make sense of things. Of feelings. To lose a few props would be good, or at the very least to try to justify them.

This bingeing will have to stop in a couple of years from now. It can't go on forever. Something will have to give. Shall I stop now? I could take the first steps tonight. Shall I?

I knew I wouldn't of course. But it felt good to tease myself.

I wanted to blow the line away. I had the power to make it just disappear, just so easily.

So I took a breath and leant over the line to blow it away. A deep breath to blow the lines away. Blow them all away.

Who loves me? Edie says she does.

Who loves me? My girlfriend says she does.

And where is the whiskey? And here is the coke.

My knuckles cracked under the strain of dependence. It goes against all that I've never known. Where does it end? I know where it begins. I know where it begins for sure. The first sniff. This is where it begins and let me tell you it never ends. It never ends. One line is way too much, and a thousand lines is not enough.

But I do it. I do my line and I go back to Edie, and I sit by her side. She speaks of our plans, and I listen but decide that we're alone in our world.

But I need her still.

And I always will.

I always will.

And then we got drunk. Both of us. Very drunk. We had a bag full of bills and we were determined to use them all up.

Eventually we both stopped staring out of the window. Edie laughed and fell against my arm as she shrieked. We took more and more coke. I drank more and more whisky. Edie drank more and more vodka.

"If you could paint a portrait of coke Edie, what would you do?" I asked her. "Describe it to me."

"Ooh, I like that," she said and gave the notion some thought.

After a few moments, she said, "It'd be a white canvas. Definitely. And there'd be a row of chairs, maybe like these," and she slapped the back of the leather-bound bench on which we sat.

"Only orange," she said, "deep orange. Almost brown. And through the middle, a train track. Definitely a train track. And on the train track you and I running away from a large suitcase," she said, "something like that. Only maybe without the suitcase, I don't know."

I smiled to myself. I knew she was going to ask me what I would paint.

"What would you paint?" she asked me.

"Oh, I don't know," I answered untruthfully.

"Erm, certainly a white canvas as well. What else? Maybe a creamy yellow one."

She smiled and seemed interested in what I was saying.

"And probably just a Jackson Pollock would do the trick. On the floor. Covered in cigarette ash!"

Edie laughed again.

She said, "Oh, come on. You can do better than that!"

So I stopped to think properly about a painting of that time in my life, and I said, "If I could paint a picture of the way I feel inside. It would be black and blue paint, splashed across ten thousand scribbled lines."

And then I said, "No. Forget that. If I could paint a picture of our lives right now it would be of the inside of a train. Probably a metro train. A subway train, you know? Underground. And it would be done from my perspective. I would be leaning up against a pane of smoked glass. I would be able to see myself on the edge of the painting repeatedly. Infinitely. But vague and ghostlike. And the body of the picture would portray a young woman standing with her back to me. I'd be able to see a cathedral or church out of a far window and there would be water, maybe water running pale blue across the bottom of the painting or through the carriage of the train. Even better! There would certainly be blue. There would be a woman with a dog, in fact two women with the same dog. Identical. Green. Blue. And it would all shimmer lightly and ..."

I tailed off as I recognised Edie had heard enough. I recognised too that I'd said enough. What began as a fun thing to do suddenly sounded too serious as word after word fell out of my mouth.

We were silent for a while.

"Don't look now," she said to revive the conviviality. "The old boy's coming back over."

She smiled at him when he drunkenly tried to buy us drinks. We wanted to be alone. We after all, had so much to not talk about.

Back at our apartment the light stayed on that night.

***

It was around this time in our relationship that I really started to fall apart, beginning to bombard Edie with some pretty unpleasant comments. Embarrassing stuff. Hurtful stuff. It was the stimulants. It had to be.

There was a gigantic irascibility eating me up and I was becoming hollowed out by my own self-loathing. My emotions seemed to be reserved solely for the pursuit of excess, and on top of all that, my dream had started to become commonplace once again.

There were several uncomfortable nights that twisted their way towards some, often uncertain mornings, and always the residue of my dream would hang with me as my new day got under way. I didn't like it. It was turning me away from Edie and forcing me back into my own self.

The train. That was the biggest thing I remember. The biggest element of the dream was always the train and then, of course, the red-haired girl.

And the station platform.

And the people dressed in tan tweed with red stitching, all lined up along the platform. The women with the dogs. The Cathedral. The shopping. The children's laughter. The voices. The general hubbub of daytime activity.

A city. A busy city in such beautiful sunshine, and then so suddenly it would be dark. And cold and then warm again. I would feel the glow of the day. I would sense the heat of the train and the warmth from the girl's eyes as she turned towards me. She looks either side of her and her expression changes, and she raises her hand to the top of her head.

The train leaves the station.

She stays on the platform.

Sometimes she gets on the train but most often she stays on the platform. Growing smaller behind me.

Small until she's gone.

She was appearing much more regularly now, and even at that time I was conscious that maybe this was because Edie and I were starting the process of drifting apart. I didn't understand that this was an entirely natural part of any relationship and that you have to work hard to pull each other back in again. I would have regarded it as some kind of tragedy that she was thinking of leaving me and I would have undoubtedly cast myself in a desperate role. I didn't know that this was a part of the process and that it was all a part of the state of being in love. I would have played the lovelorn victim. The damaged lover. I have no doubt about that whatsoever.

This is where the barbs began.

We squabbled. One morning I was reading. Edie wanted coffee. She asked me to put the kettle on.

"Fill the kettle and boil it for me, please," she said. "I'm going to take a quick shower before work."

It was a Saturday. I heard the shower as it thrummed into the tray in which she stood, naked and warm. I sensed it on the periphery of my consciousness. I had just lit the second joint of the morning and it was painful in my lungs. The book I was reading had me spellbound but I do remember the shower stopping and Edie walking, wet footed out to the kitchen. She had one towel around her head, and one around her body.

"Hey, thanks a lot," she spat, making a big fuss about taking the cold, empty kettle and filling it with water. She slammed it back down on the surface and plugged it in. Switched it on with a loud clack of the button.

"I only asked you to boil it," she said peevishly, like a child would. "I didn't ask you to actually *make* me a cup! That would have been too much wouldn't it!"

My concentration was broken. My mind, filled with smoke. I became cross in an instant and bounded up from the sofa. I threw down my book and followed her into our bedroom. My head ached then I began fighting with myself.

Edie would not listen, that would be for sure. Soon she would be at work, and I could chop out a line of coke to settle me down a bit. Instead, I chose to fight because it was easy.

"Hey, hang on!" I said loudly, directing my impatience towards Edie. "Sorry okay. I was reading." As if that were an excuse to kill the quarrel stone dead.

"I forgot," I said, "it's not a big deal. I'll make it for you now."

"Don't bother. I'm sorry to disturb you reading!" she witheringly took aim. "It's just a fucking cup of coffee."

To disarm me, she covered her chest and refused to take down her towel to dry herself. She indicated instead that I should leave the room. I didn't like this lack of naturalness. Edie nodded at the door for a second time. I stood my ground, pathetically asking her to apologise for being so bloody rude to me. Which, of course, she rightly refused to do.

"Will you get out?" she said.

And then more loudly she said it again.

I took a step towards her, threateningly. Menacingly. Last night's release from this life was still fresh in my head. The train. The laughter. The girl with the green jacket. Who the hell was this savage young woman I was confronted with now in the real world? What did she understand about my inner self? Nothing! What did she know of my secret affair with this figment of my mind? Nothing! How dare she offend me and my troubled ego like this? I became furious. Unreasonably so.

I walked to the bed and pushed her onto it. She fell awkwardly and looked up at me with soft eyes, filled with confusion. Her towel slipped and she looked then entirely vulnerable and not at all like the girl I had come to know. She looked small and shrivelled. Her confidence and her dignity entwined as one and seeming, in that moment to be so frail.

Turning to leave the room, I don't know why I did it, but I picked up a small ornament of a porcelain animal, a bear I think, or maybe a panda.

And I hurled it at the wall.

And it shattered and it fell to the floor.

For a very brief moment the whole room was silent. The air itself seemed to have run and hidden.

And then the chaos.

Edie became wild.

It was a small figurine that had been given to her by her grandmother. Her grandmother had since died; she valued it highly and I had destroyed it.

She saw me then as a devil, and she was right.

What the hell had I done? I was a poisonous, malevolent force in her life. A sickness she would need to cure. However, only I knew just how poisonous I was becoming, and I was aware that I was capable of being a lot nastier to Edie. So much that it frightened me. The horrible depth that I would stoop to in order to drive her away from me. To legitimise my loneliness. This was truly terrifying, and the worst part about it all was that I could barely control it. I was just as much a victim to this as she would soon become.

And still my dream would not let me get any peace. It was about to undermine my actual life, and along with it the very essence of any potential happiness that I might be able to carve out for myself would be eroded at the same time. Edie was crazed with anger. She was incandescent with rage, and of course, she was right to be.

That day did not go well, but by the end of the next one she would have started to calm down a little. I remember trying to sheepishly placate her when she got back from work. I'd bought her a bottle of wine and some flowers but really, this was a futile statement on my part.

I was ashamed. Hugely so.

A couple of days later I met with Yannis and told him about it. Not the entire story. Just the version that favoured me a little more and even then Yannis was unforgiving in his condemnation of me.

"What are you doing, man?" he said incredulously. "What is wrong with you?"

And then he added, "Oh, boy you've got some begging to do! Most women would leave a guy like you right now!"

I grew afraid at what my subconscious was doing. I couldn't drive Edie away. *How could I?* Not after everything we'd been through. We were close. We were a team. Did I love her? Yes, I did. Of course, I did! One hundred percent pure love for her.

I couldn't tell Yannis about this bloody dream that was now starting to become more than just an obsession to me. The dream that was now starting to dictate my actions. Like a fool I was entranced by it, and it was starting to guide me. It was starting to command my emotional processes. But wasn't I the initiator of this thing? Didn't I have control over this?

Surely, I could manipulate the dream to fit the circumstance of my life? Well, I'd already outlawed that notion long ago. I had always said, and I've said it here in the story several times, that I could never betray the dream and adapt it in any way. That would just undermine its legitimacy. Its validity. No. It was what it was. It was my subconscious, and I was in thrall to it. No matter what.

The dream had become the great driving force in my life.

Driving, and dividing.

Yannis said that Edie must really love me to stick around, and later that evening, that made me cry.

Time soon served to put distance between myself and the moment that the small figurine had hit the wall. The instant the figurine left my hand and began its journey towards destruction, I had wanted to bring it back and return it gently to the table. But I knew it was too late.

Like the regret a man might feel the second after jumping off a building. From the moment his feet leave the ledge, he will have started the clock on the final moments of his life. For ten seconds more he will be living in the certainty of his own imminent death. What a terrifying, yet blissful time that must be. Those ten seconds would be the cleanest ten seconds of his entire life. A complete abandonment to fate. A sort of nirvana. Almost holy.

Even today I still feel pain as I recall watching Edie gather up the tiny pieces from the carpet. She wept as she did so. I was outside the room, and she didn't see me, naked as she knelt. The towel was draped around her waist as she gently held the dozen or so tiny fragments in her hands.

"I love you, Nan," I heard her whisper. "I miss you. I miss you all."

I tried to keep us moving forward.

I felt such a guilt over what had happened, and I wanted

to hold her and tell her how sorry I was. But I couldn't. She wouldn't let me. I began to think that she would never let me hold her again, and that this anguish would remain with me for a long time to come. I had no idea then exactly how long I would still feel it and the depth to which it would go.

One evening, a few days later, I tried to move things along by asking her about Franck.

"Do you think we will ever be able to live without them holding on to us?" I asked.

"What do you mean?" she said. "Who is holding on to us? I don't see anyone. Except maybe you!" she added pointedly.

I ignored it.

"What I mean is," I said, reframing my thoughts, "do you think we'll ever be able to live without the possibility that we are being hunted? You know what they'd do to us if they caught us don't you."

I left the sentence hanging.

Edie shrugged. It was a gesture of resignation.

"I don't know if I even care anymore," she said mournfully.

And this was more devastating than if she had agreed with me. She looked tired then. Emotionally tired. The recent days were piling up around us like so many empty boxes and bottles. I felt that she did not want to be with me.

"Do you want to stay?" I asked her nervously, fully understanding where she was in her mind, and terrified of what her answer might be.

"I don't know," she replied. "Again. I don't think I even care anymore. Certainly, not at the moment."

"But do you want to stay *with me*?" I asked her with tears

building in my eyes.

"I don't know," she said again. Very softly. She looked straight at me, and I hurt so bad.

Edie and I continued like this for a little while longer but looking back I think I had sown the seeds of our disintegration that day. I loved her more than ever. By throwing on the light, I had uncovered a vulnerability in her that I hadn't previously detected. But equally I'd now exposed all my flaws. All of them, in one ugly scene.

Now I saw a part of her character also. A part that she'd kept hidden in the gloom and that had begun to surround us. It was heart-breaking to me that I could be so carefree with her feelings, that I could handle her gentlest emotions in the most brutal way. I was ashamed.

Today, I still am.

*

For all of that, Edie must have forgiven me to some degree. Or was at least able to ignore me in part. Because she stayed, and a normality of sorts did return. Although I would never properly be forgiven, I could only assume that Edie had seen something in me that made her believe I was worth sticking around with.

One day I opened a drawer in our room to put some of her clothes away for her, and I found a small plastic bag containing the shattered pieces of the figurine. I knew then that that would forever be a part of our lives that we would keep, but not discuss. Not openly. I put the clothes back by the radiator. I didn't want her to know that I'd uncovered this shattered part of her life.

That I'd found her secret. The bruise that she kept in a bag in the drawer.

The next evening, I was working again at the studio. There was another interview to set up and so in the afternoon I gave myself an hour before to sit and read for bit, to have a beer or two and maybe a smoke.

Some time to just loosen up and try to make some sense of who I was, or of who I was becoming.

I chose a bar at El Plaça Sant Josep Oriol and even though it was still only mid-afternoon, it was already starting to get lively as I sat there, waiting for my beer.

A juggler came and stood in front of me with a cloth cap turned upwards at his feet. From his pocket he fished out a small canvas pouch and emptied a little of it into the cap. The tiny dirty coins made a clink as they fell against one another. He rubbed his hands down the front of his birdcage chest, which was covered by a blue and white hooped Breton shirt. It complemented the beret that sat jauntily on top of a blond wig, fastened at the crown of his head.

Around his throat was he wore a white spotted, deep red, almost crimson necktie. It clashed against the mauve cummerbund around his waist. Across his shoulders he'd slung a huge string of onions, like some agricultural feather boa, all knobbly and gnarling. A gargoyle of an appendage. A horrible creation. A cliché of all things Gallic.

In caricature the juggler pulled from his deep pockets three onions that were coloured. One red, one white, one blue. He offered them around to the people in the crowd to sniff at. Each in turn refused and so he did it for them in an exaggerated vaudeville manner, feigning the smell of the onions by cocking his leg and falling to the floor.

The children in the crowd laughed, and this included a chuckle from me. The juggler stood and threw all three of the onions into the air and caught two of them to begin his routine. One fell to the floor, and he frowned obliquely. He knelt down and retrieved it as it began to roll away down a small gutter filled at the bottom with a faint trace of water. Not a part of his routine, I guessed as he rubbed it dry and left red paint on his shirt.

Again, he threw the onions into the air and this time caught them in perfect rotation. One after the other they flew about his head, up and over and down and up and over and down. The children applauded him as they shrieked joyously.

Out of the corner of my eye I thought I saw a black shape on the edge of my vision. Shifting it shifted. But it didn't. It didn't. The juggler slowed his juggling. The balls froze in the air. They hung and then they fell. He stopped and then began again.

And then this.

Or was my mind playing tricks on me? I was stoned again.

I'd recently started to hallucinate. But just shapes. Not actual forms. Shadows. The pictures in my mind were becoming jumbled.

Did it happen this way? No most definitely not possible.

Nothing happened when three children ran to him and threw coins into the upturned cap at his feet. The juggler juggled and smiled in their direction winking as they scurried back to their parents. His teeth bared like fangs, and he roared a fearsome growl. He snarled at the crowd who picked up their bags and ran screaming from their tables. His breath hot and savage. Feline.

All claws as he juggled the balls up, over and down.

The children clapped for him. He winked at them as they scurried back to their parents. He smiled at us and caught all the balls in one hand and then bowed to our applause. He said nothing.

And so again, the juggler bowed. Only this time he bowed too far, and his head seemed to fall away from his shoulders and roll down the same small gutter that was filled at the bottom with a faint trace of water.

He caught it and put it firmly back on his shoulders, squeaking it into place deliberately. Screwing it in. He tapped the side of his head to be sure that it couldn't come loose. All the children laughed again. He wiped away the blood that ran around the base of his neck in dribbles, like spittle from a baby's mouth.

His blond wig lay on the grey paving. It had come loose when his head had fallen. He picked it up, and as he did so he took three knives from a fold in the top of it. He plunged each of the three knives into the three onions and the crowd audibly gasped. He had their attention now, for sure. He returned the blond acrylic wig and the beret to the top of his head.

Awestruck we watched as he juggled the onions with the knives. I did not want to see him impale his hand on one.

And then a dark black shape shifted in the corner of my eye. I watched between fingers as the juggler threw the knives and the vegetables higher and higher. Each time: over, down and up. I was mesmerised as he caught them so nimbly, and by their handles.

He threw them then higher and higher still, so high that they flew into the sky, up into the afternoon sky. Up to the stars that were starting to appear in the clear inky mauve Mediterranean canopy under which we were all sitting. I waited for the knife to pierce a star and pull it to earth, and we all were looking up at him, now twenty feet tall.

Then he shrank to normal size and collected the knives with the onions in one hand. His left hand. Between thumb and forefinger: a knife stuck into a blue onion. Between forefinger and index finger, a knife stuck into a white onion. Between ring finger and small finger, a knife stuck into a red onion.

And we clapped and laughed.

He hushed us by laying his right-hand palm down in the air and pushing several times. We understood his gesture and waited silently for the finale to his routine. He stared intently at his left hand, the hand holding all of the knives and the onions. The silence intensified and became louder than silence. A vacuum of sound shut out the throb of car engines from behind where we sat.

He took a breath and held it in his right hand whilst staring at his left, which was the hand holding all of the knives and the onions. As the juggler exhaled and took another, sharper breath he flexed his muscles, steadying his entire frame.

It made me think of something Edie said to me the day before.

On the way to the studio, I stopped and called her from a payphone. I wanted to hear her voice.

"If we're going to do this, darling," she said enigmatically, "if we're going to build our life together then we must look out for each other, and we must head troubles off wherever we can. Otherwise, we're going to need to run again. And this time run fast."

"Are you sure you want to run again?" I asked.

"I'm thinking about it," she said.

I said nothing, just wrapped the flex around my thumb tightly until it went a bright purple colour and expanded or seemed to expand. I bent a little into the phone and said softly, "I need you, Edie."

There was silence.

And then I said, "I want to be with you. I want us to be together. I'm so sorry."

"Yeah," she said.

And then ...

"I love you, David," she said.

I caught my breath and became conscious of my insides, particularly my heart, as she said it. Her words sent pulses along my veins and into my soul. I loved her too. She had said it to me only a handful of times, but I felt that this time her words carried more significance than they ever had before. It was all too real to now pretend that I was fooling myself in the way that I had done in so many ways before. I had another chance. I would not make the same mistakes again. That's what I told myself.

Too many coach journeys, too many train rides would mean that now I could afford myself the luxury of being loved, and to feel the emotion coming back at me was a beautiful feeling. It was Edie loving me. It was her loving me. Even the way I was worrying about her seemed different. I cared for her safety. I believed in her when she said sweet things to me. Such beautiful things with a tone rich in friendship and kindness, rich in round vowels and velvet syllables. I could smell her hair down the phone.

"I love you too, Edie." It was all I could say.

And then, "I've got to go. I'll be home later. Don't worry

about us. We'll win, okay?"

I believed it. And because I believed, Edie believed it too.

"Yeah," she said for the second time.

"Bye." I said but didn't hang up.

She said, "And then I'll stay ... you know that don't you?"

"Yeah," I said.

"And then I'll stay."

"Yeah," I said again.

"Bye," she whispered and hung up.

"Goodbye," I said.

*

One evening, soon after, we were back with Yannis and Marco. Elena wasn't there. She'd gone back home for a while. I can't remember where she said that was, or if even she'd ever told me anyway. I know she was Spanish and was raised in a town to the north of Barcelona. Girona springs to mind.

Elena's absence I think irritated Edie. She had enjoyed female company and here she was again with these boys making boorish jokes about everything important and saying nothing interesting about things that weren't. Although we tried to tailor our conversation to accommodate Edie, it wasn't natural for us. There was no animosity from her. She was happy to accept us for what we were. Men. Idiots, probably.

Yannis knew about what I'd done, and I think that he thought, not without some considerable grounds to be right, that mine and Edie's days were maybe numbered. I think perhaps he was even starting to consider making a move on her. I'm not sure.

But I do know that she found him handsome and that, in turn, he found her attractive. He'd not exactly tried too hard to hide this from me. On the day I told him about my explosion in the apartment he'd pretty much told me how he saw her. It didn't matter. In many respects this was flattering. It was true, so how could I deny the fact. Edie had a great look about her.

For now, she was still my Edie. The girl I'd been with for almost a year. We were still strong, despite my dream, and despite my increasingly fragile state of mind. Unlucky, Yannis!

He gestured towards me as he stood at the counter. Did I want a drink? Well, the answer to that was always 'yes'. He looked at Edie and made the same gesture. Did Edie want a drink? Of course she did. We both nodded and smiled in his direction and gave him a thumbs up signal. I mouthed the words '*cerveza*' and held up two fingers '*dos*'. He nodded. And smiled.

Yannis came back to the table with the drinks and mine was gone in just a few minutes. I stood to get another, a process I repeated several times over the next hour. And so there we sat, in Barcelona. Yannis, Marco, Edie, and me. We were having a good evening, and like many good evenings, you don't know fully what it is you're experiencing until they come to an end. Yannis raised his glass. He laughed and blew a kiss to Edie. Edie threw her head back and pouted in his direction. I feigned indignation and protection. Yanis knew for sure this was a lie. I pretended to be jealous. Perhaps I should have tried a bit harder.

These were wonderful days again. I remember looking at Yannis as he picked up his packet of cigarettes and as he took his lighter from his pocket.

I don't know if I spotted it right away or if it was a while later, but when I saw it, a cold chill settled on my arms and my hairs all stood on end.

Yannis's lighter.

It was a Zippo. A very nice stainless-steel silver one that made such a satisfying click when you snapped it open and then snapped it shut. A fine piece of kit that smelled wonderful, a smell I now associate with dishonesty and deceit.

As Yannis snapped the lighter shut and placed it on his cigarette pack in front of us, the red and black pillar, with the three XXX's on it jumped right out at me.

Amsterdam.

The lighter was a souvenir from Amsterdam.

SEVEN

I nudged Edie's foot under the table. I had to do it twice before she looked at me, and when she did I directed her attention to Yannis' cigarette lighter. By widening her eyes, just a little, she silently let me know that we were thinking the same thing. Which was important. Was this just a coincidence? Probably. But what if it wasn't?

Yannis was talking between puffs on his cigarette. Something about nothing. Not real talk, just words. Worse, just sounds.

My mind was tumbling over itself. Should I mention Amsterdam? If I did, wouldn't I be drawing attention to something that might give us away? Wouldn't I be alerting him to something? What if he didn't suspect anything sinister? Or what if he was working for Dieter and Boaz and was looking for us but didn't know it was us? Highly unlikely, I decided. Therefore, the thought then followed that if he was working for Boaz, he'd know already that he'd found us, and that he was humouring us, buying some time. In that case we were, in a sense, packed up and ready to deliver like supermarket meat, ready for processing.

I told myself that this was all just speculation. Crazy speculation.

Even so, I didn't want Yannis to notice that I was looking at the lighter, or that I even cared about it. So, I did the opposite of what I thought would be sensible because after all, I had already started to establish that my own judgement was flawed.

I asked Yannis if I could steal a cigarette from him. He nodded. Sure. I took the packet from in front of him, and the lighter as well. I lit a cigarette and made a great show of inspecting it. Rolling it around in my hand and nodding approvingly. Edie was looking at me. Just looking at me, saying nothing. I knew what was in her mind.

"Thanks," I said. Then, raising the lighter I added, "nice lighter," or something like that. Yannis didn't drop a single beat in his conversation. In fact, he barely even looked at me. His words continued to flow. Empty. Like eggshells from which the birds had already flown. Edie continued to look at me, still saying nothing.

Later that evening she asked me, "Well, what do you think?"

"I honestly think it's a coincidence," I said.

"Do you?" she seemed surprised. "Do you really?"

I wasn't sure. She knew it. Certainly, I thought it would be wise to keep our options open, and to keep everything viable, to make all things theoretical, possible. But my positivity stalled when I started to think about the fact that I thought I had seen Franck a few days earlier.

With a large degree of increasing unease I remembered that Yannis had left the bar that evening, right before Franck appeared at the window. If, in fact, it was Franck. I still was not convinced of what I saw. But again, if it had been Franck, then the fact that Yannis had left the bar a few moments before must have meant something, mustn't it? That wasn't a coincidence as well, was it? I didn't want to mention this to Edie. I really didn't want us to become sick with it all. Not again. Not ever.

"I don't know, Edie," I began to roll a joint. Another one. "I'm just trying to use best guesses here. What do you think?"

"I don't think it's worth taking any risks," she said. "I'm worried that it could be dangerous for us."

After a few moments' silence, moments in which I was sure I heard noises out in the stairwell, like the creaking of the stairs, Edie sighed loudly and pushed her entire upper body down into the chair in which she was sitting. She looked small like that. Vulnerable.

A few moments passed in which there was just a large, difficult silence between us.

"Oh Christ! I've had about all I can take of this running around!" she cried, sitting up tall in her chair again. "If they want us, why don't they just get on with whatever it is they've been sent to get on with?"

I had to agree with her. Not knowing was the hardest thing to bear. The never-ending uncertainty was painful. I looked across the carpet. Yellow-orange and deep. Like a cornfield. Like a sun-kissed, acrylic cornfield. I imagined sitting then in such a place, with the sun beating down on us. When we were free. No burden. No financial commitments that might rise up and suck our ambition from us. I was grateful then that nothing like having any financial burden existed at that time for Edie and me. We were able to move around quickly and easily. This could be our strongest weapon. It could be our secret advantage.

"Perhaps we should leave again," I said and lit the joint. "You have always wanted to go north to France. Antibes, didn't you say to me? Or Nice. What about Nice? I could do that too."

I took a drag and handed the joint to Edie. She was shaking a little as she took it from me, but she became calmer once she'd inhaled some smoke.

Then she rolled her eyes, and said, "I can't just keep running for ever. I don't want to be scared and running all my life."

She smoked some more, before she spoke again.

"I'd rather face them. Find out how we can make things right. Maybe we should ask Yannis what he knows."

Edie reached into her pocket for her asthma inhaler. She had started to wheeze a little. She took two sharp puffs and exhaled a thin reed of air, like a tiny invisible string. This is something that occurred when she was stressed. Lately this had been more often. No surprise really.

"Wow. Do you think so?" I said, intrigued by the kind of audacity that I'd not seen from her too many times before.

Then I said, "Well, it might work." Then after a bit of nervous thought I said, "But isn't that really risky? What if he kicks off because he feels trapped that his cover is blown?"

We left the conversation hanging in the air for a few moments and then Edie said exactly what I had been thinking. This happened often.

"You do realise that he left the bar just a few moments before you thought you saw Franck the other week," she said plainly. I nodded and made out that I hadn't already thought of this. She continued.

"Seems a bit odd don't you think?" I didn't need to answer her. She continued.

"He's with us, he leaves with little reason. No reason in fact. I can't remember one. And you see Franck. Then Yannis comes back."

It was this event that was troubling us more than anything else. It was this that gave us no option but to conclude that, although we were probably over-reacting, it was still likely to be safer for us to pack up and move again and honestly, neither of us wanted to do that. We were not entirely sure if the fragility of our relationship would hold up to it, and besides, we both liked Barcelona.

And for all of this new uncertainty that was surrounding Yannis, we still enjoyed his company, also that of Marco. They were good people to have fallen in with. At least that's what we thought at one point, and we were content to keep giving them the benefit of our doubt. The recollection of that was something that we needed to hang on to, in fact more than that, it was something that we were desperate to hang on to.

However, within days we had started to look on maps again, reluctantly planning our next move. This must have been a signal to us, if only we had recognised it.

Edie liked Lyon. I wanted to be near the sea. We spoke about Nimes. Montpelier. Saint Tropez. Cannes. Nice. Antibes. France seemed like a good idea. Something about France was calling to me.

We figured that we could find work in any of those places on the Riviera. They were all tourist traps, or very near to tourist traps. We felt that we could find plenty of bar and restaurant work there. I'd miss my job in the radio studio, for sure. I liked doing that. But I knew that if we had to move again, then that was what we must do, and so did Edie.

So we soon laid some plans, and we suddenly had a date the following week when we were planning to leave. We had settled on Nice.

But then something new happened.

One evening Edie came and sat with me in the lounge in our apartment. I put down my book and I looked at her intelligent face, glowing in the evening light filtering through the curtain in front of which she was standing. She seemed then, forlorn, perhaps in some way she seemed nervous even. I sensed she was going to tell me then about the day she disappeared in Oporto. The day she came home drunk.

"Do you remember," she began, "that day when I came home drunk?" I was right, and I quickly began tremoring with nervousness, light and almost imperceptible, like the ripple of a pond under a dragonfly's wings.

I nodded, "Yes, I thought you might say that."

And she half-smiled.

And I said, "Are you going to tell me what happened? Am I going to be upset about it?"

She didn't answer me. Instead she straightened her back and made a visible attempt to control herself. It was clear. I sat up and got myself ready for what was about to come.

"I was with Maartje." She said it out loud. Right off the bat. No messing. For a moment I didn't understand. Then the penny began its descent.

"What? You mean Amsterdam Maartje?" I said, slowly growing more nervous by the moment. "What? How?" was about all I could manage. I was confused. The idea of her having an affair disappeared like smoke from a jar, and I was bizarrely feeling a small flash of anger that I'd allowed myself to think all the hurtful, self-pitying thoughts that I had at the end of our time in Portugal.

She went on.

"I'm so sorry, David," she said, and I could hear the emotion snowballing in her voice.

"But I couldn't do it," and she started to cry softly at first, and then harder, so hard she had trouble going on with her story. Tears rolled across her face now. I could see the streaks reflected in the sun. Glistening, damp lines that formed like stains across her skin. I went to her then and held her until she was a little calmer and able to carry on.

"I did see Franck in Oporto," she said. "It was him. He saw me in the shoe shop. But they didn't know we lived above it." Edie began.

I stayed silent. She continued.

"Franck saw me. And a few days later, Maartje came into the shop. She was a customer as far as Rosa was concerned. Franck didn't want to talk to me. Maartje had travelled with him to find us. She didn't say how they got to us.

"But she said they had a deal they wanted to make. You see, Dieter and Boaz ... it's you they're after. It's you they blame!" I felt right then a stab of fear. Real fear.

"Maartje said that she had a message from Dieter. She said that they would let me back into Amsterdam and that they'd overlook everything. So long as I gave you up to them."

I felt sick. It was the shock. Suddenly my nerves pulsed into overdrive. I stood and started pacing around the room. I found it difficult to resist the urge to retch. To throw up all over the carpet, the cornfield carpet.

I sat back down.

And then stood up again.

Edie beckoned me to be seated.

"David, I told them that yes, I would do it. They've been waiting for me to call them."

I was stunned. I felt betrayed. Edie wept. But then she said, "But I can't do that to you David. I love you too much!"

We held each other and cried. Edie cried the sorrow of many months of frustration, and she really meant it. Every tear was private. I felt washed out. My emotions were raw. I loved her too, very much. Her words humbled me. They had me on my knees. She had been offered a way out and she had refused it because of me. She had made an enormous sacrifice for me. How could I ever have doubted her?

So where did this leave us now?

"Maartje and I got very drunk," she said. "We had a good time together, or as good as we could. Franck didn't want to be there. He didn't want to hurt me. Apparently. So Maartje and I spoke about some old times. We didn't talk about any stolen drugs. I actually don't think she knew too much about it if I'm honest.

"I left it that I'd be in touch with details of how they could pick you up. They were going to give me a time and a place, and I was supposed to make sure you were there. Well, they did give me a time and a place, and I made sure you definitely were *not* there. In fact, I made sure that neither of us were anywhere near there."

And then she said, "How the hell do they know we're in Barcelona? It doesn't make any sense. Unless they got lucky again."

We looked at one another then. "And Yannis?" I asked.

"I don't think he knows anything," she replied. "I think the lighter is a coincidence. And I also don't think that it was Franck that you saw."

"But if it was?" I said, leaving the sentence empty.

"Well, if it was, then we're both in a lot of trouble. And we have no choice but to leave. But do we want to always be running away from everything. From ourselves?"

She took her inhaler again.

"Edie, are you okay?" I asked her as she silently pumped Ventolin into her airways, nodding her head. Holding her breath.

"I'm fine," she said finally, letting out a gasp of breath, "as long as I've got you, I'll always be fine."

She smiled and held my hand.

Okay. So it wasn't our imaginations. Boaz and Dieter had pretty much succeeded in tracking us down, and if they could do that once, I had no doubt that they could do it again. And again and again after that.

So I had to accept surely that I had seen Franck, and I had to accept as well that Yannis would have likely had a part to play in it. However, before I made any rash decisions about Edie and I taking off again, I needed to try to confront Yannis about Amsterdam. To find out what he knew. If, indeed, it was Yannis that had given us up.

Two days later I was at his apartment.

Edie was working, and it was just Yannis and I. She didn't know I was going to meet him. We had planned to go for a coffee that lunchtime, but I had decided to call in early. Catch him off guard.

"Oh, hi," he said smiling widely as he came to the door. He seemed entirely untroubled by my unexpected arrival.

"Come on in," he offered the door open, and I walked through to his kitchen with him.

"Let me just get my shoes," he said.

He was gone to the lobby at the rear of the property for less than a minute, and soon reappeared clicking his door keys in his right hand. He reached for his jacket.

"Let's go," he said, and added, smiling, "Where shall we have coffee?"

We left the apartment and before long were seated outside the same cafe where I'd recently seen the juggler. The intense midday sun was casting short shadows all around us, although the courtyard was cool. The air smelled of gardenias and apricots.

We began talking about everyday things. Some football, but neither he nor I knew much about it. We watched the occasional game, sometimes together, with a beer or two. But we didn't care if one team lost, or another won. It all seemed a bit trivial to both of us. A little bit pointless.

Close to our table, near where the juggler had recently appeared, a girl painted entirely white had set herself up on a small silver plinth made in the image of a hewn lump of marble. She'd wrapped a white sheet around herself and was standing perfectly still. She didn't move. Not a bit. In a trance, or so it seemed. She had almost stopped breathing. It was unsettling.

I stared at her as the football conversation between Yannis and myself quickly dwindled away. If a thing can dwindle quickly, that is.

Hypnotised, this girl-statue stood. I began to feel my own feet ache as I looked at her, and after a short while I began to forget about her completely. She disappeared. She simply became a statue, nothing less. She had succeeded in evolving into a piece of art and I was impressed. Her presence had become as anonymous as an item on a supermarket shelf. Anonymous, but garishly coloured, trying to grab our attention. But instead, melding into a miasma of vivid colours and hysterical lettering. Failing, in other words.

Pick and mix, I thought. Pick and mix.

At her feet was a small box with coins in it and a sign painted on the box in Spanish that I didn't understand, except the date at the bottom. Forty-nine, in Roman numerals. XLIX. I looked at the box, and I looked at the girl. I found that she was stealing my imagination. She'd cast some kind of spell over me, and it had hit me quite hard. I stared at her and then I thought that I could make her look at me, or that I could make her smile. I concentrated on staring directly into her eyes and played with the idea of standing up and walking over to her, peering inscrutably into the folds of her sheet. Trying to disturb her. Then she would have to smile. She would either smile or she would kick me, I was sure of it. One or the other. She would have to choose.

An idea occurred to me. Maybe it was possible to hide, simply by standing still. No more running.

Hiding in plain sight. Edie and me.

Hiding by standing still.

"We're thinking of moving on again," I said to Yannis. He didn't seem to care.

"Oh," was his reply. "That's a shame. Why is that then? I

thought you liked it here."

"We do. But the summer will soon be over," I said. "And we fancy a change of scenery. We want to feel a breeze on our skin. From the sea. Sure, we can go to the beach here." Had I said too much already? "But it's always really busy. We like the idea of something quiet."

He was nodding but I'm not sure he was really listening. He was sipping his coffee and seemed simply to agree with me. He was a nice guy. I already felt that I would miss him.

"Where will you go?" he asked genuinely, and of course, I sent him in the wrong direction.

"Bilbao looks nice," I said. "Or Santander," I went on, embroidering the scene.

"Somewhere along that coastline. We think we'll find some work around there, and a nice little village we can crash out in for a few months."

Finally, I dropped the telling lie: "To be honest we both miss Oporto and would like to go back there for the winter."

This lie was an easy one to tell. Because it was true.

I thought about the Mediterranean and how I have always loved it and how I have always needed it present in my life ever since I first saw the Mediterranean Sea and the flat-roofed limestone buildings that glow at the day's end. They have always stayed in my heart, and I can still feel the ghosts of the very first squat houses I ever saw, lined up along the edge of the parched, dust-filled roads that we drove through in the dark all those years ago. I can still hear the cicadas as they raised their chirruping wing cases high above the level of a whisper, still and calm in the night.

I can see all the way along the wide dirt-track pathways that led off the beaten track at Albufeira in Portugal. I see a cart pulled by a donkey smack bang in the centre, an old man twisting over on the cart, almost asleep from the soporific effect of the wine he'd been drinking almost all day. He was bathing in the early evening sun that was making him gold and crimson at the same time.

The heat in the air that I can smell whenever I think about Mediterranean countries lingers in my lungs. It fills my soul, and it makes me feel alive.

And I love it.

I savour northern Tunisia as I walk the steep slopes of blue-white Sidi Bou Said, and as I rummage through Carthaginian ruins that overlook this beautiful shimmering sea, phosphorescent and pulsing with iridescent light.

This mother of all we have known.

I can see the turquoise shutters on the white-walled buildings, and I can taste the mint tea which is lukewarm and sweetly bitter.

I can feel the sun on my back and the pain in my eyes as I squint, sitting on the edge of a boat as it cruises along the southern coast of Rhodes from one bay to the next. I can feel the fish brush past my legs as I swim from the boat on my back. Holding my breath and moving my arms in tiny circles to keep me afloat, looking up at the royal blue cloudless Mediterranean sky that hangs like a majestic canopy over this life-affirming sea. A sea that in the bays is a lighter shade of crystal blue, and the further inland you swim it becomes dark, almost violet.

This home to creatures we rarely ever get to see. With whom we share this planet. This home. And I'm fascinated by it all.

I can still see the bottom of the ocean along the Maltese coast, with tiny schools of picarel fish, maybe twenty or less, darting as one single thing, from left to right in random diagonals. Individual fish, acting as a single whole.

I can still make out the coast of Albania as I sit on the beaches in Corfu and wonder about the country and its people.

I can still taste the Sardines in the Algarve. I can still see the old man laughing and drinking Sangria from a baby's bottle.

I can still taste the paella made fresh from the shrimps at the bottom of the Portuguese well, over which I hung my legs smoking cigarettes in the late afternoon.

The Mediterranean.

It is beautiful and it makes me think of everything I was in my life. And of everything I want to be now.

"What about you?" I asked Yannis. "Are you staying here?"

"Me?" he said. "Yes, I think so. For now. I like it here. Barcelona suits me."

"But don't you want to feel the urge to travel?" I asked him. "To see new places?"

"Not really," he said. "I'm not a big traveller. I've seen a few places, but I like to settle. It's that kind of stability that gives me the freedom to think," he added.

"Where have you been, Yannis?" I asked.

All I needed now was for him to say he'd visited Amsterdam. The lighter would then be as natural a purchase as anything else. It would have cleared him and would have kept him as the friend I had come to know. I fervently didn't want Yannis to have been a part of the Amsterdam crowd. But he didn't mention the place once. It wasn't on his list.

As he ran down the names of the towns he had stayed in, I

was waiting for Amsterdam or somewhere even close by to be said.

But I heard nothing.

He picked up his cigarettes. I noticed there was a small plastic lighter now. Not the fancy Amsterdam one. He offered me a cigarette. I took one.

And then he offered me his cheaper lighter.

This was my chance.

"Oh, what happened to your nice lighter?" I asked innocently.

He smiled. "That wasn't mine," he said. "That was Iker's, you remember him? The dealer. He left it at my place the other day. I gave it back to him yesterday. He goes to Amsterdam a lot. I'm sure you can imagine!"

Iker! Of course.

Yes, he must have guessed at something. He must have! I was able to take this and use it to pardon Yannis. I needed to go to Edie and to tell her it was Iker who most probably was talking to Boaz and Dieter back in Amsterdam.

The lighter belonged to Iker! This meant that the danger was now very close and the concern I had now was enormous. I needed to get to Edie right away. This must have meant that Franck, or any one of Boaz's footmen knew for sure where we were hiding out. They were real, and they were closing in. They had to be. It would surely now just be a matter of time before they came for us properly.

I was jumping up and down inside. To mask it I turned my face back toward the girl on the plinth. She still hadn't moved. I thought about the activity in her mind. Was it churning over? Or had it been reduced to a lower level of activity? Had she the capacity to switch it off totally? Or was she perhaps thinking about an essay that she had to write that weekend? Or anything else? Was she looking secretly at the small box that no one had added any coins to in the ten minutes that she had been standing there? And was she angry with us for ignoring her? Or was it pleasing her that she was so good at becoming invisible?

I looked ahead at some graffiti on the grey corrugated shutter next to the furniture shop and then I caught the waiter's eye. I raised my finger and smiled. He came over to me and I calmly ordered Yannis and I another beer each. I would drink it quickly and go to find Edie. But first I had to calm myself down.

The waiter nodded sharply as he turned on his heels and left to fetch the beer for us. A little girl who had been throwing cake to the pigeons ran past me with some coins. She threw them into the statue girl's box, who then began to dance a tiny dance. She moved stiltedly and with definite twitches. She mimicked a statue coming to life in perhaps the only way I could imagine it, like a water nymph tipping a fountain in the air. I watched her dance her little jig and then settle back into solidity again. This time in a different pose. The one in which she had landed.

It saddened me on her behalf to see that she'd dislodged the hem of her white sheet and was revealing a patch of denim beneath it. It made the date XLIX look awkward. The little girl who had thrown in the money was jumping up and down with delight. She ran back to her parents who were standing from their table ready to go. She grasped at her mother's skirt and the father picked her up and cradled her in the crook of his elbow. He carried her away and I looked back at the statue girl.

And then I caught my breath. She was on a plinth. She was a

statue! She was a statue!

My dream! The blue? Denim! She was a statue. My dream. Was the blue in my dream was staring at me? For a long time, I had wondered what the blue bit was. Was it now as simple as a scrap of jeans?

Here before me stood a girl on a plinth wrapped in white showing blue. The little girl. Laughing. Children laughing? Shops and shopping!

I could feel my brittle mind being tested. Being tightened and stressed. Ready to break. Ready to snap into pieces. Into many pieces.

It was coincidence. I didn't feel it strongly enough. There was no train. There was no fountain and there was no cathedral. But it had given me fresh insight into the more mysterious part of my dream.

I had put a lot of emphasis on the absurdity of the situation, and I moved on in my mind. This was no revelation. It was nothing seismic.

It was a matter of flesh and being.

A matter of knowing and understanding.

I let her go. She grew bored and collected her things. She'd taken a few pesetas for her efforts and as she left, she smiled at me. She smiled the smile of like minds.

I knew her then. And I think she knew me too.

EIGHT

In an idle moment Imogen smokes a cigarette and watches the road as a late summer rain shower patters across the cobbled walkways in front of her. She takes shelter as each drop, heavier than the one before, bounces among a succession of canopies above her head.

The rain is hard and weaves a path between the cobbles, out on to the promenade and down into the river that leads to the sea. And her thoughts, as so often before, lead her to the same place, and from there they float on the bobbing waves all the way north to London.

Imogen is surrounded by words. Everywhere she looks, she sees words. Hundreds of words. So many that she feels that they are spilling out with the raindrops, across the ground, flooding the streets, and cascading into the river behind her. So many words that the river is becoming filled with them, threatening to burst its banks.

She is in London then, in her mind and soul. She feels that her life is destined to be in that city. She has always wanted to go there but has never been, and now that her summer job in Portovenere restaurant in Nice is coming to an end, she thinks that maybe this could be the time to go and see England. There's something about the country that fascinates her. Something that draws her in. She has always felt an affinity to the English. Imogen admires the humour of Londoners. She likes the down-to-earth aspect of these no-nonsense people, although she has always felt that London would probably contain too many people to choose from.

But she is looking only for one.

As she considers this in her imagination, she turns away from the words and looks out from under the canopies beneath which she is standing. Shaded on a cool day. She shudders a little. Touches her fingertips to her throat and the rain stops.

Imogen looks back at a bridge that straddles the river, and she watches a series of trains as they squeak to a halt. They are using this bridge to enter the station that sits on the bank opposite from where she is standing. There are so many trains. Too many to count. They meander in both directions. Ten and twenty at a time. She shakes her head lightly and the image disappears.

Imogen sees the cobbled walkways once again and the bridge she was watching has disappeared. The vision has evaporated. Back in the real world now, Imogen crushes her cigarette under her foot and looks up at the sky between the canopies. She sighs a small sigh. It looks as if the gloom is about to lift. This could make for a busy evening now, she thinks.

She starts to ponder on her own train ride into work that day and she thinks about how different it had felt. She smiles to herself one more time as she recalls the bald woman she saw carrying her dog and she's still smiling about that as she rolls her back off the metal support that's holding up the thick white canopy above her head. She's smiling about it still, that woman, with her toy-dog and her big red earrings, as she walks through the restaurant and back to the kitchen where the head chef, Sepp, would be sure to try to make her laugh once more.

She liked Sepp. But he wasn't an Englishman.

*

"But do you believe him?" Edie asked me. I looked at her blankly.

"Well, I guess so," I said.

"You guess so!" she exclaimed. "Fair enough. But is that good enough?" she said. "Is that good enough for you?"

I understood what she was trying to say but I'm not so sure she was right to say it. Not so aggressively anyhow.

"Look, Edie," I said. "He had a reason. He had an excuse. It wasn't his lighter. It belonged to that creepy dealer guy, Iker. That's what he said. That's what he told me. It's plausible, I guess."

"Again, with the guessing!" she said. "Guessing, and 'good enough' could be your two biggest mistakes! Sure, Iker could have a nice Amsterdam Zippo, why not? But who has he been dealing with in the Dam? He's got to have at least heard of Boaz wouldn't you say? He's definitely heard of the van Eycks that's got to be a certainty!"

She had more to say. "A creepy little *scheisse* like him would sell us in a heartbeat!"

I let this sit for a few moments. She was right. I said nothing. When I did speak, I said, "So, what is your solution?" I asked her calmly. "We go? To Nice?"

She obviously didn't have a solution. She was quiet.

"I don't know," she said.

That was the absolute truth of it, neither of us really knew.

"Let's maybe move to another apartment," she said. "And stay in Barca for a while longer yet. I'm not sure. It's difficult to second guess these people. We still don't know for sure that they're on to us. Are we just being paranoid?"

"I don't like it," Edie continued. "Even if they're not on to us, and we are imagining all of this, I still don't like the way we are living, David."

What Edie had said was the truest thing I'd heard in a long time. Regardless of whether I saw Franck, or whether Yannis or Iker or whoever else was selling us out, regardless of all of that, we were still, she and I, living captive inside of our own paranoia. It was suffocating us, and we could not have foreseen how we would become prisoners of our own actions.

If we'd known all of this, would we still have stolen those drugs? I don't think so. If we were both honest with one another, we would have to admit that we would not have done that if we could have our time again, but we couldn't give it back now, and we couldn't give him the money either. Everything was gone. We'd been living a nice life for nearly a year, but we'd been living it without once understanding that every moment that passed, every peseta we spent, then we were getting further into debt.

And into debt to some pretty evil people too.

Edie had already told me that Maartje had approached her in Oporto. She'd already done a deal with them to pick me up, and it was only because Edie felt about me the way she did that I was in any way safe at that moment. But that could all change. I knew that. And more than that, I knew that Edie had also put herself in danger by not delivering on her deal with Maartje and Franck. Our situation was getting more complicated. Which meant it was getting worse.

Edie felt she had a special status with Boaz because they had been close to one another over the years. Boaz respected her. She may well be safe from him, maybe also from Dieter. I could remember him telling me that he liked her. And after all, it was Dieter who had said that Edie was not as tough as she liked to think she was. I think that if Dieter had a say in matters, then she'd probably be able to get away with all of this. But that was not a risk worth taking. Not to my mind. Not worth thinking, and certainly not worth even talking about.

Through all this uncertainty, Edie and I were starting to fall apart all over again. It was intolerable. We seemed to have no control over it at all. The pressure of the situation, the difficulty in knowing our lives, of knowing one another: it was too much for us. We were not equipped for this kind of pressure. No one would be. We didn't understand, when we stole those drugs the year before, that we were making the odds against us building a life together impossible to beat. We were too immature. We had handicapped ourselves right from the start. We were beginning to understand that even if Boaz and Dieter didn't kill us, we could possibly kill ourselves. Or at least kill our relationship. We didn't have much of a chance.

The strength of the love we were starting to feel for one another was not going to be enough to save us. In fact, the more we loved one another, the harder it was going to be to bear our inevitable collapse. All we were doing in those days was storing up more and more pain. Pain that would, undoubtedly, be coming back to devastate us some time soon.

It is very true to say that at that time we were still discovering one another. We were still growing, and at times we were growing strongly. We enjoyed one another, but the pain and the confusion that I saw when I looked into her eyes was becoming hard to digest. It all began when I threw that porcelain animal against the wall. This was the catalyst that signalled the start of our destruction, and I hated myself for it. So much.

Perhaps we should just end it there and then? Take some pain now. But not take more pain in the future. I said to Edie that very thing.

"Perhaps we should call it a day," I said softly.

She muttered something. Very quietly. I wasn't sure she heard me, but I was crying now. That I'd even said it out loud was too much. Again, so many things were too much. I struggled to say it one more time.

Edie looked at me with a real fear in her beautiful grey eyes. Eyes flecked with orange and pale blue, filled at that moment, with an inescapable sadness and longing.

"No!" she threw herself into my arms. "Don't ever say that!" she said sobbing as well.

"Don't ever, ever say that! I don't want to hear you say that again. Never!" She looked at me closely, tears running down her face. "Never again. Ever! I love you!"

To be without her was something I could not, from that moment ever intelligently consider and I realised that I loved her then. Fully. But I knew, in an odd way, that my motive to break us up might be a sacrifice which could save her. To force us to part might be our only route to normality. I considered then that I was a toxic person. I'd not thought about myself like that before. Perhaps I was too venomous to be close to. Perhaps I was a carrier of some kind of malignant misfortune.

This was a kind of damnation that chimed with how I saw myself. It's ridiculous now when I look back on it, but what could I do? Edie had grown to become too close to me and look what it was doing to her!

If I loved her, which I truly, truly did, then I ought to cut her free.

I said, "I think we may have no choice. I think this is too much for us."

But she was crying hard now, and so was I. The despair, too heavy to hold.

"Don't," she said and placed her fingers across my mouth, burying her head in my chest.

We stayed like that for a long moment. She wanted me. I couldn't believe it. But she did. I could feel the bond between us then physically strengthening. How could I free her if she didn't want to leave me? I hadn't considered this. I would have to drive her away. It was perhaps the only way I could save her from me.

After some time, I leaned forward to roll a joint. She stopped me.

"And this isn't helping," she said. "Perhaps the drugs should be cut out for a while?"

"I know," I said, and I put the gear back on the little table. She got up to regain her composure. Whilst she was gone, I rolled a joint and smoked it as fast as I could. My head spun so badly.

The day soon dissolved into a watercolour evening. We badly

needed to escape our apartment and so took a cautious, but idle stroll among the sandy trees at the tiny Parc de Barceloneta. We each made a conscious effort not to mention Franck or to think of any of the trouble that might or might not be coming our way. The air around us was alive with the hum of conversation. People without cares. People who were free. Their words floated on the breezes that drifted in front of us. Words that flowed hand in hand with the subtle scent of red carnations and lemon flowers.

We spent time just sitting at a bench in the gardens and saying little to each other, because really there was so little to say. It was a warm evening, and we were feeling renewed by the smell of the heat. Together we watched as other people strolled nonchalantly past us, and every so often we chose to steal a glance across the northwest flank of the park towards the sand at Barceloneta.

I don't think I smiled, but I did feel a kind of contentment. A kind of closure, perhaps. And peace. I felt peace.

Spilling out of a bar nearby I could hear live music. Taking our time and digesting our surroundings, we picked up on our earlier conversation.

"Shall we look for another apartment, tomorrow?" she asked.

I nodded, "Yeah. I think so," I replied lazily. "Try to hide here for a bit longer?"

She said nothing but turned to look again at the people walking by and nodded her head imperceptibly. She looked very sad to me then, and I had to recognise that my heart was breaking.

"Edie, darling," I said. "We'll be okay. Please don't look so sad."

She didn't reply. Instead, she gazed across the sea. The evening breeze was softly fluttering her hair when she looked up at the sky that was growing redder and pinker above us. A sky that was, at that moment, reflecting apricot orange on the surface of the water that glowed and pulsed before us.

Behind where we sat there was a row of bushes stretching from one end of the small park to the other. They were tiny, squat bushes with very thick, deep green waxy leaves. I lit a cigarette. I wanted to drink some beers. I looked at the bushes. I loved them then. They made me feel the intense wonder of life.

Edie felt into her pocket, dug around for a moment, then pulled out her asthma inhaler. She pumped on the small blue plastic device and stuck it between her teeth closing her lips about its mouthpiece. Still holding on to it she exhaled until her shoulders became hunched, and then fiercely inflated her chest, firing a tiny jet of gas into her lungs. She counted to herself inside her head and after exhaling slowly she repeated the process.

I was aware that the Edie that I had come to know was embarrassed by this. It softened me to think that she trusted me enough to witness what she would undoubtedly have seen as a weakness, some kind of flaw in her otherwise invincible armour.

Then lightly, as she always did, she lifted her head and, looking skywards, she shook it gently, moving her hair like a silk scarf falling to the floor behind a closed door.

Every time she lifted her head from inhaling on her medicine, I felt that I loved her deeply.

I watched her and reflected to myself how vulnerable she seemed, and I started to wonder if I was only making it all worse for her. The stress of how we were living could not be beneficial could it? I imagined then that I saw Franck. But I knew of course that I was playing cruel games with myself. This was a fatalism that I could not explain.

I smiled at her and said, "Are you okay? What's the matter?"

She said, "I feel a bit down, that's all. A bit blue." And then she said, "I'm going to go back to the apartment. Let's move out tomorrow. I don't feel safe here."

She stood and said, "Something's happening."

I didn't give thought to it at that precise moment, what she had said. Instead, I just asked, "Shall I come with you?"

She shook her head. "No. Stay here for a while. I want to be alone for a bit."

As she walked away from me, she stopped as if she'd forgotten something. She came back to where I was sitting, and she kissed me and said simply, "I love you."

That is a moment that I will never forget. Not ever.

Not for all of my life.

*

I watched Edie walk away from me that day and it felt as if she was going forever. Briefly, I became concerned for her safety and thought to follow her back, but I decided against it and instead stretched my arms out along the top of the bench. I rested my head backwards, looking up at the cloudless sky.

I looked at the flickering stars as they began to appear, and I can remember looking at the brightest one as it seemed to change colour from yellow to pink and back again. I thought of those bushes that ran behind me, and I thought for a while of the vastness of nature and then I wondered if nature was a regular, or constant, thing. I knew, of course, that in all things created or evolved, there lay a certain rigidity, but I also knew that essentially in all matters of nature the defining element was itself one of chaos and disorder, and that it was from such a disordered soup of electrical charges and chemicals that the majesty and beauty of nature had revealed itself to those who cared to look.

I was thinking all of this to myself, as I breathed deeply on that park bench in Barcelona. It was also dawning on me that my own personal failings that had been haunting me were simply a symptom of my own chemistry. I figured that I too was a by-product of this chaotic maelstrom. I found that then I could excuse myself my indulgences and pass them off as an unfortunate phenomenon, albeit one that would need to be controlled. Either way I was blameless. It wasn't my fault that I was the way I was. Blame nature. Don't blame me.

I thought then about the Conscience thing again and this introduced another element to my contemplation. I felt relieved to have remembered the Conscience thing. It was as if a friend had arrived to ease the joyless soul searching that I was already starting to indulge in. The reflection was intense as I began to think that maybe my conscience simply didn't allow me to do the things I wanted to, and I wondered if someone like Martin Heidegger was able to justify the thoughts he had through means of his conscience. I concluded that yes, without knowing much about him or his work, he probably could. I figured that any sentient person could.

Behind me, a throng of bit players took their parts seriously. Nameless faces were milling about on the periphery of my story, on the edge of my own imagination, as indeed I was on the edge of theirs.

I fixed my gaze on a distant, tiny point of light suspended in the deepening violet sky. It was beginning to shimmer, gently, as if reflected on the surface of boiling water. I stared at it until all else was crimson. A thin almost imperceptibly static buzz grew inside my head, and the star had the effect of intensifying. Out of earthbound proportion.

I looked at it. I looked at nothing else.

And I thought about Edie. I could think of nothing else.

I lit the joint that was in my pocket and threw it on the ground. Suddenly I needed to be with her, above all else, so I stood and walked quickly back to the apartment. It had grown quite dark around me and I was thinking then about the auburn wig. I was thinking about the green jacket. I was thinking about my dream. Could she and I lose ourselves inside my dream? Could we find a place for ourselves in there? If not there, then where?

As I climbed the stairs to the apartment door, I had a sense of unease. They knew where we were. I felt it. But why hadn't Franck made his move? If it was him that I saw, then why had he not pounced? My paranoia, enhanced undoubtedly by my overwhelming dependency on the drugs, took a firm grip on me and I thought about the joint I had just thrown away and felt that I wanted to go back and get it. But I resisted this.

As I hit the top stair, I became hot and afraid and my skin began to prickle, and a light sweat broke out on my face. I was aware that I was breathing fast now, and shallowly.

"Edie!" I called. But she didn't come.

I fumbled with my keys.

"Edie!" I called again and I rattled through the fob to find the right one. I shook as I fought to insert the key into the lock. In my heightening state I rattled the door to try and get her attention.

"Edie!" I called loudly. I shouted her name now. "Edie!"

I opened the door and Edie was walking towards me. Behind her the sofa, and at the foot of the sofa a wine bottle tipped over. An empty glass by its side. I rushed to her and held her tightly as she slurred my name. I held her hard. Her tiny form, like a baby bird. Her ribcage so delicate and so frail, containing a heart so strong.

She pushed her face into my chest.

"What are we going to do?" she sobbed. "What are we going to do?"

On a chair in the corner of the room was the wig. And hung over the back of the chair was the green jacket.

I knew exactly what we were going to do.

NINE

A couple of days later we moved our stuff from one apartment to another, still in the centre of Barcelona, but a little closer to the sea. In fact, not far from the Parc de la Barceloneta where we'd sat a few nights earlier. It was an easy decision. We didn't have a lot to move and most of our things went easily into our backpacks and three or four rubbish bags. We needed to really watch the money now, we were almost broke, and this place was a lot cheaper. We soon found out why.

So, we paid up the remainder of the week in rent at the place near the top of La Rambla and walked our belongings down La Via Laietana, and then around the northern edge of Port Vell. We stopped along the way for some wine in a small bar made from dark wood and grey floor tiles, with pictures of matadors and footballers from the seventies peppered all along the back of it.

From there we strolled along the Passeig de Joan de Borbo to our new apartment above a textiles warehouse, nestled three streets behind, in the thin and rather Gothic looking Carrer de Sant Miquel.

The area that we now called home was far more anonymous than the one we'd left, and it had a definite vibe about it, not really a good one. We had a feeling that we were nestling in more shadow there than anywhere we'd been up until then. It felt cooler here, but with the coolness, came gloom. It was darker and quieter than at the top of La Rambla where we'd been sequestered in a back street filled with busy shops and busier people. Our new place was less fussy. A lot less fussy.

Naturally, with all that shadow came a different kind of darkness, and with that came an inability to see people clearly. To understand their motives. Their faces were hidden in the shadow. Their personalities too. In fact, a lot of the life in this area was obscured by blackness, and this extended to facts and events, not just the people.

And because of that the whole neighbourhood very quickly added to the feeling that we were living unreal lives in an unreal situation. Looking back, it did nothing to lighten the load for us.

I remember very clearly how distended crowds of kids congregated every evening in the small plaza directly across from our apartment. They hung around the door that led to where we were living and going out meant walking through the centre of this group every time we passed through our front door. And since we were two foreigners in a local neighbourhood, it meant that we often got singled out for all sorts of cat calling and ridicule. A lot of it good-natured, and not at all threatening, it's just that after a while it became hard work to keep smiles on our faces.

It was just as well that I didn't fully understand what they were saying about us, although I definitely knew enough to get the gist of what was being said, and although most of it wasn't good, it wasn't all bad. They were having laughs at our expense.

I got that. Why wouldn't you, I guess. I did the same thing when growing up on the estate in London. None of us then would ever actually hurt anyone. Not physically. And so of course, I felt that this was these kids' rights, in many respects. They were poor kids and in a poor area, and we were seen as privileged foreigners crashing in on their patch. Like I say, I'd do the same at their age.

But for sure we had now shifted from light into shade, and it became an effort to keep paranoia at arm's length. It was never going to end well. We felt paranoid, so we moved into a paranoid area to remedy this. Illogical. All it served to do was to drag us further down. And it so continued.

By trying to hide, we had cut ourselves off and 'normality' had begun to be a movable thing. Edie still had the shop where she worked, so she did get to see the outside world, but we both knew that this was probably not going to last. She was nervous every time she went there, desperate to return home from the moment she left the apartment. I still had the radio job, but the work there was ad-hoc and they were calling me less and less. Money was now getting really tight, and the dwindling supply that we did have was spent almost exclusively on drugs and booze. On getting out of it.

Days were becoming lost to Edie and me. In fact, it was much more than that, only we hadn't properly seen yet that it was our lives that we were losing. Our soul, in fact. I would often get back to the apartment and she would just be sitting on the floor watching the door, waiting for it to open and as soon as I walked in and put the thin blue carrier bag on the kitchen table, she'd be on me to open a bottle of wine. She hardly even waited to pour it into a glass. She would soon simply raise the open bottle to her lips and suck it down.

Meantime, I'd be rolling a joint and getting myself ready to cut out a line of speed. The coke days were well and truly gone. Speed was less than half the price. Pretty soon all the glasses would become broken and drinking from the bottle became normal. From the bottle, or from old coffee mugs. We never drank hot drinks anymore.

"Give me that fucking bottle," I said to her one day.

She turned away, shielding it from me. Then she saw that I was serious, and she gingerly handed it over to me. I grabbed at it and snatched it away. She was pouty, hurt almost. To anyone looking in we would have appeared like monkeys fighting over fruit in a cage.

Edie had started to understand that she shouldn't deny me when I made demands. I was becoming unreasonable towards her. It was how I behaved towards everything now. On so many occasions, too many to remember, I thought about how we were becoming hyper-violent versions of the people that we used to be. Edie and I were a long-forgotten memory. Edie and I, the people drinking cocktails by the pool in Albufeira, were unrecognisable. The worry and the fear had destroyed us. The optimism was now gone.

We both knew this. We found it hard to discuss.

"I'm worried, Ede," I managed to say to her one day. She looked up at me with hurt in her eyes. The girl was really suffering.

"Me too," she said softly. Almost a whisper. Timid and tiny.

"I don't even care anymore," I said. "That's the biggest problem. I don't care about Franck or any of them."

"Me neither," she said. Softer still.

But I knew this was not true. I cared deeply. But it was exhausting. So I tried to pretend to myself that it didn't mean much to me, and although I had started to reason that if they were truly looking for us, if they really wanted to pick us up, then they had had plenty of opportunity to do it. But they hadn't. Was it a game? To torture us in this way? Did they know that we would do this? That the guilt would eat us up from the inside out?

After all, it had now been year since we stole their coke, so what was keeping them? They'd found us twice, or so we figured. Certainly once, that was confirmed. But, of course, Edie hadn't led me into their trap. So now she was on their list of enemies too.

Double-crossing. Serious for her.

By stealing those drugs, Edie and I were undermining everything good that we'd done for ourselves. We were effectively holed below the waterline. By shutting ourselves away, we were now disintegrating from society. The kids outside our apartment door could sense this. We were like prey to them, and they were making a great sport of it.

One evening, Edie was standing in the centre of them. I could see her from the window upstairs. I was looking down and one of the kids noticed me. He laughed and pointed up. All the others joined him and were starting to howl obscenities in my direction, flipping gestures and all the rest of it. I hid a little behind the shutter.

Edie was trying to find her door key. She looked small then. Frail and hollow. I was trying to hide. Not going to help her. I was, instead, hiding!

My heart felt as if it had been pierced when Edie dropped the keys and, from where I stood, I could almost hear them hit the pavement. She was holding her handbag and a carrier bag with two bottles of wine in it. As she bent to pick up her keys, she nearly dropped the bottles and one of the kids nudged her with his knee and she almost fell over.

I was incensed. Heartbroken. Confused. Helpless.

It was so sad to see her kneeling among these kids looking for her door key. They all gathered around her in a circle and made like she was about to blow them one after the other. The boys grabbed at their cocks and thrust themselves into Edie's face.

It was too much.

I bolted down the stairs and threw open the main door just as she found the keys. She dived into the apartment and the kids all backed away as I slammed the door in their faces, with Edie now safely inside with me. They started kicking and banging the door and a chorus of jeers served as our backdrop for the next twenty minutes.

Edie and I drank one of the bottles of wine. I rolled a joint.

I looked around the kitchen. There was a half-bottle of brandy, two more bottles of wine and a few beers: it wouldn't be enough to see us through to the morning. Edie opened another bottle and poured nearly half of it into one of the remaining chipped enamel coffee mugs.

A little later that week, she came home early from the shoe shop.

"You're early," I said, looking up from the book that I was trying to read, when all I could really think about was alcohol.

Even reading now was becoming difficult. If not impossible.

She said nothing at first and seemed to be struggling with the right words with which to form a sentence. I knew something was coming.

Then she said simply, "They've let me go."

It took me a few moments to understand that she'd been fired from her job.

"Oh," I said. "I'm so sorry."

And I was already thinking about how we were going to get money in. How would I be able to get drugs? It was such a selfish thought. I was ashamed.

"What happened?" I asked her.

"They wouldn't say why," she said vaguely. "But I think ..." and she found it hard to finish the sentence. She tried again, two or three more times. I went to her and held her.

"I think ... I think ... I think I smell bad!" and she started to cry hard.

I embraced her more tightly. Poor Edie. Not the strong willed, confident, ambitious girl that I had met in Holland. No longer the strident beauty that I knew so well.

She felt tiny in my arms. Skin and bone. Baby sparrow.

We had to stop what we were doing. I think we both knew then that we had to find another way. But could we? Was our love strong enough?

I rolled another joint. This one was for Edie, and I still had a little bit of speed left, so I cut her a line as well. She sniffed it between her tears.

Without her income things were now looking bad. My studio work had all but dried up and we were running out of money fast. When I next saw Yannis I asked him if he could let me have some speed on account. He wouldn't do it, he said he didn't have any. Only weed, he said. But even then, he wanted to make things clear to me first. He wanted to set some ground rules for the inevitability of our new junkie/dealer relationship.

"David," he said in his thick, endearing accent. "You guys are not in a good place, huh? Can you tell me what's wrong?"

I falsely assured him that we were fine. There's no way he believed me.

"No!" I exclaimed. "We're okay. Edie's lost her job, that's all. They didn't need her now the summer is ending, and I've been a bit tight for cash. There's a lot less studio work. But we'll be okay. We'll find something."

He seemed unconvinced. As unconvinced as me.

I was a good liar. I didn't know it until that point. I've always hated lying, and liars. I find lying to be too exhausting to try to do it successfully. I guess lying for necessities sake is different, and perhaps that's what this was. What do they call them? White lies? Is that it? Maybe that's why I could do it that day. Because the drugs were so necessary.

"But you seem..." He paused to choose his words, changed the angle of his comment. "You don't seem like yourself," he finally said.

"It's fine," I snapped at him a little bit. My patience was dry, and later, walking back to the shadows, I felt bad that I'd spoken to him that way. I patted the bag of weed that Yannis had let me have. I had a strong feeling that unless we found work, this would be the last one, and inside myself I felt small fires of panic igniting all around.

I started to think that maybe Edie had something that the kids outside our apartment might want to trade some drugs for.

Maybe I could ask her to blow them for some gear? My God! Was that what I was thinking? Honestly? What kind of a monster was I becoming!

I thought then how Yannis wouldn't let us have any powder when I asked him. Only weed. Even friends were starting to not trust us.

Back in the apartment on Sant Miquel, I told Edie how Yannis only let us have weed. She was furious. With him, and with me. With everybody.

"You're kidding me!" she shrieked. "Why?"

"Because he said he only had weed. We both know that's not true." I replied, putting two carrier bags of wine down on the kitchen table.

I looked around me and on the floor I counted eight empty bottles left free to roll around the lounge on their sides.

"I wanted a lift," she said. "It's a Saturday night and we can't go out, can we? Even if we could go out, we haven't got any money!"

"I know," I said, feeling that familiar hollowness of failure in my stomach. "Let's have a drink and think about what we should be doing."

Against some swiftly multiplying odds, we still had enough wit about us to plan an escape from all of this. We might be losing the ability of good judgement, but it hadn't completely gone. Not just yet.

Instead of pulling ourselves up, we started to squabble about what we should do. Edie wanted to go to Nice. This had become almost a totally implausible thing to consider. We could barely walk to the end of the road these days, how on earth could we collect ourselves to go to another country?

Even though a couple of weeks before it was a decision we'd pretty much already made, I was now starting to lose the fight. To lose the will.

"We've only just moved," I said as an excuse.

She said that if we don't go now, then we soon might not have any more chances. She said that it was because the neighbourhood was poisonous. She said that it would destroy us like it had destroyed the kids that lived there, the kids that were at that very moment hanging around in the plaza across the road waiting for us to show. They knew that we'd have to go to the supermarket soon enough, to buy more wine. I thought I heard the ping of small stones on the wall outside, close to our window.

I tried to get us off the subject by asking her to put the red wig on. We'd found it in the move recently. She did, and it looked good on her.

"Nice," I said, smiling for the first time in a while, becoming excited by it. She looked complimented for a moment and returned my smile bashfully. It was the Edie I knew looking back at me, and for a brief moment I felt hope as I recognised the flash in her eyes.

"And the jacket," I urged her.

"Later," she giggled. "Not right now."

"No, now," I insisted, becoming impatient.

She stood to refill her cup. "Later," she teased, comically exaggerating the wiggle of her backside as she walked to the kitchen.

I followed her.

"Edie," I pleaded. "Do it now! Put it on now!" It sounded too much like a command. I didn't mean for it to. Our nerves were so shredded that we were never more than a few comments from a meltdown.

She backed away from me, appearing justifiably anxious at what I might do. Our moods could turn so quickly. I had no control over my emotional mind. She backed into the living room, passing the jacket as she did so. I picked it up and waved it in the air between us, clutching it aggressively.

"Put the fucking thing on!" I demanded then.

All the kindness and good humour now gone from the room, she stood and faced me. But before she spoke, I pushed her, only lightly but she toppled backwards over the small table that was right behind her. She lost her balance and fell to the floor, her face rubbing against the wall as she went down. I stooped over her. Not knowing what to do.

Edie looked up at me from the floor. Her cheek was already starting to smart. She looked sadly at me, and then more sadly at the coffee mug that she'd dropped on her way down spilling wine all over her lap. She started to cry and reached out gently for the mug. She picked it up and held it above her mouth as if to capture any drops that might remain.

We were an utter mess. I looked down at this girl whom I loved. *Whom I once loved*, I told myself, but I knew full well that I still did, and quite probably always would.

And now she was going. Soon she would be gone.

Holding the empty mug above her head, the wig slipped. Her eyes hidden beneath its fringe, soulless now. Lifeless. All vitality evaporated.

We were in a lot of trouble.

That night I slept on the floor in the living room. Edie took the bed. It was only a small bed and we needed to be close to one another to sleep in it and there was no way I could be close to her that night. Not after what I'd done.

Still I pretended to play the big man. She wanted me, unbelievably, to share that bed with her that night. Still. After everything.

I'd told her to fuck off and she had cried, and I had made a scene and I threatened to hit her if she didn't leave me alone, although, of course, that would have been the last thing I would have done.

She backed away and the anger quickly petered out.

In the morning we silently occupied a small corner each and went through the bottles on the floor until we found one that had some wine still in it. We shared the contents equally and considered this as some kind of gesture of reconciliation.

We then walked outside to catch some air and realised how bad we must have looked when the kids outside our door all backed away from us. No longer sniggering.

I stole two ham baguettes, and we went and sat in the plaza.

"What are we going to do?" I asked her. I didn't apologise for my behaviour the night before. I arrogantly didn't feel that I had to.

"I think we've got to go now," she said. "While we can. This place is going to finish us, David. We're going to finish ourselves."

I looked sadly at the food that I was trying to eat. Food held no interest for me. If it didn't make me feel high, then I didn't want to know about it.

"Running again!" I said sarcastically. "Look, they're not after us. If they were, they would have us by now. We agreed to hide by standing still. Remember?"

I gestured at the plaza around us by waving my arm in a silent arc. I tried to reason with her, but my patience was thin. I wanted to goad Franck, or whoever, into taking us.

"They're not here Edie!" I pleaded with her. "They're not following us!" I said as I stepped up onto the low concrete wall that ran around the perimeter of the plaza. Holding out my arms at right angles, I made like a crucifix, and I faced up to the sky and shouted with all my voice, "Come on, Franck! Here I am! Come and get me you fucking bastard! Come and get me, Franck! Fuck you Boaz!"

All around me people were watching, afraid to approach. Edie grabbed my coat and pulled me down from the wall.

"Fucking hell, David, what are you doing? You mad man. Jesus! You're out of your fucking mind!"

She held on to me as I calmed down. A few moments passed before she said, "I want out of here. There are too many memories. Too much sadness. I'm falling out of love with you."

I felt myself collapse a little more inside.

She continued, "And I don't want that to happen. I've always enjoyed our time together. Especially when I was getting to know you. And the love I have felt for you has been real." She started to sob a little. "And I want to keep it real. I honestly do."

I felt sad, but this was a chance to get her away from me. She had to leave me. It was her only chance. Why couldn't she see that?

That's when I said the cruellest thing I could think of.

"Well, Edie. I fell out of love with you a long time ago. In fact,

I don't think I have ever really loved you at all!"

I felt sick when I said it. Edie did too. I couldn't believe I could be so cruel. We pulled our food apart and threw it to the pigeons and then we walked towards the beach until we passed a wine store. We went in and Edie kept watch while I stole a few bottles and then bought a bag of potato crisps.

We went back to our apartment and finished the lot within the next couple of hours. By the evening, the cycle was ready to begin again. It was exhausting.

*

Our days passed like this. Edie got some work on a hot dog stand at the bottom of La Rambla. Any hot dogs that were left half-eaten, she would put in a little plastic bag and bring them home for us to eat together. Again, this job was out in public, but by now we both knew that forcing ourselves to hide from invisible people with no tangible or apparent reason was unsustainable. I'd had the studio call me a couple of times to go and help out, so there were still a few small lifelines out there for me and I chose to grab at them wherever I could.

For a while we tried to pick our lives up again. We went up to see Yannis and Marco, exactly like we had when we met them in the early days, back at the tapas bar. We had spent some pleasant evenings up there and we wanted to rekindle those, but I think Yannis, and Marco had now all but given up on us. I think they saw us as leeches.

Nonetheless, I'd made a little money, and I used it to pay Yannis fully what I owed him, which wasn't much to be honest.

I think he let me off some of the money. I wasn't keeping count. Elena came back for a few days and Edie enjoyed talking with her. But something had died. Something between Edie and I was gone, and it was, in the end, Yannis who made me see this.

"Edie," I said, tapping her on the shoulder and interrupting her conversation with Elena. "Don't you think we ought to make a move?" I asked her, or maybe more demanded. I was trying to mask the fact that we were now completely out of money.

But Edie was enjoying her time with Elena and felt that so long as she had good company, she didn't need any more alcohol. I, on the other hand, was totally the opposite to that. I needed the alcohol to have a good time. One without the other wasn't possible.

"No," she said. "I'm fine."

She fixed me a determined look.

"Yes, I know you are fine," I said with sarcasm in my voice. "But I'm not."

I said it as if I were the only important part of the equation.

"You go then," she said bitterly and quickly. "I'll be home soon."

"Fuck you," I hissed close to her face. "I will!"

This exchange was heard by all. Edie and I had become accustomed to speaking to one another like that when in our apartment, and so to us it was quite normal, but to the others, this would have been shocking.

I picked up my jacket and said my gruff goodbye to everyone around the table. Their polite protestations for me to stay, drowning out my farewell. I simply walked out of the bar. Away from them all as quickly as I could.

I don't think I have ever really loved you at all!"

I felt sick when I said it. Edie did too. I couldn't believe I could be so cruel. We pulled our food apart and threw it to the pigeons and then we walked towards the beach until we passed a wine store. We went in and Edie kept watch while I stole a few bottles and then bought a bag of potato crisps.

We went back to our apartment and finished the lot within the next couple of hours. By the evening, the cycle was ready to begin again. It was exhausting.

*

Our days passed like this. Edie got some work on a hot dog stand at the bottom of La Rambla. Any hot dogs that were left half-eaten, she would put in a little plastic bag and bring them home for us to eat together. Again, this job was out in public, but by now we both knew that forcing ourselves to hide from invisible people with no tangible or apparent reason was unsustainable. I'd had the studio call me a couple of times to go and help out, so there were still a few small lifelines out there for me and I chose to grab at them wherever I could.

For a while we tried to pick our lives up again. We went up to see Yannis and Marco, exactly like we had when we met them in the early days, back at the tapas bar. We had spent some pleasant evenings up there and we wanted to rekindle those, but I think Yannis, and Marco had now all but given up on us. I think they saw us as leeches.

Nonetheless, I'd made a little money, and I used it to pay Yannis fully what I owed him, which wasn't much to be honest.

I think he let me off some of the money. I wasn't keeping count. Elena came back for a few days and Edie enjoyed talking with her. But something had died. Something between Edie and I was gone, and it was, in the end, Yannis who made me see this.

"Edie," I said, tapping her on the shoulder and interrupting her conversation with Elena. "Don't you think we ought to make a move?" I asked her, or maybe more demanded. I was trying to mask the fact that we were now completely out of money.

But Edie was enjoying her time with Elena and felt that so long as she had good company, she didn't need any more alcohol. I, on the other hand, was totally the opposite to that. I needed the alcohol to have a good time. One without the other wasn't possible.

"No," she said. "I'm fine."

She fixed me a determined look.

"Yes, I know you are fine," I said with sarcasm in my voice. "But I'm not."

I said it as if I were the only important part of the equation.

"You go then," she said bitterly and quickly. "I'll be home soon."

"Fuck you," I hissed close to her face. "I will!"

This exchange was heard by all. Edie and I had become accustomed to speaking to one another like that when in our apartment, and so to us it was quite normal, but to the others, this would have been shocking.

I picked up my jacket and said my gruff goodbye to everyone around the table. Their polite protestations for me to stay, drowning out my farewell. I simply walked out of the bar. Away from them all as quickly as I could.

I was growing irritable. My ability to be patient was entirely eroded by the onslaught of so much alcohol. I heard a voice behind me and turned sharply. It was Yannis.

"Hey, David!" he called. "Wait up."

Within moments he was beside me.

"What's up, man?" he asked with genuine concern in his voice.

I shrugged. Indicating that I did not want to talk about it.

He went on, "You and Edie, man. What the hell is going on?"

I think Yannis would have probably been secretly pleased if Edie and I were to break up. She found him handsome. She'd long ago told me so, and he had pretty much said the same thing about her. So perhaps that was behind his actions that evening. After all, I'd now left her in his company hadn't I. What a fool! Perhaps I should go back?

"Oh, it's nothing," I said, unconvincingly. "We're just having a rough patch that's all."

But it was much more than that and Yannis could sense it too. Anyone could have sensed it.

"Well, it looks like more than that if you ask me," he said, before continuing, "I wanted to say something the other week. When you came over for the credit. Man, you guys look fucking awful. Tell me buddy, what is wrong? Maybe you should cut this shit out for a bit. Just a short while, no?"

I didn't say anything to Yannis. I felt it was none of his business, and I flatly refused to go back to the bar. I didn't tell him we'd run out of money. I didn't want to admit that to even myself. But I did suddenly feel that leaving her with him was not a good idea.

But why should I care? If I had said to her, as I had, that I never even loved her, why would she want me to remain? Why shouldn't she let Yannis make his move on her. If only to teach me a lesson or two. I had some bad shit coming my way, as if this weren't bad enough already. I could feel it building up. Maybe I should just go and throw myself into the sea. If I drowned, wouldn't it be better for everyone?

I hung around outside the bar for about an hour. I watched the door. It was a very lonely hour that I spent standing there in the late summer drizzle. People came and went. Laughing.

Were they laughing at me?

At least they all seemed to be laughing.

Maybe it was in my head.

That's how I remember it now. I began to wonder what the hell I was doing. My behaviour, if I were able to divorce myself from me for a moment, was completely irrational, and even more unreasonable. It didn't strike me as odd that I should be standing in a doorway across from a bar where my friends were enjoying one another's company. I was completely welcome among them. They even didn't want me to leave! But I couldn't go back in now.

Almost half an hour had passed, and I should by now be back in our apartment in the shadows. Drinking and smoking pot. Instead, like a fool, I was standing in the gathering rain and feeling the laughter and warmth that was spilling out from the tapas bar eating me up from inside.

Eventually Edie and Elena stepped outside. Edie waved her goodbyes to some people inside the bar that I couldn't see, presumably Yannis and Marco, and she kissed Elena on her cheek.

Was it my imagination, or did Elena hold Edie to that kiss for a little too long? Edie began to walk in my direction, and I stepped back so she wouldn't see me.

But then Yannis called after her and did the same to her that he did to me. He certainly looked like he might be asking Edie the same questions. Are you guys okay? What's going on? etc. But then as she turned to walk on, he tapped her shoulder, and she turned back to face him.

He went to embrace her, but she pushed him back and lowered her head. I recognised the look she gave him. It was one of shame. Coquettish. Coy. I recognised it well and I could only guess at what she might be saying to him. I could always read her expressions, and this was one of guilt.

I guessed that she'd rejected him at that moment, and that nothing had passed between them. But I knew also that things would happen if I didn't act fast to save our relationship. I would need to act right away. Certainly, standing in a doorway spying on her would not give me that opportunity.

I needed to get back to the apartment before her.

Once she passed me and I had remained unseen, I chose to run via the backstreets, south to La Rambla and back along the Passeig de Juan de Borbo. I got to the apartment ten minutes before I heard Edie arrive.

We'd done a decent job of trying to cut back on our growing dependencies, but that night we relapsed in a big way. My resolve, to try to be nice to Edie, was not being properly repaid. In short, I think I had maybe lost the ability to be nice to her. To be nice to anyone. Me included.

I was still harbouring this bizarre idea that to save her from

Boaz and from Franck and from me, then I needed to drive her away. It was, after all, me that the Amsterdam gang was after.

Then I had a significant thought.

If I went back to Amsterdam and gave myself up to them, then they'd probably stop looking for Edie. After all, I was the one they wanted. I was the one they blamed.

That, I decided would be my ultimate sacrifice for her. That could be the only true way that I could show my love to her. That was it! I felt that I'd had some kind of revelation!

I'll go to Amsterdam and give myself in, I said to myself. *Then Edie will be free of all of this.*

Free of me. Free of Boaz.

Free to live her life again.

And that night, again, I had my dream. Maybe something, at last, was becoming unblocked.

TEN

Out of the sun, at a hundred miles an hour, we plunged into a darkness so deep and so intense, that it was like a fantastic star. The rush of the wind blew cold in my chest, too fierce to ignore. From the comfort of La Rambla we were now moving toward a far more sinister world, and toward the apparent uncertainties that seemed to lurk there.

My back was aching. Because my spine was arched.

We smiled a lot to try to offset the anxiety. We were both tired of running and we needed to rest, but we couldn't rest. The unease was coming in waves now, and real fear came with it. I felt it too keenly, and at times I could hardly move as an overwhelming depression descended all around me. I often sat in a catatonic state, able only to stare into nothingness, unable to move or communicate. My senses completely anaesthetised. I was looking over the edge. Shutting down.

The shadows on the periphery of my vision became regular visitors to me, like daemonic shepherds that were steering me to a place that I didn't recognise. A place I could never go. Finally, it would pass, and Edie would look at me and say, "You okay?"

"Can't you smell it?" I answered her one time. Elliptically.

Divorced.

"Smell what?"

"Fire," I said, and I looked out of our apartment window. "Like hair. It's disgusting."

Edie scrunched up her nose. She flexed her nostrils. She said: "I can't smell anything." She sniffed and said it again.

But it had passed as quickly as it had arrived.

Every day began with a depression like this, together with an all-consuming sense of remorse. I think the same was true for Edie, but I couldn't be sure. There were times when I thought she was coping a lot better than I was. There were other times when I knew she wasn't. And it was in those times that the animal in me sought to exploit her distress. To make her feel worse. To push her away. To try and save her from herself. In order to be free of me, she first had to hate me. I was certain that *that* would be easy.

The apartment on Carrer de Sant Miquel was a place that permeated deep sadness, and as individual people, the grief that we absorbed took on its own peculiar characteristic for each of us. Whether we had made it that way, or it was the other way around, is hard to tell now. But the narrow, tobacco-yellow walls and the small rooms with their worm-eaten wooden shutters and web-covered plastic plants, emitted such extreme anxiety into the air we were breathing that it was hard for us not to be profoundly affected. My memories from living there are heavily weighed down with a deep, deep melancholy. It's as if the place was haunted by blunt emotions.

Mornings were spent trying to clear our heads and we did this usually by walking along the beach at Barceloneta. Truthfully, they weren't even mornings. It was rare that we'd be out of bed much before midday, and always we were nursing hangovers. Our lives had become so dysfunctional. Our despair was suffocating. We were trying to rid ourselves of it. But it appears now that we weren't trying hard enough. Something had to give.

I walked down to the harbour wall quite a lot. I liked to walk out to where it reached the spit that jutted out into my beloved Mediterranean Sea. I remember one time standing there on the cold, windy, late-summer wall and I remember watching the sea churn angrily below me, all of its power and violence, all of its might, untrammelled. Uncontrolled. I wondered what I had to do to tame my own turbulence. If indeed it was possible.

I looked at the sea and, at first, its motion appeared random, but I soon recognised a kind of pattern to the chaos. This, to my mind, was the perfect example of nature controlling its own violence. Could I do the same thing? I understood that I had to. More for my sake than for Edie's.

The idea of going to Amsterdam and giving myself up to Boaz and Dieter became convincing and the more I thought about it, the more I realised it might be the most correct solution to our situation.

I could save Edie.

They wouldn't need her if I gave myself to them. Boaz would leave her alone. She would be free.

Standing on the wall and looking at the sea as it folded over and into itself a thousand times, I understood that this could be my gift to her. I realised then how strong my love for her was. In many ways, unconquerable. I would die loving her. I would die *because* I loved her.

I was thinking about photographs of water then, and I was

contemplating that every photograph of every moving body of water was completely unique, like snowfall, or cloudscape. The split second that the camera lens captures that movement the image becomes a totally different thing. Never, ever to be replicated identically in the whole history of the planet. A photograph of the sea would be unique for all eternity. The shape of the waves, and of the foam. Never again to be repeated in that exact same way. Not ever again. Some things remained impossible.

I felt that relationships could be like that as well. The intricacies and the dynamics between people were every bit as complex as the elements that make up such truly unique photographs. Take each individual, how many billions of thoughts and emotions would that person experience in a lifetime? How many cells would disappear and reappear in even a single day? How many ideas and dreams were predestined to occur during the night? How many fantasies, influences or ambitions would cause how many actions to be made?

Consider these numbers.

And then multiply all of it by two. The complexity of how two individuals can interact is phenomenal. In many respects, this is like music, or even literature. Music is, in the western sense of the word, predominantly made up of only twelve notes, distributed across five or six octaves, in varying combinations, juxtaposed against a rhythm or time signature.

How many songs have been written? How many can you sing? How many can you name? All from twelve notes! All of them. Astonishing. This is where nuance plays such an important role. Nuance gives colour to music, and nuance in relationships does exactly the same thing.

Books too. A book essentially is, to my mind, and assuming each language is comparable, a collection of the same letters except in a completely different order each time. So when broken down this way, every book is basically the same book. It's just that the letters are in a different order.

I tried to superimpose these thoughts on to my attitude towards Edie, whom I adored. Was I trying to make all emotion, all feeling, all experience, and sensation ... was I trying to make those things all the same in every person? Trying to make out that we were no different to anyone else, and that because we were no different, then we didn't deserve to act as anything new or special? Nor even unique.

Not anything. Nothing. Not even worth saving.

In the scheme of life, we were utterly nothing. I was utterly nothing. But my dream? My dream was *something*.

The girl in my head held me captive. I was enthralled by her. She was the one I loved more than anything. I needed to bring her into my life. I needed for her to be real. If she didn't exist, then neither could I. And I think I felt a guilt that Edie was moving in on the real object of my affection. Maybe this was the real reason why I felt that I needed Edie away from me.

Just by travelling on any train I could feel a sense of anticipation, an excitement that one day the girl in my dream might become real and that I would be so ecstatic and happy when I finally met her. Every church or cathedral that I passed held hope. Every blue object that I sensed. Every green jacket that I saw. Every shopping plaza that I passed. Every child's laughter. These things all contained hope so real that it made my soul feel alive. Every single body of water, be it river, lake, fountain, or sea, they all contained the potential of an epiphany for me. The prospect of this girl's possible presence sent my mind soaring.

Where was she? Where was she?

Maybe I had to forget it all now. Maybe I had to draw a line under my life.

Out over the open sea I watched a burst of rain crash into a thin ribbon of mirrored glass. It fell in the way that I imagined a heavy velvet curtain would fall across the stage at La Scala Opera House in Milan.

One motion, magnificent and impressive.

I entered into a deep dream as I stood there, and I had the most vivid thoughts about a woman standing close to the balcony of a hotel apartment that we were sharing in a block in Cyprus or somewhere like that. She is sipping a long drink, possibly a vodka or a gin with tonic or lemonade. But a clear drink, nonetheless. I see a column of ice threading the length of the glass. I see two slices, or maybe only one. Cleanly cut lemon or lime.

She smiles at me affectionately, and then she opens her smile wider to show me her laughter. I delight in the sound her voice makes as it breaks into fragments becoming a rapture. She is tall and she sports a fluffy feathered haircut that tumbles in big platinum rolls down either side of her head, curling upwards like springs on both of her shoulders.

This is nineteen seventy-five and she is elegant. Her breasts seem oddly out of keeping with the rest of her body. And although they are possibly too large for her frame, she clearly enjoys them, and takes great comfort in her sexuality, which is both abundant and understated. She likes herself and she likes her skin, and she takes good care of her appearance. She touches herself whenever she feels free or effervescent. It is her right, and it is her place to do so.

Tonight she is wearing a light white cotton dress which hides little of her body. Entirely on purpose she stands in front of the balcony, between me and the illuminations of the hotel complex behind. She knows how the light is playing with her figure, and she knows how much of her I can see. She smiles and half turns towards the view across the concourse below us leaning heavily now on the balcony rail.

And then she is gone. Suddenly. Gone.

I peel an orange and hold one of the segments between my thumb and forefinger and, controlling my breathing now, I squeeze it gently, feeling the small flesh of the fruit burst below the skin until it becomes a soft pulpy mass robbed of its structure and form. Below me, people are screaming and have gathered beneath the balcony. Some are calling up in my direction. I compare the crushed orange segment with a fresher one and I lay them alongside one another on a glass-topped coffee table as I stand to answer the knock that has started at my apartment door.

I looked again at the rain cloud across the sea, and I recognised with disgust the horrible daydream that I had been having. Was this some kind of subconscious mechanism designed to make me distinguish sentiments of well-being from those of distress and upset? Were these self-inflicted images some kind of controlled stimulation meant to channel the difficulties that Edie and I were experiencing? Was it, even, an illness? Or the germ of an illness? Was I perfectly healthy? Was I totally sane?

*

On the day that I was having such horrible, disjointed thoughts while standing on the harbour wall looking into the tumult of the breaking waves beneath me, I was completely unaware that, in Nice, a young woman was clearing tables at the end of the season at the restaurant Portovenere, where she had been working all summer. Soon she would be asked not to return the next day as they would be closing for the winter. They will tell her that she would be welcome to go back in a few months' time, and that they would keep her job open for her. Only, if she could let them know as soon as possible, they would appreciate it.

But she didn't feel that she would be going back.

Her thoughts about England had recently been growing more vivid and she was thinking that she might visit London in the spring. Her time in Nice was, she felt, crawling to a natural end. She decided that she was going to stay there for as long as they wanted her to, but then she would be taking a train north to meet up with her parents and her brother at their home in Normandy. She would spend the coming Christmas with them, and then in the new year make plans to go to London.

Imogen was brought up in Benerville-sur-Mer, a small town close to Deauville. This was where her family still lived. Naturally, her life had been lived inside the shadows cast by the events that took place all along the Normandy peninsula at the close of the Second World War. Maybe it was because of that that she had developed, over time, a profound respect for England that few others in her community seemed to share.

That evening, after she'd cleared the tables, she walked down to the beach again and stood looking out to sea.

A gust of wind blew her jacket around her, and she felt a chill cut through. Her little blue hat nearly flew from her head, and she instinctively put her hand to her head to hold it down on her shoulder length, auburn hair. The sea fascinated her, and she stood in awe of its power, and she began to think about how every photograph of water was unique.

The sun began to drop behind the horizon.

The moon began to glow more strongly.

Pretty soon it would reflect across the surface. She liked that moment in any given day. When the light changed. Softened. The stars began to flicker in the violet evening sky, a sky that seemed to now be lowering across the bay, sending pomegranate clouds scudding across its entire surface, from Portugal to Spain, from France to England.

Orange, crimson, red and purple.

She knew that soon her chance would come, but for now she had a little more time in Nice. Maybe a week. Maybe two.

She'd enjoyed the summer and she'd made some nice friends. She had even, on occasion, attracted lovers. But none of the friends or lovers felt substantial to her, they were all temporary people on the edge of an intransigent plane. People who were flitting in and out of her life. But all of them were visitors. There seemed to be no one that wanted to stay. To become a resident.

But she was in no hurry. And she was happy that evening as she turned her back to the sea. She leaned on the railing that ran along the perimeter of the Quai des Etat Unais and she looked up then at the hotels that lined the Promenade, across the wide heavy road in front of her. She liked Nice. She would always remain fond of the place.

She felt an overwhelming sense of contentment then, and the strong feeling that her chance was soon coming took her over completely.

*

When I got back from the harbour Edie called to me from the bedroom. She was still in bed. She looked awful.

"Did you go to the shops?" she asked me. "What did you buy?"

"I've not been to any shop, Edie," I said. I was irritated by the way she asked me one question, and then a second that assumed the answer to the first.

"I've just been by the harbour," I called to her.

She came into the room and asked me again, "What did you buy? Did you get wine?"

I was becoming tired of our focus on booze. I sat and rolled a joint. It was one o'clock in the afternoon and this was going to be the first of the day. I was doing okay. I'd already been awake for nearly two hours. I considered this an improvement. Two hours and no smoke already. This was progress.

"No, I didn't get wine," I said. More progress.

"We'll have to get some later," she replied. She went to count out the coins from her coat pocket. She threw them down on the table.

"We're going to have to steal some again," she declared.

I had some money in the bank at that time. Not a lot, but enough for wine, so I wasn't concerned by what she said.

"I'll get dressed and we can go out again. Is that alright with you?" she asked me. I nodded as I licked the cigarette paper's gummy edge, folding it over and twisting it as I did so.

I went to the stereo and played Sylvian, *'Pulling Punches'* beating into the room. Edie walked to the stereo and turned it down. She left the room. I stood and walked to the stereo and turned it up. She immediately came back, and we began our first squabble of the day.

That afternoon, with my dream bouncing about in my head, I asked her to put on the green jacket again. I waited until she was drunk. I didn't have to wait long. And she did put it on. The red wig too. We fucked like art students. Later we chose to take a walk up to La Rambla to see if anyone we knew was around.

We had grown tired of hiding now and quite often we tested ourselves and flatly refused to continue doing it. Besides, we had figured out that, when we were walking, we were not drinking and so, therefore, walking was something doubly good for us.

Something we should be doing more of. Something to encourage.

It was a Sunday, and it was quiet in town. We sat in our usual tapas bar, just the two of us, and briefly it was like sitting with an old friend. Edie was relaxed, and cordial. We laughed even. Smiled a lot.

Yannis called in for one beer, he said that Marco was working late, and that he was bored on his own. He was happy to see us, and he said that we were looking really well. He kissed Edie lightly, and she smiled at him. I remember now how happy she was that night. It was like a cloud lifted whenever we left Sant Miquel, and beneath the cloud Edie appeared visibly younger.

Her whole demeanour improved whenever she was out from under the shadow cast by the gloom in that place.

Yannis picked up on this and when she went to use the toilet, he said to me, "Edie's looking great, mate," and he tapped my arm with a shine in his smile.

"Yeah," I said bashfully, thinking about how she was my girl. Mine. Not his. Thinking then about how much I still needed to do to keep her with me. Did I have the patience?

I'll never know now.

Edie came back and Yannis left to go home. He said that he had things to do the next day and so Edie and I decided to head back as well. As we walked and got nearer to our apartment, the fog again began to descend. As soon as we turned the corner, and we saw the kids gathered near our door, the depression intensified. Instantly. Like a switch had been thrown.

From the moment we were inside, we were transformed.

I'd managed to steal about four bottles of wine earlier in the day, from two different stores. I could afford to buy it again now, but I had to use the excuse of having no money to sometimes give me a way out of constantly supplying it. We also had plenty of brandy and enough weed for a dozen smokes.

We didn't mean to do it. It just happened. We snapped. Like always.

Our feelings of contentment towards one another, feelings that were so strong not even one hour before, automatically dissolved when we entered that bloody apartment. The way it would happen, so unbelievably quickly, was terrifying.

After the first bottle of wine, and our second joint, we started to attack one another. She called me some terrible names. I shouted some horrible things. Over nothing! We fought like crazy.

Edie hid in the bedroom at one point that night, and she took a bottle of the wine with her. She moved the wardrobe in front of the door so that I couldn't get to her. I think she wanted to give herself some security that the whole bottle would be hers and hers alone. She knew I'd try to get it from her, and that I would down it if I did. She was right. I was a fucking monster to her. It's awful to recount all of this.

I knew that once she'd finished the wine, then she'd be out to fetch another, so the only way to spite her would be to finish the rest of the bottles myself. So that's what I did. Edie was incandescent with fury. Almost possessed by it. Haunted by it.

By midnight we were so angry with one another that we began to shout incoherently as our inhibitions completely dissolved. I tried to grab her, but I fell over. I was too drunk. I stood up and swayed on my heels, standing in the middle of the room. Edie escaped to the bathroom and locked herself in, again clutching a bottle of wine.

I tried to calm down, but after a few short moments I went and beat my hands on the door calling to her to come out. The people in the flat above us started banging on the floor, and pretty soon I was shouting back up at them. Pointless.

It was a horrible scene.

I kicked and kicked at the bathroom door which quite quickly started to break loose. My rage on this night was like no other night before it. There was more banging on our ceiling and then at our door. Someone shouted at me in Spanish, but I was too drunk to be able to understand. Edie was virtually screaming now from inside the bathroom.

"Please can I come out?" she sobbed hysterically. "I need to come out of here and get some sleep."

I agreed, and I told her this in a voice that was the calmest and most reassuring that I had sounded in a very long time.

I don't know why I did it. But the moment she left the room I was on her. I pinned her to the floor and raised my hand as if to slap her face. It was so fucking awful. I loved her so much. Why was I behaving like this? I didn't hit her. At least I can say that I didn't hit her. It's nothing, I know. But at least I didn't do it.

Instead, I grabbed one of the several empty bottles that was rolling, stray across our floor, and I threw it as hard as I could against a table leg. It shattered dramatically, sending glass shards across the carpet.

Edie rolled on to her front and pulled herself up on her knees, crouching now. Then she was sick all over the floor. I remember it smelled strongly of wine. There was probably an entire bottle of it all over her knees and all over the carpet. She remained crouched and cried like a small child.

And all I did was watch as this poor wretch blindly stretched out her arm and began fumbling around, trying to find something. Sobbing, she was grasping for her purse. Once she had it, she scrabbled inside, scratching to find her asthma inhaler.

She was heaving hard. Struggling for breath. The stress was attacking her. I walked away. I didn't help her. I got up and walked away. It was possibly the worst thing I've ever done.

The anguish was incredible. My arrogance: indescribable.

Edie tried to stand and fell against the table. She picked herself up and went back into the bathroom. We were silent now. The storm had passed.

A few moments later I heard the shower running and then shortly after she came hobbling out to where I was sitting in the lounge. I was rolling another joint. I could barely focus on what I was doing. I was swaying backwards and forwards. It was all so terrible. Really terrible.

Edie tried to go to bed. But I wouldn't let her rest. Instead, I stood in the doorway puffing on my hash and telling her how much I hated her and how much I wanted to be alone. I didn't want her. I didn't love her. She made me feel sick, I said. Physically sick. I told her she repulsed me. She revolted me!

What the fuck is wrong with me?

The absolute truth was the complete opposite, I loved her so much that it hurt me. It made me afraid of how much anger I had inside me. The stress of living our lives on the run was destroying us completely. It was monstrous. Maybe I simply wasn't made for relationships. Maybe love was too big a thing for me to cope with. I was too immature. Love was simply something that I could not handle. Maybe the only love I could ever feel was for a total fiction. A fiction of my own making. This could explain my reluctance to commit to anything real. At any time.

Edie cried herself to sleep that night, and I finally stopped haranguing her when I realised that she was unconscious and couldn't hear me anymore.

I crept close to her and looked at her face close up. God, how I loved this woman! There was a bruise on her cheek, and a graze from yet another fall she had had a few days earlier, after I had pushed her over.

I hadn't even seen it until now.

There was another bruise on her arm, a huge one that was turning yellow. It must have been a day or two old already. I couldn't recall bruising her arm like that, and then I remembered how I grabbed her tightly a few nights before. It must have really hurt her to make a mark like that, and that girl didn't complain to me once about it. I think that even after everything I'd said and done, and the way I had behaved, she still loved me.

I think that perhaps she *had* loved me. But not anymore.

I'd made sure that night that she could never love me again. There was no way any woman would tolerate the man I had become. I sat on the edge of our bed as she slept and I cried so hard as the night grew cold, and very, very lonely, all around me.

Eventually I walked to the living room and tried to sleep on the sofa. I was trembling and sleep did not come easily, but when it did, I didn't move until I heard the door quietly open in the early morning. The click of the latch was a tiny sound from out on the furthest edge of my consciousness. Barely registering, I collapsed back into sleep.

Empty, cavernous, and very, very black.

No dreams.

No memories. No light.

When I finally awoke, I felt a revulsion sweep over me in a hollow wave, a disgusting empty wave that made me feel sick. I became aware of how hard the front of my head was throbbing. I felt the need to throw up and instantly stood, wobbling and unstable. I had to hold down the vomit as I gagged and tasted stale wine and brandy in my mouth. I held it all in until I managed to stagger to the bathroom, tripping on empty bottles on the way. All over the floor.

I puked into the sink and then I heaved a whole load more stale booze in straight away. From my gut. Deep.

Edie.

I thought of her and of how I had behaved. Oh my god, the shame! How could I ever tell her the depth of my sorrow. I needed help. I told myself that first. It was a step, and now I needed to apologise to Edie. To hold her and kiss her face and tell her how I felt. How sorry I was. How much she meant to me. That she must pay no attention to me when I'm like that. We would have to leave the apartment now. That was clear. I would tell Edie these things. I would get help. We could try again.

So, I went to our bedroom.

But it was empty.

She was gone.

I thought at first that maybe she'd gone to work at the hot dog stand. I checked the time. It was midday, too early for her to be there. I thought then that maybe she might have gone to get some air, and that she would be back soon. I decided to wait for her, but one scan around the bedroom told me something was permanent.

A quick search showed that she'd taken her clothes. I checked. And then I did the same thing again. Everything was gone. Her make up. Her clothes. A couple of her books. Gone. I looked again, for a third time. Even the small broken figurine that I had destroyed. She'd taken that too. I checked the living room. The wig. The red wig. And the jacket. Gone.

She'd taken everything. She had left me only the memory of her in our wig and jacket. I remembered the fun we had choosing them at the market up at Calle dels Encants. How we'd laughed on the day she wore them outside the café at the top of La Rambla.

I thought of her stern demeanour on the day we met outside of the movie place near The Grasshopper in Amsterdam.

I thought of her and I running from Timo's place, carrying his coke and then giving it to the guy in Paris on the motorbike.

I thought of she and I in Oporto, and the day she came home drunk. I was so afraid. I thought of her smiling warmly at me in the sunshine and I heard her whisper that she loved me.

I thought of her carrying two orange drinks to our poolside loungers at the hotel in Albufeira, and I remembered how proud I was to know her. I could see her smile, light on her lips as I leant in to kiss her softly in the evening breeze in Barcelona.

I thought of her sitting opposite me on the train into Germany, and I thought of her feet resting in my lap. I thought of her canvas shoes, the black and white ones that I never told her I liked.

I could smell her scent then as I pictured the sunlight that flickered across her face as she slept in front of me, back in the days when we were falling in love.

I thought of the two stars that appeared on the blue horizon, when the sky was both day and night at the same time. I'd said to Edie that we should be like them.

I believe that, for a while, we were as eternal as those stars.

But even stars don't last forever.

And I realised then that I had destroyed the most precious thing I could have ever wished for in all of my life.

What had I done? Why had I done it? I wanted to die now. I loved her with all my heart.

Very soon it became clear that Edie had gone for good. This was never going to change. The part of my life that had her by my side was now over.

There was no more Edie and David.

It was now just David.

It was now just Edie.

PART TWO

ELEVEN

I sat for the rest of that day in the apartment at Sant Miquel, vacantly looking at the walls and then at the floor. All of it empty of everything but shame and anguish. My emotions left me unable to stand. I felt ill if I tried to sit up. The sorrow and shame were too heavy for me, and I simply couldn't move. But my thoughts, they were the greatest of all of my torments. They were more than I could bear.

Disgust pulsed through me in waves. Why had I done it? How could I fix it? Or even, could I fix it? Could she forgive me? Did I want her to forgive me? Did I deserve to be forgiven? No. I didn't.

I understood perfectly well how I'd been steadily undermining our relationship for weeks, trying to push her away in a weird effort to make her safe somehow. Did I now think she'd be safe? Did I think she would be better off without me? Yes. I must concede I actually thought that she was now better off.

But did I think she was now *safer* without me? I didn't know. Probably not, not yet. Did I think that she would soon be safer without me? I think that maybe yes, I did believe that could well be true.

I figured that if I left her alone now, she would quickly find her own space. But I wouldn't be there, sharing it with her and that realisation cut me wide open. Right down the middle. I wanted so much to hold her and treat her well. I wanted to cloak Edie in love and affection, do nice things for us. A pleasant evening, a nice meal. A few drinks and some laughs. Nothing excessive. But I couldn't. I felt such harsh bitterness and I was suffocating in the thought that I knew we could never go back.

I needed Edie. I loved her. I wanted her.

Would she forgive me? No.

Should I go after her? Maybe.

But where had she gone? Did Yannis know something? And then a shudder. Was she with him now? How far away was she? I tried to stand to go to and see him, but my sorrow pulled me back down again. Too heavy. Too heavy. Down into hell. I looked around the living room. I looked around the kitchen. The place was a horror show. If the landlord came now, I'd probably be evicted. I thought about the neighbouring apartments, and of the residents banging on the floor and on the door in the night.

I thought then that there was a strong possibility that the landlord would arrive. If they'd called him to complain, as they must have done, then it was not unreasonable to assume that he might just turn up unannounced. I decided to clear the place up and get out of there for a few hours. To put some distance between myself and that desolate scene that I had created. To go and find Yannis. To see if Edie had been in touch him, or with Elena.

So that's what I did.

I limply moved bottles to bags, and bags to bigger bags.

Bottles containing booze were poured straight down the sink. I told myself, with conviction, that I would drink no more alcohol. Not ever. What a joke!

I straightened the furniture and gave the place a bit of order. I cried as I made the bed look tidy when I caught Edie's perfume from across the pillows. I felt that I would never get into that bed again. She'd left some hair clips and a small hair band on the bedside table, and I picked them up and put them in my pocket. I still have them today. Somewhere.

The place looked better. I carried two large plastic bags down the steps, hoping for all the world that I wouldn't see the neighbours. I didn't, and it felt a little bit like progress, as if I was purging myself. The bags were filled with empty bottles, and they clinked loudly as I placed them out by the plaza for the lorry to collect in the morning. The kids said nothing to me as I pushed through them. In fact, they barely noticed me pass. It was as if they were too disgusted to want to play anymore, or maybe they were finally bored with us. With me. There was no more 'us'.

I'd been in the apartment all day, and it was already growing dark. I walked mournfully among the sailing yachts moored at Port Vell, and then on up Via Laietana cutting across the Placa d'Urquinaona to the intersection with Ronda de Sant Pere. From there it was a few minutes to Yannis' place where he lived above a bakery on the Carrer de Girona.

When I arrived, Marco answered the door.

"Oh, hi David," he said, and it seemed as if he was annoyed that I was there. He wasn't his usual self. Had they heard?

"Yannis is in the tapas place," he said.

"Okay, thanks Marco," I said. "Is Edie with him?"

Marco shrugged and looked at me directly, his brow furrowed slightly, creasing like the spine of a well-read book.

"No, I don't think so," he said. "Elena is with him."

I didn't want to see Elena. I've no doubt that Edie would have told her about my hidden self, and I could not take any kind of criticism at that moment, especially criticism that I deserved. So, I walked to the bar and saw Yannis sitting at the back with Elena, and I carried on by and stood in the same doorway that I had stood in a few nights before, my shame and humiliation crippling me.

What was wrong with me? I needed to get it fixed, whatever it was that was broken.

Eventually they left the bar. I'd waited not even half an hour, but nonetheless was about ready to abandon my vigil when I saw them. I slid out from my cover, walked around the block, and met them coming the other way. It looked like a chance encounter.

I was right. Elena was very cold to me. She physically backed away and turned a little to Yannis as I approached them both, almost as if she was doing it for protection, a reflex reaction on her part, one for which I could not blame her.

He, on the other hand, seemed genuinely pleased to see me.

"Hey!" He smiled warmly. "No Edie? Where is she?"

I said nothing. I believed he was genuine. Elena gave me a dark look and turned to Yannis and said goodbye, saying that she could walk herself home now. She grunted a goodbye to me and hastily disappeared. I ignored her completely. I don't think that was intentional, it was just that my mind was packed with events, and just wasn't working properly.

"Yann," I said, "something terrible has happened." I held

back the tears. He read my anguish straight away and he walked me back to the bar where I ordered sparkling water. We sat and I looked at the empty space on the bench at my side. The loneliness was too much. I was crying hard now but trying to conceal it. My face a mess.

"Edie has left me!" I said, actually crying now, struggling to control myself.

"Tell me," he said.

I couldn't be sure if he knew or not, but I honestly don't think he did. So, I told him it all. I told him everything. I didn't hide how bad I had been. I didn't cover a thing. I needed to exorcise myself of the daemons inhabiting me. I needed absolution from a friend. I needed to find some kind of comfort, some kind of peace. And more than anything at all, I needed to rediscover the hope that had been lost to me.

"It's not good," he said. "What you're telling me is not good."

"We've been through so much together," I sobbed, and continued, "I love her, mate. I really do. I think I need to get her back. I miss her smile and her laughter. When we first met, she was cold. I liked it," I sniffed, "only I didn't realise I liked it. And we went through so many obstacles to come together..."

Yannis looked at me. He was being patient. Allowing me to talk. He felt it would be a benefit to me. But of course, I couldn't tell him about the drugs we stole from Boaz. I had to make sure I didn't breathe a word. For Edie's sake, as well as my own.

"At first it was easy. We had money. But then it finally ran out. A couple of keys don't get as much as you imagine they would."

And I stopped immediately, realising what I was saying, and what I was about to tell.

Yannis waited for me to go on. When I didn't continue, he said, "What do you mean?" and he tilted his head quizzically.

"Nothing," I said, too late. "Forget it."

There was a silence in the space between us. A big silence. A bigger space. Yannis knew. I swear he knew. Or, at least, I'm sure he suspected. That's why he didn't push me to say more.

Eventually, I said, "Just ... let's leave it. I'm sorry." But I couldn't keep myself under control. The pressure was making me lose my mind.

"They'll fucking kill her if they get her mate!" I said then, more to myself than to anyone else. I leant forward, crying hard and he put his arm around my shoulder.

"They'll kill her! I'm not kidding Yann. They're serious people. What have I done?"

His embrace at that moment was honest. Whatever else happened between us, at that moment I genuinely believe that Yannis was being real.

He wanted to comfort me, his friend. He could see what a wreck I had become, and he wanted to help me. I know this for a fact.

He was not a bad man.

I was not a bad man.

After a while I calmed down a little and Yannis went to the bar and brought back beers.

"Have one of these," he said. I looked fearfully at the beer. "One is fine," he said. "Two is fine, okay. Three is not fine, not for you."

We drank in silence for quite some time. When Yannis was sure I was calm again, he said, "I did think something."

He let the words drop.

"I did think maybe there was more to you guys than we all knew, but I didn't think you two would be stupid enough to do something like that. If you're messing with dealers, then man you must have a death wish or something. And if they're Dutch dealers ..."

He didn't need to finish the sentence. I started to shake and drank my beer in one go under Yannis kind eye.

"The lighter," he said. "Amsterdam." His eyes widened "Ah, now I get it! Iker knows plenty of those guys. You'd better get out of here, mate."

And then he said something else.

"Don't beat yourself up over what you did to Edie. You know it was wrong." I nodded, and he continued, "But she was leaving you anyway, you know that don't you."

I looked at him, genuinely shocked.

"What?" I mumbled. And again, "What? What do you mean? How would you ..."

"Elena," he said. "She told Elena last week that she was going to leave you."

"Did she say anything else?" I asked, feeling suddenly betrayed. "Did she say where she was going?"

I had hope again. It felt like lightning.

"I'm not sure I can say, David," Yannis said.

He was a solid guy and a genuine person, and he would keep his word, but I begged him, I pleaded with him. I shouldn't have done that because I put him then in a difficult place and he didn't deserve that.

"Please Yann, tell me! I need to be with her. I need to find her!"

I started becoming frantic that he might be holding on to a key that I needed so desperately, but could I trust him?

"Yannis, please mate. Where is she going?" I asked him, my voice breaking.

He looked at me then with a kind of pity in his eyes, as if I were an animal that had just been hit by a car.

"France," he said. "She's gone to Nice."

After some more time passed, I asked Yannis, "What can I do now? Should I go to find her?"

He shook his head.

"No," he said. "There is nothing that you can do. Just get yourself straight again. Only then will Edie even look at you."

I stared at him as he continued, "You have lost her now, David. You have to face up to that. There is no way she will come back to you after what you have told me. No way."

He said it sadly, as if someone had died. And in many ways, someone had.

Me.

That was the last time I ever saw Yannis. I liked him, but I was never entirely sure that I could fully trust him. I always suspected that he may tell Iker the things that I had said to him, and even if he did, I'm not so sure that Iker really ever got any of that information back to Amsterdam.

But maybe he had, and maybe Franck was there at the window that night because he'd been told we'd be there. I didn't know, and the constant unravelling of these mysteries was crippling me emotionally.

But one thing that I was very clear on was what I did next.

On the day that Edie left I was inconsolable, and that night was unbearable. I left Yannis and walked slowly back to the apartment. Alone. Half hoping she would come back, but knowing full well that it was never going to happen.

I arranged to meet him the following day. I was hoping to pick up some drugs. But I didn't go. Instead, before I could change my mind, when I got back to the apartment, I packed up all my things.

I left a lot of it behind and hoped the landlord would sell it all and take the money in return for me not paying him the final weeks' rent. I'd lost the deposit, but I didn't care. It wasn't much. Not as much as it should have been.

I left Barcelona that night and even though I didn't know where I was heading, I knew roughly the direction. The thought that Edie might have a change of heart barely even crossed my mind.

What if she were to return after I had gone? What if she had told Elena she was leaving, but only so that this information might make its way back to me. To make me consider what it would be like to not have her in my life. What if Yannis was lying? How would he know she and I had spoken about Nice? Through Elena, probably. I think Yannis was telling the truth, even though he would like to have had Edie all to himself.

And then, what if Edie herself was planning to stay away just for a day or two, just to teach me a lesson. Just to give me a proper taste of how life without her would feel. I barely considered any of this. I had to get out of there. I had to get out from under that dark shadow, and to save my brittle mind. I think I knew in my heart the truth of it, and that was that there was no way that Edie would come back to me. We were in a bad way, and together we were out of control. We had to be apart, even if only for a while, because I knew that if she did return I would only do it all again. What I needed then was to try to find her, and above all, to keep hope alive.

It was about four in the morning that I walked up to Colom to catch a bus to the Barca Sants train station. I couldn't stay in the apartment a moment longer and I didn't even look behind me as I closed the door on where Edie and I had lived together.

We could have had a beautiful life if we hadn't stolen that coke. If we had done the right thing, and delivered it to Boaz, we could then have left and built something real, something without the pressure of constantly thinking that we were being followed, constantly looking behind us and hiding in the same shadows that were trying to claim us. Shadows that were trying to eat our souls.

We had lost control. It would have happened to anyone living under a cloud like that one. It was a symptom of our circumstance. A sickening one. We shouldn't blame one another. What was done, was done and truthfully, the odds were against us from the start.

But now, all of a sudden, I had hope. Now I had to find her, and if I couldn't find her, then I would have to go to Boaz and give myself to them.

Above everything else, I had to make life safe again for Edie.

One way or another. I owed her this.

There was a train to Nice that day, but it didn't leave until the afternoon. I was at the station by five o'clock in the morning so had a lot of hours to kill. I tucked my backpack up under my head and lay down across three blue plastic seats. I was exhausted and fell into a deep sleep and when I woke up, there were people sitting either side of me, eating and drinking coffee. They paid no attention to me at all as I swung my feet to the ground and rubbed my eyes. I needed a wash. I can remember well how badly I smelled.

The ticket to Nice was cheap, and I didn't think twice about paying for it. I was encouraged that I'd still have money for at least three nights if I found a cheap enough hotel. The train ride was a long one. Seventeen hours. Every stop, virtually. And it had a horrible overnight stay in Marseilles, so I planned to stay in the station all night. The train arrived at roughly ten-thirty at night, and it left for the final leg of the journey at about six the following morning.

That's what you get with cheap tickets, I told myself. I had little choice. So I got myself a croissant and waited for my train. I still had a long time to wait.

By late afternoon I had arrived in Girona, just about ninety minutes after I had left Barcelona, still numb from everything that had happened. The withdrawal of the speed was starting to bite, and I understood that I had probably given myself a problem. I knew then that I would need to face up to some unpleasant things in the coming weeks.

I turned my attention to watching Spain slip by as my train pulled out and continued its journey to Port-Bou on the border with France. All in all, I'd need to change three times, the first at Port-Bou. I cracked open a small window and breathed deeply. The air was warm like warm water. I caught sight of a large clock that told me that it was coming up to five in the afternoon.

When I arrived at Port-Bou about an hour later, I stepped down from my train feeling lighter on my feet than I had for many weeks. I had fifteen minutes in which to find my connection, so I walked along the platform and up a small flight of steps out on to the station concourse. I passed some small placards advertising biscuits and beer and made my way towards the information office where I was directed to platform six. I stopped in the lavatory to splash water on my face in an attempt to wake me up a little. It worked fine. The cold water made me gasp and my eyes felt fresher and instantly less dry.

I patted my pocket and felt inside for my tickets, then I headed up to the platform. The train to Narbonne was about to arrive. I climbed aboard and took a Marquez novel from my pocket. It was a collection of short stories. But I couldn't read. My mind was too frantic.

In my imagination I started to pretend that Edie was with me. She smiled at me, and then at herself and then into her chest. I thought again of her on the train to Germany. How she'd looked that day as she read a thin book with the sun throwing dapples across her face and shoulders.

Beautiful Edie. Would I ever see you again? Then, in the back of my mind I could see Boaz slamming his hands on his desk in the office above the pizza shop. I could see the yellow standing lamp in the corner of the room and the little blackened out windows, masking his expressions and hiding the obscenities that he was spewing.

I looked out of the window. I was looking for my dream. I lit a cigarette and simply stared at the passing terrain. How different it was to anything I had seen up until then. It looked hot out there. It looked clean and dirty at the same time, and I liked it. Mountains had sprung up on the horizon and great balls of fluffy cottonseed blew thickly and was obscuring the mountains a little bit. The cotton drifted like snowflakes in a light blizzard, and I remember thinking that it was like hot snow.

I saw dark green fields nestling comfortably alongside barren swathes of sun-scalded grasses, hemmed along two edges by dusty crumbling roads leading nowhere. I saw delicate and dazzling fields filled with poppies stretching across ditches away to the horizon. I had never seen so many poppies. They were beautiful. Abundant. I saw road signs flash by to places I knew nothing of. I saw the familiar, relentless advertisements for San Miguel beer.

I saw the same giant-sized cardboard cut-out of a black bull at the top of three or four enormous hills as I journeyed across an increasingly verdant landscape, and I saw the same petroleum and oil company signage that had followed me across Europe from the day that I had left England and had sat on the ferry out of Dover.

I thought about how the power of consumerism in the west meant that this cycle of consumption couldn't be broken.

Petrol. Oil. Gas. Modern civilisation had been built on the availability of these things.

Power. Energy. Almost everything we touch today has a plug attached somewhere at the end of it. Electricity is commonplace in the western world. It is endemic. It is everything. Without it we wouldn't have the telephone, the computer, the radio, the synthesiser, the lights, the screens, the fridge, the music, the toaster, the view at Piccadilly Circus, Times Square, Tokyo, Hong Kong. We wouldn't have the aeroplane, the high-performance car, or the power to drive the turbine that creates the electricity.

And I wouldn't have been there at that moment, on a train drifting through France, on a train going nowhere looking out at the tumbling landscape as it grew, fertile and immense, in all directions. The world turning blue again.

The Pyrenees were making their presence felt.

I looked out of the window of the train as it began to rock gently away from the border and through a small village station. The station was nothing more than a junction box and then a raised level at the side of a dry, grey pot-holed road.

All around were small houses. The track rose above them for a few moments, up and over a small bridge. I looked out over the roofs of the houses as they softly glided beneath me, and in spite of everything bad that had happened to me, I felt a fervent tranquillity as I gazed at the blue-yellow lichens that spread across the tiles, and far out to the edge of the horizon, beyond the houses. The valley began to dip away into the distance until it met with another poppy-filled plain dropping down through a vast, protected nature reserve.

I looked silently at marshlands then that buzzed with the wings of dragonfly hovering cobalt and silver-green over stagnant puddles. A mound of earth sprung up that was filled from top to toe with small hollows, out of which flew kingfisher birds, and I watched as a heron come to rest at the top of a massive silver fir tree, its wings beating the moist and fragrant air beneath it. I saw donkeys tugging at dry grasses near the edge of the woodland, braying as they did so and looking dolefully at the train.

I imagined a thick line of black ants tracking their way across the sand gravel path and down into their nest. Several of the larger ants would be negotiating the passage of freshly cut leaves on their backs, some ten or fifteen times bigger than themselves. I saw a pheasant, with a bright red collar that ran toward the train as it now approached the sea. The pheasant disappeared as quickly as it arrived, and it disappeared into the fallow marshland that was now becoming drenched with the saline waters of the Mediterranean to my right.

On the approach to Argeles-sur-Mer, I saw the beach at La Racou, empty and perfect, remote and free. The surf lifted gently like the flap of a curtain as it lay itself down over and over again across the sand. Small, cool waves rolled over one another and it smelled and looked like a kind of paradise to me. I gazed tearfully at the horizon as I thought about how far I had come. Maybe I should go home to London and forget about all of it.

The train would soon change again in Narbonne. I had about an hour until that happened, so I thought I could steal a couple of hours sleep before the final change at Marseilles. I doubted I'd get a lot of rest overnight in the station there so I wanted to grab a couple of hours where I could.

I was right, and the night in Marseilles seemed to last for an eternity. I stretched out on a series of plastic seats, my head once again on my backpack, and slowly people began to gather around me, and I knew they were looking to steal my things. It was like these were people back from the dead, their eyes glassy, like the eyes of junkies, thin and silent. Ghouls from another world. The routine was the same. I slept, they gathered. I would sometimes wake to them stroking my hair. I picked up my stuff, went to the other end of the station and did the same thing. An hour later, I'd wake again with them gathered around me. Eventually I spoke to a French guy who offered to buy me a coffee. He seemed genuine. I can still see him now. Black, wide glasses. Black hair, perfectly parted, like a man with money. He was older than me and he had good advice about how to keep the ghouls at bay. Just shout at them, he'd said. He was right. It worked.

"But," he also said, "do not leave the train station whatever you do."

Marseilles, he told me, was not a good town.

"You'll be stabbed if you go outside while it's dark."

Train stations, he pointed out, were always in the busiest parts of a city, and at night those parts were the most haunted. It was good advice.

He bought me one more coffee before he went.

Finally, after a deeply uncomfortable night at Marseille station, most of which I'd taken head on as some kind of penance for my behaviour, the dawn arrived, and with it, my final train connection to Nice, where I would disembark at about nine in the morning. So I settled in for the final part of my journey, my head filled with images of Edie.

All along the coast I counted pylons as they fluttered by. I gazed over fields that were filled with livestock, mostly cows and sheep, mottled and rough. The fields stretched out to reveal a sea in the distance, a sea that melted into the morning sky, blue and beautiful already. At only six-thirty I could taste the ozone of the late summer dawn.

I passed yet another Parc National, this one at Calanques and soon approached La Ciotat, and with its yacht yard pulling away behind me, my train began snaking its way along the shore and around the coastline. The views were an inspiration. The sea was cobalt and mauve. Purple sea. Blue sky. Lavender in the fields. Violets and bellflowers for as far as I could see.

France. All around.

Finally, north of Toulon, the train turned inland once more. I went back to watching clouds form in the sky above me and I can remember now how I was starting to feel clean now that I had left Barcelona behind me. I felt, in France, that I was at home.

Edie, I said to myself, *will I find you again? Can you ever forgive me?*

*

In Nice that same morning, Imogen leaned across her bed to silence the alarm that was loudly buzzing by her bedside. She smiled faintly as she remembered her dream, and she allowed the alarm to wait another nine minutes before it tried again to wake her. Her job at the restaurant had finished, but today she had promised to go back to do one more shift as a favour to the owners. They were going to give her cash for it, so she was happy enough to oblige, but she needed to be there earlier than usual.

Just after nine-thirty.

There was plenty of time before then for her to wake up slowly, stretch out in her bed and take a warm shower before a breakfast of yoghurt and apricots. She listened to a lighthearted radio program, two young men clowning around and playing popular music of the day, none of which she was overly impressed by. Finally, she stood and noticed that the hour was already escaping her if she wanted to make it to Portovenere on time. *Funny how that happens*, she thought, *I had all the time in the world and now I'm in danger of being late.*

She used the toilet one last time. Checked her make up, and then checked her face in the mirror, her grandmother perpetually looking down on her which caused her to idly think about her family in France and how she would shortly be seeing them all again after a long, free summer away from home. A warm glow of contentment began to rise in the small of her stomach. It was a nice feeling.

Imogen held nothing but a great respect and deep affection for her parents, who had always been very popular in the village back home. The family lived on a farm, keeping mainly chickens and pigs and she remembers visiting her papa at the market on Saturday mornings where he would be working with her elder brother, Thierry, selling pork cuts and pâté's and saucisson and eggs to the villagers, always smiling and always joking as they went about their business. Often there was a song or two as well.

Her papa made such a fuss of his little girl when she appeared, picking her up and lifting her high above him, proudly exalting her talents to anyone who would listen. She felt like she was flying when he did that, and it filled her with so much joy that she would feel surges of pleasure flooding through her entire body.

Saturday evening on the farm, especially in the summer, was a time for them all to sit outside in the courtyard, drink wine and play cards and she suddenly thought then of her parents' friends who used to come over to visit. She doesn't remember them all clearly, she was too small, but certain characters have stayed with her through all the years. There were a lot of musicians, she remembers that the most. In particular she recalls a tall guitarist, who wore thick lensed spectacles that magnified his eyes to twice the size they ought to have appeared. Alarming for a little girl. And memorable, of course. He always wore a necktie, no matter how hot it would be. He had a girlfriend. Imogen can't remember her name now, but she had very black hair. There was another guy, also a guitarist, with an enormous brown moustache and a sparkling smile and he sometimes sat in her room and sang a song to her as she went to sleep. Probably only once, but she liked to think it was a regular, bohemian kind of thing.

Then there were the twins, both of whom were strong lads and often helped out as hands around the farm. They were some fifteen years older than her, handsome boys. They fascinated her. They looked so alike it unnerved the little girl and fired her imagination.

How could they look so alike? she asked herself in wonder whenever she saw them, and then, *How can I have a favourite when they are both the same?*

The twins used to help her parents with the pigs and seemed to continually be fixing things up, hedgerows and barn doors in particular.

Imogen's thoughts went on a journey, and she saw herself in school then, remembering fondly the friends she had, and it seemed to her that she didn't have a negative memory in her head about her childhood. Life on the farm was good to them all and she loved her days at school. Everything felt unfussy. Uncomplicated. Simple.

She remembered the games they used to play outside at school breaktimes. She thought about the chalk drawings that they made on the ground, and how they would hop from one foot to the next as they went first up the ladder, and then back down again without touching the ground outside of the chalk marks. And the skipping. There was a lot of skipping.

She pictured then one of the nicer assistant teachers, but again, she couldn't remember her name, although she knew she wasn't French, and she laughed to herself as she pictured in her mind's eye the six-year-old Imogen, gabbling away at her in a language the poor girl couldn't fully understand. In spite of the communication barrier they got along well, and Imogen remembered how this pretty teacher used to make a fuss of her vibrant ginger hair, sometimes falling silent as she held it in her hands. Looking long into the distance.

She remembered how they would laugh that autumn and joke about the leaves of the trees that were slowly turning the same gold and orange colours as each day passed, and her teacher would say to her 'be careful what you do, Imogen,' although of course she could never understand her properly.

That teacher got married that Christmas and moved away and they never met again. Imogen simply turned up for school at the start of the following year and her favourite teacher had gone. Married, she heard, and starting a new life in the south. It taught her a lesson in accepting that things would sometimes not make sense, and that she could only ever take a deep breath and keep going whenever she felt that way. Although of course, she was far too young to articulate it like this.

Back on the farm, only one of the twins used to turn up for work now, and although she had never really joined these events in her mind when she was small, her parents did tell her some years later that yes, her favourite teacher had married her favourite twin, and had moved south and that they now had two children of their own.

Even now that thought made both the grown-up Imogen, and the little girl inside her, feel happy and she smiled as she picked up the metal brush and ran it once more through her copper-coloured hair.

My hair is too red, she thought to herself. *Perhaps I'll dye it or something. I wonder if my teacher would approve.*

She put on her little black ankle boots and pulled the zip to the very top, enjoying the rasp of the teeth as they clasped together. She put on her jacket. Green. An old canvas army coat that her brother had given to her two Christmases ago. It suited her. She turned to tighten the belt around her waist and looked at her reflection in the standing mirror. It wasn't too windy today, but nonetheless she still decided to pin the little blue pillbox hat in place, and when she'd done that, she stood back to look at herself. Ready for her day to unfold.

Who knew what it would bring?

Often, she walked the whole route to the restaurant, but today she had inexplicably not given herself enough time, which she felt was a shame because it was such a clear and pleasant morning. Pulling her coat tight, and shutting the door behind her, she walked up the little hill to the train station which was only two stops from Nice-Ville. It was eight-twenty, and her train was pulling in already. She had to run up the stairs to make sure she caught it, and she jumped on the small, three carriage train just in time. It was busy, as usual, only this particular morning, something felt different about it.

The air carries a different optimism, she thought. *The air is different today.*

Her train rumbled out of the station and soon stopped at the next one down the line. She stood and looked through the arms of the other passengers, out towards the packed platform filled with people who would shortly be fighting their way to pack themselves into the carriages either side of her. Imogen reminded herself of how much she didn't like this kind of claustrophobia and she looked then and noticed how many of the other passengers wore sepia coloured, tweed jackets.

Blood-red stitching seems to be the fashion, she thought.

She felt that to get off early might be an option but instead closed her eyes and surrendered herself to the fact that one more stop wouldn't be too much to endure. As she had her eyes closed, people around her all seemed to assume she wasn't there, and they started to push against her as they packed themselves into the train.

Not long, she said to herself. *Not long now.*

At Nice-Ville she really couldn't wait to get off, but even so she allowed all of the other passengers to disembark before her, allowing herself to be dragged along by this human tide, finally being spat out on to the platform in front of her. But still she stood back as she waited for the platform to clear.

As it did so, another train pulled in. This was a much larger train, and it was finishing a long journey that it had begun in Marseilles several hours earlier. She stood back from the crowd that was emptying the platform as the big train pulled to a stop barely a few metres in front of her. She looked at it once. There was something about it. She didn't know why she was looking at it for so long. And then she looked at it again. One more time.

A gust of wind caused by such a large train nearly took her

hat from her head and she raised her hand to catch it. She became aware that she'd pinned it in place that morning and so stopped holding the hat straight away.

The train stopped.

She turned and tucked a lock of her auburn hair behind her ear and began her descent down from the platform. The sound of children laughing was hanging in the air behind her and as she took her first step on the down escalator, the bells from the church behind the station began to chime.

She glanced at the clock, suspended above the platform.

It was 09:00.

She'd better get a move on.

*

My head was filled with Edie as the train arrived at Nice-Ville that morning. I couldn't think of anything else. Would I find her? Where should I look first? I guess I'd get a hotel so I could get some proper rest and drop my bag. Edie had said that she'd find work in a restaurant or a bar, I remember her telling me that, but the season was ending.

It was only because the late summer was so mild that there were any open still, and I suspected, in fact, that many had already closed. So maybe she was in a hotel bar? Yes, that'd be it. That's what I told myself. I'd look in hotel bars. Trying to keep myself off the booze didn't feature in my plan.

I was going to give myself three days. It's all I had. If I couldn't find her, I'd have to go to Amsterdam. I'd made a promise to myself.

I had to somehow make her free.

I owed her that.

As my train slowed coming into Nice, I noticed how busy the platform was.

And then I stopped.

The hair on my arms stood on end.

A church. A shopping plaza. I could see children over the high wall of the platform. I saw a fountain. The platform sign. Blue. Purple. There was a pond. A green pond. The railway bridge had passed over it as we approached the station. The bridge had been blue. The doors of my train hissed open. I felt something happening.

Or was I just tired. Could this be ...?

I grabbed my bag, stepped out on to the platform, and straight away I could hear children laughing. I could see crowds of people shopping in a plaza almost exactly like the one I had imagined in my dream for so many years. Could this be where she is? Could this be it?

I looked around me for a girl with red hair and a green jacket, my body alive with excitement and anticipation. Something was happening and it felt so natural, like I was supposed to be meeting a friend. *She has to be here somewhere*, I thought to myself. I could feel her presence. I know that sounds odd, but it felt so strong as to be completely real.

I scanned the faces of those around, almost in a frantic way. I saw a woman carrying a small dog disappear down the escalator. I felt droplets of water in the air, spray from the enormous fountain over the wall that ran along the top of the platform, a fountain with dozens of shoppers milling around it. I felt the thrum of all these people going about their daily lives. The hubbub of their days.

I started to move towards the woman with the dog, but she was quickly swallowed up by the crowd, before she silently glided beneath the platform. There were too many bodies between us for me to reach her and so I ambled in the same direction, along with everyone else, as we all patiently waited for our turn to join the queue at the top of the escalators.

I felt the warmth of the sun that was breaking through the clouds now and I smelled the scent of so many flowers on the back of so many breezes that drifted through the morning air, which carried with it a note of coldness and a tiny chill. Subtle. Non-threatening.

It was a beautiful late summer morning, and my senses were all at a great height, finely tuned. I was susceptible then, and I was very aware throughout those moments of the church bells that now hung in the air as they finished chiming.

I looked at the station clock.

It read 09:01.

I'd missed something then, but I didn't know what it could have been.

It was nine o'clock. And I had nowhere to go.

TWELVE

Nice felt welcoming and for a while I was almost able to put the horrific scale of my unforgivable behaviour to one side. But it couldn't last. I knew it couldn't. My plan, in as much as I had one, was first to find a hotel. It had been a long night, especially the punishing wait for the connecting train at Marseilles. Punishment that I felt I deserved. A kind of penance. I figured that a short rest before I set out to try to find Edie would be sensible, and 'sensible' was the new word that I was hoping people would one day use when describing me. I didn't really believe it then. I sure as hell don't believe it now.

So I wandered down the hill from the train station and walked past the same fountain that I saw from the platform. I paused, taking it all in. There was a school across the road that had a low fence surrounding it, with little purple flowers poking through the cracks in the stone wall in which the fence was set. I could see children gathering in lines, all preparing to go into the red brick building to start their day. The school had pale blue shutters across tall windows. The same colour blue that I had seen in my dream for years now. Azure light, sea blue. It had become my favourite of all colours: optimistic and clean.

The children's laughter was infectious and, combined with the sunshine, it made me smile involuntarily to myself. Wry and ironic, the air was thick with innocence which I found intoxicating. I remembered innocence then, the simplest of states. Good times.

The town had an honest old-world charm about it, and I felt sure that I could easily learn to adore it. In spite of opening out on to glass and cement-clad side roads, all of which were filled with designer boutiques, wineries, delicatessens, and the like. Nice was in parts prototypically French. Even the more modern aspects of the architecture had an allure infused within. *It's a good balance*, I thought.

Figuring that there would be plenty of hotels down by the seafront, I allowed the air to guide me there. Without seeing it even once, I could sense in which direction the sea would be. I literally followed my nose. The clouds above the sea were high in the sky and they puttered lazily over the horizon. At the bottom of the hill, turn left, and then right, through the shops and past the restaurants. Down the narrow, winding hillside shaded by vines that created a covered boulevard, charming from every angle. I passed all kinds of food places, from several countries across Europe and twice as many regions across France.

I passed dozens of bars lining either side of the walkway and I passed art shops with huge canvasses, mostly nude studies painted from real life models, confidently assembled with strident and aggressive colours. Portraits in purples and pinks, landscapes in lime and blue yellows. Purple and blue, like the light that had been hanging over the horizon from the moment my train left Spain.

I continued to walk, passing a train of low-slung signage on poles, in the mediaeval style. Images of cats cut from wrought iron and painted black: 'Restaurant de Le Chat Noir'. Mock-Monet paintings of bucolic sun-dappled fields heralded the entrance to 'Le Cafe des Impressionistes'. That sort of thing. It was that kind of place. I liked it immediately. None of the restaurants down this road were open, it was too early. None were even serving breakfast and it was not until I got on to the promenade at the bottom of the road that I saw a cafe where I could get something to eat.

I stopped at the first place I passed and sat down under a blue and white striped canopy, shielding my eyes from the late summer sun which was still strong down here by the coast even at this comparatively early hour of the day. I ordered a coffee and a pastry and sat with my eyes closed, just drinking everything in and allowing my mind to settle before I did too much more. Edie was right, this was a beautiful place, and I reflected again on how we should have arrived under much happier circumstances. If only I could have controlled things more confidently. I smiled internally. The story of what my life would become would be down to learning the meaning of control. Eventually. But at that stage I didn't know it for sure.

When the coffee came it was good. Strong and bitter. It gave me energy. Intense energy. I liked it and I drank it quickly and ordered another. I lit a cigarette then and blew smoke into the air, looking all the while across the road at the Mediterranean Sea, alive and vibrant. Purple, lilac and blue. Glistening before me. Glitter across its surface. I felt such a deep contentment looking at the sea, it was like a drug to me. A free one. The smell. I love it.

The freshness of the water hits every pore. This Mediterranean. The cauldron of all modern civilisation. The font from which the western world was baptised.

I finished my cigarette and pastry. I ordered another coffee, then I smoked another cigarette and my thoughts dwelled upon Edie. Was she here? Could I feel her presence? I wasn't sure. I didn't think I could. I had to concentrate. Could I feel her near me? No. I couldn't. If I had to concentrate, then I was forcing the issue. I knew I was not going to find her, but I had to feel that I had tried before I turned myself in to Boaz and Dieter. One last chance, Edie? One last chance?

It was in this frame of mind that I resolved to begin my search, so I told myself that I didn't have the time to rest right at that moment. I'd three days only and if I couldn't find her, I knew that I would have to make a huge sacrifice to keep her safe. This was decision already made, and it was about the only one I could look toward as any kind of anchor.

After paying for my breakfast, I crossed the road and stood by the railing that ran around a part of the beach there that I now know is called the Plage de l'Opera. I stood with my back against the railing, looking away from the sea and back up at the hotels that lined the promenade. There were so many of them and suddenly the scale of my objective became clear. Was she even in this town? Yannis had told me she was, or at least, he told me that was what Elena had said to him. But could I trust him? Really? I told myself there had to be some truth in it. How would he have known that Edie and I had been discussing Nice? Unless Edie herself told him on the night that I left her in the Tapas Bar with them. I decided to push that from my mind. There were too many possibilities. I could send myself insane trying to hypothesise every single one of them.

So I abandoned the idea of finding a place to rest; I could deal with that later. Instead I set about looking for Edie straight away and walked to the far end of what I could see of the Promenade des Anglais, which was approximately half of the entire length of it. I began eyeing the hotels all the way up to where I'd had breakfast and I noted that beyond that was the old part of town, a place called the Gambetta. Many French towns have one, in some form or other. It's common apparently and is so-called in tribute to a liberal-minded lawyer at the time of the Franco-Prussian war. Often these Gambettas are areas lined with restaurants and tourist bars and cafes. Liberal areas. Kind of like how Soho is to places like London, Hong Kong, Sydney. New York. Nice had its own liberal quarter. The Gambetta.

I was destined to go there.

Relying on little more than instinct I began to ask in each hotel about a room. The cheapest rate, the view, that sort of thing. I quickly discovered that the places along the Promenade were going to be too expensive. For finding a simple place to crash, I was definitely in the wrong part of town, but for finding a bar or restaurant where Edie might be trying to find work, the opposite was true. For that I was maybe in the right kind of place. It was a start.

As I walked from door to door, I soon realised that it was unlikely she'd even be working so soon after arriving. If she was in town, she would only have arrived two or three days before me, and it would be surprising if she'd found work that quickly. Looking back along the road, at the sheer number of hotels, I thought how ridiculous I was being. Trying to investigate the places she might be working was pointless. She probably wouldn't be working anywhere. I put myself in her place. What would I do? What would Edie do?

She'd be trying to find a place to stay. Of course she would, and she'd be looking in the same places as me. That would be the number one thing to do. I would just go with my natural instinct. Do what I thought was sensible. That word again.

Somewhere to sleep is more important than somewhere to work, although there's not a lot in it. I didn't call in to any more hotels after that. Instead, I ambled back up to the railing at the Plage de l'Opera and leaned on it again, only this time looking out to sea. I allowed the breeze to blow salt onto my skin and closed my eyes as I ran my tongue along my lips.

I was tired. Very tired. I could taste the salt in the air and my eyes grew heavy in an instant. I wasn't thinking clearly. I could have fallen asleep standing up.

I stayed there for a while, almost welded to the railings and then I impulsively turned to enter the Gambetta, allowing my feet to take the lead, wandering in a state of fatigue-induced catatonia. My mind was wrapped in woollen blankets as I ambled among the many shops nestled beside the cobbles.

Edie, where are you?

I looked to my right, out across the beach and then back down the wide, red-plaster coloured promenade along which crowds of people were jogging and walking. In the distance I could see small white porticoes under which people sought refuge from the late summer sun. It was still warm enough to suck on flavoured ice, or to pour water from a bottle down the back of your neck and as I walked further into the Gambetta, I instinctively lowered my head, looking down at the floor as I made my way through the old town.

It was a negative way to pass through life, I knew that. Too much self-pity. Looking down when I should be looking up and looking forward. The weight of my guilt was forcing me to slump forward, and I tried to remember a time I'd had a drink or smoked a joint in a carefree way and without any need attached to it. But I couldn't. At that time, it seemed to me that every indulgent action I made was out of necessity, as if I didn't do it, I would die. But if I did, it might kill me.

I stopped and looked at the street ahead.

Were you out there Edie? Were you in front of me?

"I'm sorry," I whispered to no-one. "Please forgive me."

As I said it, a dark cloud arrived and hung across the town, grey and black in equal measure. Rain began to fall. It was a strange moment. From out of nowhere the sky turned from blue to purple, and I remembered then the painted rooms in my childhood home and the empty cans spread out across the front garden of our small house. I thought of my mother and suddenly I wanted to see her. I wondered to myself why I hadn't felt that need before now. Perhaps the way I had been living really had become all too much and now I had to stop. Go home. Unload. Recuperate.

The light from the horizon was now all about us and in a small handful of moments, the scene intensified. It was as if I had made it happen. It was odd how it perfectly reflected my emotional state. Blue to purple and back again, just as quickly. In no time at all the rain was falling heavily enough to send everyone darting for shelter. It cascaded like so many metal shards being guided by magnets. I stood under one of the white canopies that hung outside a restaurant whose name I can't recall now. I remember the word Porto was in it though because it made me think of our time in Portugal and I remember feeling strangely close to Edie at that moment.

It was clean rain. Very clean. I held out my hand and licked my fingers to taste it. It was salty. Sea water. I lit a cigarette and stood looking out at the others around me who gathering in clusters, sheltering. I looked at the sea and tasted the rain again.

The emptiness that had invaded me could only be filled by Edie. Now I knew what people meant when they said that they didn't feel whole. That they needed to feel complete. Like they used to be. When they said that only one person could make them feel that way. I felt this too. I needed her. It was more than just wanting something. It was a need. I guess need is only ever born from experience. If you don't experience anything, you'll never know if you truly need it.

All around me the rain fell in heavy drops and spattered against the cobbles, then gathered, and ran in rivulets under my shoes. The air smelled metallic, and I breathed it in deeply. It complemented the cigarette smoke that I was enjoying. I looked down the road toward the sea and although the rain was steadily falling, the sky was already brightening. I was looking out for a rainbow. Ever hopeful, always looking for rainbows. It could be a sign perhaps that things were not as bad as I imagined and that things would recover, and that Edie and I could find one another and find some peace. Maybe even find love again. I had to be optimistic that my time was coming. I would find her here in Nice. I told myself that.

I looked again at the sky. There wasn't any rainbow.

Leaning my back against the restaurant I sensed someone standing alongside of me. I turned and a young boy was looking up at me.

"Bonjour," he said.

And then he said something else in French that I didn't understand but I smiled at him instinctively as he darted out from under the canopy outside the restaurant. I watched him run along the road toward the seafront, looking to find shelter under another canopy further along the front. His innocence invaded me. To have such a simple life. I envied him.

When does it disappear? I wondered. *Innocence. Does it actually disappear or do we just learn to ignore it? Does society condition us to not see our innocence after a certain stage?*

Yes, I thought. *It is society that ruins it all for us. Other people. Peer pressure. Without other people we could have a chance to retain a certain wonder at the world. Cynicism is the enemy of all of that. Cynicism is like a disease,* I considered, and quickly concluded that it was a disease that was instilled in me at an early age. I would like to have been less cynical. I loved life. I loved the world around me. When did it happen that I grew to be bitter? I didn't want to be bitter.

Should cynicism equate to bitterness anyway? I wondered. *Can it be healthy to have a part of all of these things? Can my life not be made up of a rich tapestry of colour?* And then, *Does anger and violence and aggression feature as a part of that palate? Is timidity good? Is submission good too?*

I thought then about my family and about my brother going

to prison after being prosecuted for dealing for the fifth time. No more chances.

"Fuck the drugs," I would have whispered to myself then, and I would have meant it too.

I watched the boy as he drifted along the street. He passed all the bars and the restaurants, but no-one seemed willing to move over to give him any shelter. So he did something I still remember to this day. He accepted that he wasn't going to be helped, and he looked the situation right in the eye.

He stood in the rain.

Staring up at the strengthening sun, he started to laugh, just a little at first, and I thought to myself that this was a small revelation. Once you accept that you are wet, then you no longer need to concern yourself with getting soaked.

This taught me something. If you're afraid of something, then immerse yourself in the problem, and the fear of that problem must then disappear. This could allow you to focus more clearly on what is the core issue: putting the problem right. Not the problem itself.

The boy smiled back at me and the look on his face as he stood in the rain was joyful, and we, under our shelters, were all miserable. Our concern about getting wet was driving this misery.

So, take away the concern, I thought. *Take away the problem.*

I decided there and then to join the boy, to go and stand with him. To get wet. I stepped out and walked towards him and everyone was watching us now. He turned to me and held out his hands. I took them both in mine and we leaned backwards, supporting one another as we did so. He looked up at the sky and let the rain wash across his face. I did the same. We both laughed at the clouds above us as they began to drift away and very soon the sun arrived as quickly as it had disappeared. *Like my life*, I thought again.

I was wet now. But soon I would be dry again. No harm done.

The boy let go of my hands and waved as he ran off towards the beach, calling something in French back at me as he went. Everyone around us now was coming out from their retreat and the strong sun instantly began to peel back the thin veneer of water from the alleys and walkways. Within seconds, puddles began to shrink and then, quite suddenly, the air around us was warm again.

I decided to go and grab a beer. Fuck not drinking. I could rest later.

The air shifted and began to carry on it a chill as it blew in from the sea and later, after several hours of ambling through Nice like this, the day began to fade from my grasp. And I still had to find some digs. A chilly evening was stepping in to replace the day when I finally walked slowly back up the hill to a cheap hostel that I had spotted when I left the station that morning. I was so tired by then. I hoped they had some room for me.

I was struggling to order my thoughts properly. I just wanted to get my name on a bed and then eat something bad before falling asleep. I'd had a few beers that day even though I had told myself that I wasn't going to have any. So, I had lied to myself. Again. Like so many times before. I think maybe I was beginning to obsess about it. Which, I figured, was also bad.

The only space the hostel had was in a shared dorm. This didn't bother me because I simply planned to hide under my blanket and to let the night pass beneath me like the tracks of a railway line. The place was clean. I was thankful. That was all that mattered. I had to sleep.

But before I did, I went outside to grab a pizza and started to walk around the roads adjacent to the railway station. I was looking for Edie. Still looking for Edie. Always looking for her. Even in my subconscious I was scanning the roads, gazing up and down along the line of shopfronts. No wonder I was tired, I was always active. My mind was not even realising the stress it was placing upon itself, my eyes darting from side to side feverishly, my head filled with regret and self-loathing, not to mention shame for what I had done; sadness for what I had lost. My head obsessed about being obsessed. No escape.

I was constantly searching in doors, peering through windows. Trying to be a better person. I was staring past my reflection at any kind of movement coming from inside. I saw myself reflected in glass, folded a multiple of times, and through my own reflection could I see Edie? Was that her? Could she be in there? I ambled my way in a lethargy, past one road after another. Many buildings were a beautiful limestone yellow, like butter. Wrought iron railings, black and stark against the soft looking brickwork. I walked in and around the area, never going too far, but always trying to come back on myself. Rue Paganini. Rue d'Italie. Rue de Suisse. D'Angleterre. Pizza. Grill. Kebab. Burgers. Car hire. A small park. A closed bank. Boulangerie. Fashion and Mode. A laundry.

I soon began to realise that I didn't know where the hostel was, or even what it was called, but I did know it was by the station and I knew that was nearby. That would be enough for me.

I chose a pizza restaurant and went inside. I had some food at a small plastic table and suddenly felt very lonely. I rarely feel lonely. I have always been able to tolerate my own company. Just about. But at that moment I was overwhelmed, and I knew it was mostly because I was tired.

The table at which I sat had a plastic covering on it with prints of small, richly coloured houses and trees in each corner, and in the centre stood a bottle of hot sauce, some mayonnaise and two salt and pepper pots. Wedged between them were thickly laminated, plastic menus that displayed photographs of the food on sale. Falafel, pizza, burgers. It was cheap. I was clearly out of the way of tourists down in that part of town. I liked it. I liked the natural rawness of it. Nice was getting under my skin.

The evening was still small, but I was beyond ready to drop. It had been a long few days and my mind was creaking as I sat there staring out of the window. I had a compulsion to walk back through the Gambetta to the Old Town, but I resisted it. That could wait until tomorrow. In fact, I felt a vague sensation of optimism when I thought about the Gambetta and, in particular, the restaurant where I had sheltered earlier, where I had been watching the boy go from door to door, looking for cover. He still impressed me, and I afforded myself a weak smile.

Staring through the heavy glass to the road outside, I could make out the station behind me at the top of the hill. I ordered another coke and instinctively felt in my pocket for some of the hash that I usually kept there, but this time there were only crumbs. A vague panic started to build inside of me, followed by a kind of relief. I closed my eyes in an effort to bring everything under control when the guy behind the counter brought my pizza and placed it in front of me.

I ate the pizza in less than five minutes and as I allowed the food to digest, I simply sat looking out of the window watching the road empty out. A couple came in and sat at a table adjacent to me and I remember thinking that, of all the tables that were empty in that place, and that was all of them, why had they chosen to sit so closely to me. I checked hesitantly to see if it was Franck. Or Maartje. To see if I recognised them at all. No. I didn't.

They were young. About my age. He wore a black leather, biker-style jacket whilst she sat with her back to me, wearing a purple woollen coat, pulled tight across her shoulders, accentuating her spine. Her red hair clashed against the purple, and I thought that Edie would never wear a purple jacket. I began to feel my loneliness all over again. It kept coming in waves. Where was my friend when I needed her? She'd gone away.
It was time to go. My river of emotion, tumultuous and angry, would be easier to navigate after some rest, so I stood and walked to the counter. I never looked back at the girl now that she was facing in my direction. Instead, I paid what I owed. And I left.

*

The following day when I woke, I had an unsettling sense of my own mortality; an unusual feeling that thankfully soon disappeared as I began to walk the streets of Nice again. There was something promising about the day, and I knew that I could learn to survive in a place like this. I often started those days with a stifling sense of the ennui which was hanging in the air around me and I knew fully well that it was one of the downsides of alcohol. Depression. I rarely let it get its claws into me, and if it did, it was not for long. Like then, the feeling of hopelessness would always pass, and on that day it did too although, I told myself, I couldn't be sure it would always be that way.

So I had some breakfast, strong coffee again. Another. Two cigarettes. Two more. An ordinary world unfolded around me, and I walked the same route as the day before, down to look at the sea where a light mist was beginning to burn away. It would be another good day.

To counter that, I had a feeling that my search was stacking up against me then, and that it was not going to give me what I was hoping for. I was placing my faith in blind luck. I was placing my life the hands of fate, which was exactly the same as the very reason that had I left London in the first place. If this didn't work, I was determined that I would go to Amsterdam and that I would face up to what I had done. My sense of guilt was so strong that to live with it each day was worse than any amount of pain that might follow. I convinced myself that I had little choice. And I was very scared about it. You can be sure of that.

So I gazed out across the water and allowed all these things to float through my mind. Above all, I told myself, I needed peace. I needed something to silence the whistle of the winds that were blowing through my heart. Alcohol did that, but only for a while. I liked exercise, simple walking. That also helped.

Standing there, leaning on the railing at the top of the Plage de l'Opera, I felt that God himself would understand me. I had to make do with that for now and it helped to breathe in the overwhelming serenity of the sea. The Mediterranean had been a constant in my life for the last year.

Perhaps today is the day I find her, I thought.

And then something else ... what if Edie was thinking the same way as me? A horrible notion I hadn't considered until that point. What if she herself had gone, not here to Nice, but to Amsterdam? What if she had thought that she was going to give me that comfort that she knew for certain I desperately needed? Maybe she was gifting Nice to me. This thought made me both humble and afraid. My body stiffened and I stood up straight. What if Edie had gone to Holland to sacrifice herself to Boaz? In an effort to try to keep *me* free!

No, I thought. *Boaz would be determined to find me, no matter what Edie did*. I decided that it was unlikely that she'd have done that. Sure, she was generous in spirit, generous enough to make that kind of gesture, but sensible enough to know that it would fail. Not like me, I'm the dreamer of the two of us. The idiot, many would say. Edie would have known that even if she had gone there, it would make little difference. I was a marked man. That much was clear.

And then I had a second thought: *what if Yannis told them I'm in Nice? Can I really trust any of those people?* Or maybe Elena told them. I certainly couldn't trust her; I was sure of that. She hated me. She must have done. She would have known Edie was here, if she *was* here, that is. And after all, didn't Yannis say that Elena had told him she knew this was where Edie was headed? Well, what if she only said that to get me to go to a place where Edie definitely wasn't hiding out, so that she could tell the Amsterdam guys, via Iker, where I actually was?

These were all scenarios that I considered possible, but unlikely. Was I safe? Yes, I reckoned that I probably was. But was 'probably' enough for me? Yes, I reckoned again. Probably. However, there was still doubt. I perhaps needed to keep Franck in mind as well, or even Maartje. Any one of them, in fact.

Turning right once more I walked back into the Gambetta. I felt that I was living like a tourist and that made me a little bit uneasy. In fact, I think I felt guilty to be living like that. When this was all over, if I could persuade Boaz to let me pay off my debt to him, if I could persuade him to leave Edie to live her life freely, then maybe I would go back to England and find something I liked doing. Something that I could use to make a living with. Peace and contentment. No more danger. No more excitement. To be bored for years on end, that was what I wanted at that time.

Walking further into town, the buildings began to cling to the hill as if they were putting down roots all the way up the incline, across the brow and over and down to the other side of the peninsula. I came upon Old Nice with its labyrinth of narrow alleyways, cool and claustrophobic. I was charmed by the disintegrating walls, their colourful plasterwork peeling away to reveal stone and cement, patched up facades, crumbling like anything old that had been exposed to so much sun for so many years. Crumbling like the faces of people that have spent their lives out of the shade.

The buildings held a great deal of character. Salmon red, alongside mint green. Marine blue and mustard yellow. Shuttered windows aqua blue and cobalt, green, all bound by thin narrow strips of anonymous greys. The sun was high and strong again and I turned right and made my way down towards the sea once more, down towards the Gambetta.

Just down from the corner of the street was the restaurant

where I had sheltered the day before. There was a girl laying cutlery on the weatherproof cloths that covered the tables outside. I told myself that I would eat there before I left for Holland, but I would need to be sure that I could afford to, so I walked across to check the menu that was held in a glass display case sitting at an angle on top of a flimsy, weatherworn lectern. I ran my eye down the list of items. Yes, I could do that. It wasn't too much, and it looked good. Some nice fish, clean and fresh. The fact that I had already started to think about a trip north, alone, to Amsterdam, was as if I was preparing myself for the inevitability of what was to come.

I walked on down the hill and smiled as I passed the point where the boy and I had stood in the rain washing away our hang ups; or some of them anyway. I turned left and saw even more shops, more tourists. Edie, if she were in Nice, would surely be out in town at this time of day. She is not someone who would stay inside. *She could be nearby*, I thought. It was an odd feeling. I could almost sense her when I thought like that. I turned and walked back up the hill and back past the restaurant where the girl was still laying tables. I turned left and ambled around Old Nice, close to the Jardin Albert 1er.

And then suddenly I saw it.

I stopped and caught my breath before backing up and retracing my footsteps back around the corner. Of course. Why hadn't I thought of it before? I looked back around. There was a shoe shop. 'Suffern Massena'.

I walked back and gathered my thoughts once more. I lit a cigarette. Yes, she'd take a job in a shoe shop, wouldn't she? That would be obviously easy for her. I doubted very much that she would want to, but we were not living in a world filled with what we wanted back then. I doubt we ever actually do, do we? Not ever.

I decided to try to see inside and so I approached nonchalantly and began browsing in the window but, all the time looking further beyond the glass. I felt then like Franck must have felt back in Oporto. An observer through thick glass. Inside it was almost empty. I could see two girls standing at the back silhouetted against the display cabinets behind them. One of them might have had Edie's slim build but I didn't think it was her. The other was not Edie. She was heavier than Edie. I looked again at the first girl. They were completely oblivious to me. I could look for a while, and I did. But no, Edie was not here. However, I now began to consider that shoe shops might provide the right kind of stone to look under, and so I ambled around the cobbled streets for a few more hours, stopping here and there for coffee and as the day wore on to the point when coffee became replaced by beer. I drank Pastis with water. The aniseed soothed me. It made me feel contented and I liked it. It was like a warm embrace.

I looked in about six shoe shops. No, nothing. Once or twice my heart skipped a beat when I thought maybe I had seen her. But no. Each time I was setting myself up for a fall. A crushing fall.

The evening came and there were no signs. I was beginning to realise what an idiot I had been. Only one week before, if I had been nicer to her, then this simply wouldn't be happening now. Did I seriously expect to just see her? Out of nowhere? No, in truth I really didn't think it was going to happen and so I set then out to numb myself against what was about to come.

I had very little cash, and I would need to travel soon otherwise I actually couldn't make Amsterdam. As it was I had only barely enough money to get there. I wouldn't even have money for food. Twenty or more hours on a coach with nothing to eat or drink.

I drifted into one bar after another, telling myself I should be conserving the cash that I had, and each time I sat outside so that I could watch as the relentless crowds shuffled by. I tried to make my drinks last for a long time. Each person I saw was wrapped up in their own life, and each face was scored by its own concerns and considerations. I remembered then the coach ride close to Breda on the day my adventure began over a year before. If only I could have known then all that would happen.

I remembered Sand-and-Shell from the petrol station, and the girl, Haircut, who checked me in on the boat hotel and I remembered the guy in the jeans who had been with her. I thought about the house on fire, and Oliver that Canadian guy who was with us, and the woman jumping out, first throwing her shoes to gauge the height she had to fall. Where would she be now? Out there, someone was telling that same story but from a completely different perspective.

I thought about Dieter, and of course, Boaz. They were never, ever far from my mind. I remembered the woman that Dieter and I shamefully laughed at when she tried to tempt us into her booth in the alley that ran behind the semi-circular road outside the Oude Kerk in Amsterdam. I remembered the Grasshopper, and I remembered meeting Edie there for the first time.

I became sad at how things had ended between us, and I realised then, that with that thought I had crossed a line. At how things had *ended*. I said it again. Past tense. It didn't feel right still. So I said it out loud. The people at the table next to mine looked at me. I must have appeared crazy to them.

I realised then that I had been talking to myself for quite a while.

"How things ended," I said regardless.

One more time.

It made me sad. Of course, it did! I had fallen for her, and I was still in love with her. Truthfully, I probably always would be. Certainly, for a long time I would, in some form or other, either with or without her. Nothing could stop love, a great immovable force. I would always carry her with me in some way or another.

I decided then that some food would be good. I didn't want to go to the hostel yet, it was still early, and I was becoming drunk, so I ambled back through the Gambetta and made a route that would take me back to the corner restaurant where the girl was laying out cutlery earlier in the day. My head was full of it all. I had to shake it out. Simply reading a menu could do that.

I found the place sooner than I expected and I asked the waiter for a table.

"Solo?" he enquired, without showing the slightest hint of disappointment. I have always felt guilty about this. An entire table but for half the amount of revenue it could potentially sustain.

"Sí," I said and then corrected myself. "Oui, pardon," and we both smiled.

He asked me, in English, "Inside or outside? I think it is a little chilly, no?"

But I wanted to be outside, and I told him that.

"I'm English," I said. "This isn't cold."

He smiled and pulled a chair out almost exactly alongside where we were standing and lit the adjacent heater. I took my seat and made sure I was facing the crowd. It continued to ebb and flow like water across the stones on a shoreline. Backwards. Forwards. Rise and fall.

The waiter returned to take my order and bring me a beer and a basket of bread. I opened the book I had with me but couldn't read it once again, so I closed it and left it sitting face up. I was looking, after all. I couldn't look and read at the same time.

I was completely convinced that Edie was out there. In fact, I felt her near me. Very near me, somewhere among this crowd. I just needed to see her and then I could try to begin my life with her again. My food came. I ate it. It was okay. I turned to look back into the restaurant. Idly I wondered if the girl that I had seen laying tables earlier in the day was in there. I was looking for her, but I couldn't see her. Why did I even want to see her? It was madness.

When the waiter returned to ask me if I wanted dessert, I almost said to him, "The girl in here earlier today, is she working this evening?" But I decided against it. *It would sound very odd*, I thought. Very creepy. I declined dessert. Settled for a coffee. He brought me an almond liqueur.

"On the house," he smiled as he put it down before me.

It smelled good and I thanked him, perhaps a little bit too keenly. I ordered a Pastis to go with it, and I asked for my bill. I considered running before the bill arrived, but I couldn't do that. It was not my thing.

I drank the almond liqueur in one go. Amaretto, kind of. Homemade. Delicious. I then savoured my Pastis and smoked two cigarettes, one after the other. I looked in the pack and was disappointed to see that I was running out. I tapped my pocket. I had some money, but not much. Maybe enough for one more pack but I would need to ration them. I was easily smoking a pack every day, and things were now really tightening up for me. Financially, things were becoming beyond serious now.

I stubbed out my cigarette and drained my glass, and then left. I had one more day to find the girl that I loved.

Or for her to find me.

THIRTEEN

It was going to be my last day in Nice and I figured that the best thing to do would be to start it by buying my ticket to Amsterdam. That way, I couldn't spend the money on booze or drugs by accident. And also then I would already be committed to travelling. Kind of.

So I went first to the ticket office at Nice-Ville station. It was going to be a relatively simple journey. A train was leaving the following morning that would stop in Paris, and from there it was just one change to Amsterdam. About ten hours in total.

I had to ask myself how serious I was about this. The danger, and the irrationality of it all combined into a single whole, and I was compelled to risk everything for just one more hare-brained adventure. I fully recognised, of course, that I would be walking into a world of trouble. That was clear. But I had almost started to not even think about how dangerous it was going to be. I was practically giving myself to them. *It was like suicide*, I thought. Suicide without the certainty.

But more than anything, I thought about how I owed this to Edie, and I thought about how much I missed her, and about how badly I felt over the way I had behaved towards her. I considered then that this act now, going back to Amsterdam, was in many ways actually quite peculiarly selfish of me. I thought that maybe I was only doing it to make myself feel better. And that was probably true, so I accepted it, taking on at face value all possible outcomes, the most likely of which was, of course, anguish. I was making a selfish gesture in some regards. I couldn't find Edie and I needed to keep her present in my life somehow. I construed that, one way or another, this was keeping her alive and keeping her in my thoughts.

It would be enough. For now.

To do this for her was one way I could keep her with me for just a few days more. Unless I could find her. Unless I could just see her again.

Where were you, Edie? Where did you go?

I bought my ticket. It wasn't at all expensive. Much less than I thought it would be. Then I walked into town and passed all the boutique shops and bakeries as I went. I walked further on down to drink coffee and hang out by the railings at the Plage de l'Opera. I liked it there. It felt comfortable. I'd been there a few times in the last couple of days, just looking at the sea as it sparkled in the late summer sun. Fresh and tepid at the same time.

Inviting.

As I walked, I thought about the dream that I'd had again the night before. It was the same dream, over and again. I felt that forever I would be on a train, travelling over, or near, a large body of water. I'd be hearing church bells for all eternity, and often, quite inexplicably, there would be a bald woman walking a dog through the carriage. But above all, my train would be pulling into a station near a fountain and a shopping mall, and I would hear children laughing. Calling. Playing.

And then she was there. A red-haired girl in a green, olive coloured jacket. A star and something blue. In all of this time I'd never been fully able to discern the something blue. Was it the Ocean? Was it a hat? Was it a bag? Was it something else? It was close to the girl. It was personal to her. That much I thought I could be sure about.

Maybe it was the sky? Maybe she was close to the sky? Maybe this is what my dream was trying to tell me. Maybe she was ascending to the sky? Perhaps that signified separation. Distance. Death. Maybe the girl in my dream has died. Maybe she died a long, long time ago.

I didn't like the way my thoughts were heading and so I suspended everything and looked across at some birds that were picking remnants from off the rose red boulevard. Scraps of wafer I think, or maybe some small nuggets of bread. Maybe some cold, spongy frites scattered across the walkway.

The sun was high, and our shadows were short. The sea was, again today, an electrifying cobalt blue fringed with a thin veneer of foam made from the salt that bubbled as the sea licked at the shoreline like a lion licking its paws. In the distance palm trees sat in beds of light grey stone, fringed by paving that complemented the pink asphalt of the boulevard in which they nested.

I felt how this walkway had, down the ages, been witness to a million romances. How much love had been forged across its surface? How many lives had been inextricably altered whilst walking along it? Or by simply standing there beside the Plage de l'Opera? It was beautiful. Running like a thin ribbon around the edge of the land. A thin ribbon that laid out the boundaries of grandeur that the ocean before it possessed in abundance.

How could you fail to fall in love in such a place? I asked myself. The Promenade des Anglais, named after perhaps the least romantic nation on earth. I noted the irony, and it made me smile, something I realised I was doing more of as I spent my time in Nice. We English were not romantic. Not in the classic sense of the word. This was especially true of those of us from London which was, on the whole, a fairly gnarly, tough, and cynical sort of place filled with generations of hard-bitten people. Twisted and inflexible, but accommodating and generous at the same time. Especially to their own. *Londoners*, I thought, *were a fascinating mix of stark and very real contradictions.*

As I was looking out to the sea I was thinking of love, and I was thinking about how much I needed it then. I wanted to love. But I *did* love, I told myself. Except that I had betrayed it. I had abused it. Edie had loved me once. But I didn't feel that she loved me still.

If she did, I oddly thought, *then she will appear before me right here and now*. She wouldn't let me suffer any longer. She would know that I was in Nice. She would know that I was looking for her. She would know these things by instinct. The kind of instinct that two people that were close could communicate. She would know that my heart was going to burst if I didn't see her again. It made me feel desolate to think about her then.

We could have been standing there together, laughing at who we were and how foolish we could be. Laughing together at things we shared in our happier times. From that bench in Barceloneta, we could have carried our love across Spain and on to France, and we could be standing on that boulevard together right at that moment. As one. Without knowing a need for anything. Without understanding this true sadness. And then, I figured, our story could have been added to the millions of others that I considered had been born on that tiny red strip that ran the length of the Promenade des Anglais. But instead, I stood alone.

I stood watching others living contented lives. I stood watching families eating ice creams and pushing pushchairs in which sat small people who haven't known disappointment yet, or at least don't know how to convey it, to identify it even. To know it as intimately as I felt it then. I guess I was destined to always suffer that way.

But for how much longer? I didn't know.

Going back to Amsterdam was a mad move, but for some reason I simply blocked it out and didn't allow myself to be weakened by the insanity of it. I didn't allow myself to give too much thought to it. I felt over all that I *had* to do it. It was a fatalism for sure, but I had such guilt, and all the while Edie was out here, somewhere, she was at risk. I had to try to do something to protect her at the very least.

And yes, it did make a kind of sense to me that if I could at least see Boaz, or Dieter, then I might be able to reason with them. I was sorry, I would say. I wasn't thinking, I would plead. I would be in their debt for a long time and that was the worst that I thought would happen. After all, it was only two kilos of coke. It wasn't twenty-two!

I wasn't thinking straight. No way was I thinking straight. I had allowed the trauma of Edie's departure, for that was what it was, to completely dominate my logic.

Yes, a trauma. That describes it accurately.

I think.

I stood looking out across the sea for a long time that morning. I glanced across at a clock that was nestled among magazines that adorned a newsstand slightly to my right. It was eleven o'clock. I thought two things in that moment. In twenty-four hours, my train would have just left Nice. And then I thought that it was too early for Pastis. But only just.

The gulls had taken all the scraps that they were fighting over and had now flown a little further down the promenade. I watched them as they spread out, some gliding high above the shoreline, looking instead for small fish to pluck from the water. It looked calm today, and the life that it contained felt motivational to me. I wondered how truly idyllic it really was and I quickly concluded that what appeared ordered and calm, particularly on a day like this, was in fact a universe of violence, deception, threat, and anger. A giant, dystopian chaos. A colossal fight for survival was going on right before my eyes, under the surface of the sea laid out all around me. The sea. This place that all throughout my adventure across Europe I'd sought solace in, and by which I had experienced deep serenity simply by gazing at it was, in fact, a cauldron of biblical upheaval.

There, for as far as I could see, was a world where creatures attacked and devoured each another. A world from which entire communities were scooped up in a single net and subjected to a slow and agonising suffocation in the open air. A place where predators ruled, where aggressors were king. A place where to be a savage was a default. A place where violence was a virtue. Where violence was a benefit. A good thing to possess.

Was it the same on land? I asked myself. Of course it was. As I was about to find out, I assumed.

Nice. I would miss it. Why had Edie and I not gone there sooner? This is something I would regret for a long time. I thought we would have been happy there and that I would have loved to have shared it with her. But I doubted if she was there now. I had, in fact, pretty much abandoned any hope that I would find her. In hindsight I can see that it was a flawed idea from the start. Maybe it was a subconscious delay to what was about to unfold. I was giving myself one last chance to catch my breath. I started to tell myself then that Yannis had betrayed me, and I started to make him the focus for a lot of what was wrong with my current circumstance. *That is typical of me*, I thought. Always looking for someone to blame when all along I knew only too well that it was myself that was the architect of all that was wrong in my life. But more than that; all that was wrong with my personality. With my character. My identity.

Conversely, I thought, *could I not also be the architect of all that had been right as well?* Lately there had not been much of that. That was an understatement. But if I was optimistic then there could, one day, be good times again.

Had Edie, in fact, betrayed me or had I betrayed her? I was sure it was the latter. But at the time we finally collapsed, she was already planning to leave me, at least that was what Yannis had told me. But could I trust him? I mean, really trust him. Of that, I wasn't sure. I doubted him. Sometimes I felt that he was playing me in some way, that he might be setting me up. Worse, perhaps he was undermining me all along. But why?

If he was, then what was his motive? To make his own move on Edie? It seems a bit far-fetched. To go to all that trouble just to steal my girl from me, well I was sure that she would be flattered by that. So, perhaps then I was the victim in all of this. In which case, did Edie deserve to be the beneficiary of my forthcoming suicidal benevolence? My mind was made up. Despite all the logic that was contrary to it, I told myself that there was no alternative, I had to return to face them. Besides, I had bought a ticket now and the ball was starting to roll.

These are all the things that I thought that day. Standing by the sea.

I walked some more, and on again into the Gambetta and up to the old town. This time I went further and ambled up across the hilltop and out around the front, down on the other side of the peninsula. I walked around the port and watched the boats drifting in and being tied up for the autumn. It was a little more overcast now and a sense of the season's end was in the air. Less people were out and about, and the town had a definite feel of an impending hibernation about it. I wandered along the Quai des Deux Emmanuels and then down among the boats, stopping once to have a coffee.

I lit a cigarette and walked some more, taking in all that was calm and at peace around me. The calm before the storm. A backdrop of rocky white cliffs, densely populated with thick carpets of foliage and cropped with verdant trees that gave the scene a deep tranquillity. The pavements were clean and well cared for. Everything was just in exactly the right place.

In the distance, overlooking the harbour, I saw a series of apartments evenly placed in their respective blocks. Hanging baskets adorned almost every balcony and behind me, above the shopfronts and stores, more balconies all with plants and flowers hanging from them, or plants on small tables with any variety of accompanying wrought iron chairs. Mopeds were everywhere. Fewer cars. A town built seemingly around people and not convenience. Everything well kept. Everything kept well.

Bars and cafes and restaurants everywhere. Cocktails. Viandes. Grillées. Restaurant L'Ane Rouge. Restaurant La Barque Bleu. Edie could be working in any one of these. There were so many.

I walked around the harbour to the Quai Lunel. It took me about fifteen minutes, and again, here it was even cleaner. No litter, all straight lines. All in order. Immaculate roads. Soft white clouds deftly puttered against the tops of the mountains beyond, and patches of sand peppered the thick brush that covered the horizon behind me. High above, sat a light, blue translucence that covered this part of the earth, as clear as the waters below. One or two planes sat high, trailing twin columns of thin smoke in their wake, columns that spread and became indefinable as the minutes passed, billowing outwards until they were gone forever. Dissipated.

Naturally I was, all the time, looking for Edie. I had to concede that it was now too hard to sustain, and that I had spent two days simply ambling among strangers and not finding her. Not finding even a clue. Apart from the shoe shop, I'd got nothing. Nothing at all.

I was also now becoming keen for company. I was starting to hunger for conversation, and I felt that I needed a friend. I was hurting badly. I'd hardly spoken a handful of words to anyone for about five days. I was aware of an ache in my throat where I'd not been using my voice. I had stopped reading as well. I couldn't focus on reading. I had too many thoughts that haunted my mind, a mind which was frenetic and disjointed and becoming distressed and ragged at the edge.

My thoughts were forming at random, without any construct or any lineage about them, like little mushrooms sprouting in an autumn field. My thought process was random and inarticulate. Disordered. Small scale chaos.

Walking helped me. I liked it, and it was a good town to walk around in. I strolled then around the back of it. When I got to the top of the hill, I stood for a while in the Place Garibaldi and marvelled at his statue that stood imperiously assessing the road beneath.

And there was a fountain.

And there was the plaza that appeared in my dream. Almost. A vast, porticoed building with the same mustard-yellow painted frontage that demanded my attention. In fact, it demanded the attention of anyone that stood there, it's arches and columns in a pristine white plaster very much like the icing on a massive cake. White framed windows contrasting with the yellow of the walls. I counted sixty of them, each with grey shutters, and in the centre, a clock.

On top of it all, a weathervane. *Very French*, I thought. Older men, retired possibly, sat in some shade, as they read their newspapers. They were dressed in jackets and trousers. These were proud people. Rightly so. Proud of their town. Proud of their society. Proud of who they were and how they got there.

I turned left then and made my way once more back to the sea. I was aware that I was consciously moving now toward the restaurant where I had eaten the night before. I was aware also that it was twenty-fours before that I'd seen the girl laying tables there, and that twenty-four hours before that I had stood with the boy in the rain, laughing for the first time in a long while. It felt like the right place to be.

I suddenly needed alcohol then. It came upon me very quickly. I could sometimes feel it rising in my soul, this need to drink, this need to be mollified. I began to get excited at the thought of a drink coming my way, and so I stopped in a small courtyard at a place called La Rossetti. I took a seat among others and ordered a beer. I lit a cigarette and looked at the buildings around me. So characterful. Again yellow, but this time older, less clean. Not like the harbour. Less order. I liked it. It was rougher.

There were tables all around me. It was hard to tell which set of tables belonged to which bar, and in truth it didn't matter to me at all. Not one bit. I soon had my beer in front of me and I closed my eyes as I took a long pull and let its crisp bitterness cover my mind with its comforting numbness. Thoughts of nothing invaded me.

It was good to be thinking of nothing for a few moments.

I sat there for about half an hour. I smoked my cigarette, and I had another beer and then I had another cigarette. I looked at the shops across the square. I looked at the postcard rack. I looked at the gaudy plastic chairs, blue and brutal. I took it all in.

The red canopy of the restaurant at the far end of the square. The plinth in the centre of it. The ice cream shops. Closing now. Summer was closing too. I looked at the clothing hung from the balconies above, all left out to dry. Sheets and blankets, jeans, and button-down shirts. I let my mind wander down the side streets as I smoked my cigarettes and drank my beer.

I took a private peek inside the apartments that surrounded

me. It was like Barcelona in very many ways, and this made me think again of Edie. Was she there? Was she somewhere above me? Maybe someone else?

I couldn't explain it. But I didn't feel alone just then.

I stood, left some coins and a couple of notes on the table, and continued my walk to the restaurant. This was a conscious act. No matter what I was trying to tell myself, I was wilfully walking back toward that place. I don't know why especially. It wasn't as picturesque as where I had just left, but it felt good to be there.

Within twenty minutes I was standing outside and looking at the same place that today appeared empty. I asked the waiter if it was open, and could I get a beer or two? He was happy to let me take a seat. I figured it was quiet enough that he would let me sit for a while, and he did.

It was noticeable how much emptier the town was that day. Especially in that part. I think it was a Monday, I can't remember exactly now. But it was definitely quieter. The waiter was busy around me taking covering off the tables, precisely the opposite of the girl that day before.

"Are you closing now?" I asked him, keen on conversation, no matter how small.

"Yes, monsieur," he said. "It is over for this year."

"When do you open up again?" I asked with a little interest, but not too much. Maybe he'd have work for me next season?

"Easter next year. Usually, we close for the winter, and we all go back home."

"Where's home for you?"

"I live in Menton," he said. "Not too far. I will help my parents in their grocery shop for winter, and then come back here next spring. Every year it is the same. I prefer to be here."

I don't know why I asked him about the girl laying tables then.

It just seemed quite natural.

"There was a girl here yesterday," I ventured. "She was here," I said pointing at the floor. And I raised my hand to my head then, "*Cheveux roux.*"

He smiled and softly told me, "Yes, I know who you mean. She has gone too. Back north. She leaves tomorrow. The summer was long," he said and puffed out his cheeks raising his eyes skywards as he did so.

He shook out the white linen tablecloth and then folded it across his chest. I smiled in return and nodded just as softly as he had spoken.

But said nothing more. That girl had gone. Oh, well.

Then he said, completely unexpectedly, "She goes to Paris in the morning." Maybe he'd picked up on my dejection.

"Oh," I exclaimed lightly. "I do too! I have a train booked for the morning."

"A coincidence," he said, smiling, "then maybe you'll see her on your train."

I stayed in that restaurant for perhaps an hour, and, as it grew slowly darker, I felt then that my time in Nice was ending. I needed to simply board that train in the morning and leave. Edie had not turned up. I would have to admit that it was over.

I had failed and I would need now to do what I thought was right. No matter how wrong it actually was.

So, I went down to the sea one more time. I didn't plan to stay out that night. I wanted to have some simple food and get some rest. I would need my strength.

I was going to go back to Amsterdam!

I couldn't believe I was planning such a thing.

As I walked back up to the apartment, I started to trick myself, in my mind, by pretending I could sense someone following me. I pretended it was Franck. I was keeping myself in a state of alert, a state of tension, agitation almost. But in truth, I had now given up completely. On everything.

I started to give myself a feeling of foreboding, as illogical as it seemed. My head now spinning with everything that had gone on, I would not allow myself to rest until I'd done the right thing and had been to see Boaz.

I had to try to explain myself to him. It was a crazy move.

And I knew it.

I went back to the pizza shop in which I'd eaten two nights before. I ate a small pizza, had a small beer, smoked three cigarettes, and went to my bed. I checked my ticket before I bathed that night. I checked it again before I fell asleep.

Nice-Ville to Paris Gare du Nord. Ten fifty-five.

Paris Gare du Nord to Amsterdam Central. Five thirty-five.

Tomorrow was going to be a big day for me. Something was about to happen.

I don't think I had my dream again that night. But I might just as well have had, because the next day, it was going to come true.

FOURTEEN

Pushing myself back into my seat gave me a real sense of the speed at which the train was running, propelling me to my destiny. I closed my eyes and counted to sixteen and then I opened them again and the landscape was exactly the same. I wondered how much distance equated to sixteen. With southern France now disappearing behind me, I knew that within the hour I would be coasting through the suburbs of Lyon and that the centre of France would be upon me, and I would be hurtling towards a great uncertainty. In my headphones I had repetitive electronic music as my soundtrack. Thin beats keeping time with trees that flashed by. The rise and the fall of power cables came endlessly then, and I gazed at them as they dipped and folded their way across fields filled with cows, the whole scene bathed in cloud-dappled sunlight.

The track over which I was suspended was chewing up the miles and drawing me on towards Holland. I took off my headphones. The rhythm of the train as it rocked imperceptibly, slicing through time like a scythe through wheat, began to feel hypnotic. Trance-like. I watched across the fields as the sun grew brighter on this crisp, late autumn morning.

I was sad that I had lost Edie.

I had dared to start thinking about her then in the past tense, but I knew that I had to be positive and that it was the wrong time to be thinking negatively like that. I had to start being kind to myself. I had to. For every moment of the previous week, I'd been beating myself up with how poorly I had behaved towards Edie. I needed this to stop now. Yes, I was wrong. I was very, very wrong. I told myself that we all made mistakes, big ones too, but that it was no good living my life surrounded by the wreckage of what I had done. I simply had to move on. Like the train on which I was travelling. Whether I felt it was appropriate or not I had to feel then that I was doing something good for Edie so that I could ignore my nerves. Or at least try to.

I thought of beer, and of cider as I looked across the apple trees and the hedgerows and out towards the sky. I thought of how much I wanted to drink. Of how much I thought I needed to drink, but I couldn't let a drop past my lips. Not yet. I told myself that I'd have a little later that day, when I finally made it to Amsterdam. I knew also that it was a lie. I had promised myself that I would not drink to excess anymore. It was a sacrifice I wanted to make for Edie, but I knew deep down that it was a sacrifice I needed to make for myself.

I closed my eyes again. Counted to sixteen again. Felt the sun warm on my face. Four hours out of Nice-Ville and approaching Lyon, and I felt the time melting away before me. I thought about the mornings. Tomorrow and yesterday. One bathed in optimism. One bathed in gloom. I couldn't decide which was which, and I counted the goats in a field alongside which the train was now passing. Above me the sun was lighting the clouds from behind which it had slipped. Grey in the middle, the edge of the cloud was a blaze of light, like a brilliant corona pushing hope out into the entire world. No wonder people believed there was an omnipotent God, I told myself, when there was beauty in nature as strong as this.

At the other end of the carriage in which I was sitting, a door was constantly opening and closing, bringing a succession of people from the carriages further ahead. They were coming down to use the buffet car located right behind where I was sitting. I was in a busy seat. Presumably that's why it was cheaper than most. Every time the door behind me opened, it let out a violent hiss. A compressed spurt of sound, low and resonant. Hydraulic. Followed by a 'thunk' as the door sealed itself shut, as if air was being expelled from bone. For some reason, everyone that passed me seemed to look down at me as they did. Did I appear alien in some way? There were no discernible expressions of disapproval, but neither were there any discernible expressions of approval either. I simply existed. And so did they. And the many people that passed me were simply registering that fact. They bought their drinks. I closed my eyes.

I tried not to think about the alcohol, and it wasn't easy, but counting the goats helped. After the goats came trees again. And after the trees, more roads and cars. And road signs. Towns I vaguely knew of. Cities that filled me with small-scale awe, almost humbling.

We sped through countless local stations, all of them empty. We sped through towns that seemed closed. Schools with chairs on the tables. Lights off. Empty playgrounds. Factories closed. Car parks empty. Shops not open. Where was everyone?

Occasionally, as the train glided through stations, one or two people flashed by, often standing too close to the edges of their platforms. I thought about people who threw themselves in front of trains. I could understand how that would be an efficient way to make sure you didn't make a mistake in pursuit of your own death. I couldn't imagine that there would be any coming back from an act so decisive. I also couldn't imagine there being much time to regret what you'd started.

I watched the crowd that was thickening around me, spilling out now from the buffet car behind. It was late morning already so it was reasonable, I figured, that those who might be disembarking would be getting their drinks in now. It was growing to be very busy around me. I looked at a selection of the faces and I leaned my head against the cool glass of the train window, seeing my eyes reflected back at me. My breath on the glass made this image distorted and I pulled back a little and wrote Edie's name in the mist on the glass. I watched it quickly disappear.

Edie. Disappeared.

Across from me the seat was empty. I had my backpack stored in the luggage rack above it. I put it there so that I could see it easily without having to look straight up above me. But at that moment, I was more interested in the world outside. It hadn't even occurred to me that Franck might be among these people, intent on getting to me before I could get to them. And the truth of the matter was that I no longer cared. Not one way or another. I blamed the stress of all of that for making me into a monster that did such unspeakably bad things to the girl I loved.

I replaced my headphones then, and I sighed, and the music intensified. It was hypnotic and exciting. Metallic sounds began to ring in my head. Rhythmic pulses of clanging and grinding and screeching and I was lost inside of it all. I became then a part of the big machine on which I was travelling. I felt like a part of the engine itself. And then a mid-pitched, single note arpeggio and a solid, reedy tune. Six notes. No more. And then, one harmony. And still the arpeggio. Fantastic. Empty. Like the towns I was passing through, like the fields beyond them. Like France. Nothing at all like Barcelona, or Nice. Or Oporto. Or Amsterdam. I reached up for my backpack and pulled it close to my chest. I cuddled it and thought of Edie. She was never far from my thoughts. Then, despite the loudness of the music in my head, I fell asleep for a while. Truly exhausted. Mentally. Physically. A mechanism to make me sleep. To rest.

*

The countryside began to unfold a blanket of damp, mud-green grass about twenty minutes after the train had left Lyon. Small lakes and deciduous trees spread for miles. On that day they would have looked no different to how they had looked for thousands of years before. Perhaps a little less populous, perhaps a little bit stronger, but essentially the same. Controlling their environment, and calling the shots, the trees dipped and rose in the light autumn breeze, their leaves whispering like children telling secrets out of school.

It's her! the leaves were whispering. *I can hear her crying! She's coming to get us!*

One after another the trees stood, singing stories that had drifted across the millennia. Creaking in the wind. Someone was coming. Someone was coming.

When I woke, I looked into the distance and imagined all of the wildlife nestled in and among the trees that stretched far off to the periphery of my vision. I couldn't see them, but I could sense them. I knew there would be spiders and flies and ants and snakes and mice and rats and voles and badgers and rabbits and hares. An entire world teeming with life that I couldn't comprehend. A world far, far removed from that of ours. Of man's. Wrong or right didn't matter. Just different. That's what it was. I could feel the serenity take hold of my spirit, but I knew that mine was not a pastoral existence, and neither was the nature that I currently surveyed. Out there among the trees there was a war. The snakes would eat mice, the spiders would eat flies. As serene as it might be to me at that moment, I knew that the stakes for natural wildlife were always every bit as high as they were for us in our buildings among the cities and towns, with all of our jobs and all of our dreams and ambitions. These pointless dreams and ambitions that we subconsciously deploy to act as a futile distraction from the vacuum created within our time on this earth. Blink and it's gone. It really is true.

Acres upon acres of quilted, bottle-green patches spread before me rising and dipping over burgeoning hillocks beginning to start their ascent to the centre of France. Blue greens, purple greens. Salmon greens and bottle reds. Side by side fields were nestling and converging, creating and all the time multiplying in a spectrum still to be defined. In twisting undulations from back to front, and from side to side to side and the colours began to sway together in clustering vortices, swooping through ninety and back through ninety more. Curling in billows and laying down to sleep in the afternoon when it grows too hot to stand.

And all around: the silence.

The silence heavy and hard to carry. There are no ears to decipher the noises of wildlife. Without the ears the noises are obsolete. They simply don't exist. The grasses can't hear. The grasses can't see. The grasses simply are.

The silent countryside nestles into its own inexorable state of denial. Slightly, it breathes, and I imagine the fields lifting slightly as they do so. Once every thousand years it takes another breath. But all the time its level rises and falls lung-like to bury and expose the secrets of hidden years. A penny dropped six years ago. An ivory pipe fallen from a farmer's pocket.

Previous lives.

In this part of France, a tree, and by this tree, in nineteen forty-four, a young *maquis* firing dipped bullets at the shadow of his enemy. Bang on the leg, the invading soldier drops to the road sucking in handfuls of earth as he rolls into a ravine. Here he finds shelter. A little respite. The stricken soldier's colleagues train their aim on the tree behind which the young *maquis* has hidden.

Fifty years later a limping soldier returns to that spot and stands back to look at the tree which is much wider than it was back then. Thicker it stands, stronger it feels, and how lonely it appears. He understands the arduous trials of nature and still, he can feel that bullet deep in his thigh always ever too deep to remove. He rests his arm heavily on his cane as he runs a moist eye up and down the trunk of his tree. If only the bullet had missed his leg, even by just a fraction, it could have saved him from being in pain for all of his life.

It could have saved him the embarrassment he suffered that time he made love to Ilse Brunner who giggled as he slipped taking off his trousers in a hotel room in Milan in 1954. It could have saved him the humiliation of not being able to chase after the boys who stole his wife's handbag as they left a cinema in Basel in 1972, having just watched *Last Tango in Paris*. It could have saved him the sadness he felt every time he looked at the scar that remained when he took a bath or lay naked in bed.

It could have saved him the hurt inside his soul, a hurt that pulled at his gut when he saw his grandchildren staring at him one year on the beach at Sorrento after he had fallen in the sand and couldn't get up without his stick. Their shocked silence still caused him to not sleep deeply over many, many nights.

He looked at the tree for a long time. He looked at the tree and was able to translate the rustling of the grasses that sung about him. The grasses, among which his story had been told for generations, passed down from harvest to harvest.

The tree recognised him. The tree knew him. He picked at its bark and uncovered a hole. He told himself it was a bullet hole. But whether it was, or wasn't, he still smiled his distant melancholic smile, far away and all knowing, the smile for which he'd become known to his family and friends.

At his feet as the earth around him imperceptibly exhaled, the empty shells, tarnished and crushed as they flew from the young *maquis*' rifle, scalding the brittle grass into which they fell. A faint smell of burning cordite. The shells of the bullet that nestled deep inside his leg all those years ago. The grass had been holding them for him all that time. One day, somehow, they knew he would return.

Hardly anyone else has passed that way since him. Hardly anyone else before.

The grass tells other stories now.

The tree can continue to grow untroubled by its past.

The old soldier can now die with some of the peace that he's been trying to find for half a century or more.

But today is a silent day. No visits. No thunder. No rolling tanks or rhythmic marching, no thuds, or booms. Just nothingness. A lot of nothingness. An all-encompassing, overbearing heavy bout of weighty nothingness.

Tranquillity.

A tide of tranquillity that washes the fields for miles around.

In the distance, more cows. Dotted along the horizon lies a broken fence over which they have stepped, rotten and neglected. Deep violet, almost black mosses cling to stones and an empty line of railway track cuts around and along the field from which we watch as the sun rises higher into the sky laying sheets of heat that frees the odours of the damp earth.

Crickets rub their wing casings silently together. No ears can decipher their vibrations, they chirrup to no one. They sense that there are others, and they sense a distant wave coming in from the east. Long before the field mice smell the wave, the crickets and cicadas can feel it. They sense it coming. The rain is coming.

Crows sit in trees and watch for grubs in the tall field below and marionettes march like clockwork in the night around the fence and out to the village that lies close to Belleville-en-Beaujolais, where the children go to bed at seven o'clock in the evening and read books before they sleep. Staccato marionettes that move in stilted snapshots like a film missing every other frame. They lead a pilgrimage to a world free of unbelievers. Their journey takes them every night to the place where the children dream at eight o'clock in the evening. Where the day becomes night, they usher in peace to the village. When the church bells ring at sunset, the marionettes begin their nocturnal march through the fields carrying the children's dreams with them as they go, and even in the darkness the creaking of their rusty limbs is left unheard for they too live in the silent world.

Thrushes peck at the foot of the stones where they know they will find insects and snails, all trying to find shelter there. At the bottom of the ravine in which a German soldier once lay injured there gathers a nest of grass snakes that writhe in a heaving mass of coolness, slithering but dry and firm to hold. Cold to the touch.

An owl at night will again attempt to break into the ravine and snatch away the youngest of the group, and a hare bounds across a field as it too senses the wave coming in from the east. It stops in the distance, close to the cows, and lifts its head then skips, randomly leaping left, right to right, then right again and then left twice and away from the wave that is coming in from the east.

A hum breaks the silence that no-one can hear.

The sun presses harder against the grass, purple-yellow and blue-yellow, bottle-red, and fire-green and the hum that no one can hear grows louder. Grasses sway in anticipation of the wave from the east. The cicada's song grows in intensity as if all sound is being heightened by the introduction of a now even louder hum that seems to be emanating from the train track that cuts around and along the field from which I am watching. And the grass sways in anticipation of the wave from the east. The wind drops and stills the grass as the sun then cries and moistens the earth. The sun pulls out the crow's wings that fan the hot bird and the silence of the cicada's chirrup is now drowned by the greater silence of the mysterious hum that has pitched itself now as a note.

Without warning there is a squeak as the rail track moves and noise is all around. The speed is deafening the silence that no one can hear and the wave from the east becomes the wave to the west as the train hurtles through all the grass that is now cooled by the breeze from the noise that is sending the crows into the sky. Out across the open fields the mice scurry away from the vastness of the sound that has cooled the grasses, and they move as if a wind has uprooted their stories of soldiers, returning to find shells by which once they were felled.

The train speeds on like a demon. Slowly it hums again. It hums one more time and then no longer, and the breeze has decided that it is probably safe to return languidly back to cooling the grass now that the imperial metal tube has breathed its diesel over the silence that no one can hear.

As the grass settles back toward the thrumming of their natural rhythm, they remain unaware of the relief inside the metal tube that I was feeling at that moment.

An insurmountable relief now that I had chosen to be kinder to myself.

I thought about Edie, and I afforded myself a smile. I thought about when she and I had left Erkrath after we had stolen Boaz's cocaine. I thought about us drinking to celebrate and then being still drunk one morning on a train in Portugal, each of us carrying tempers tightly stretched out from the night before, our hearts beating a little more slowly as we relaxed into ourselves. United we sat side by side clinging to each other. Clinging. I tried to speak to her, but I couldn't. My tongue felt elated and electric. My soul pulsed and throbbed with excitement and the uncertainty of not knowing. Edie was relieved to be through it all as well, but we didn't know that it was only just beginning. I knew on that very early day that I needed to be careful, because I could fall in love. And I did. I truly did.

Edie was happier then, sitting alongside of me. She had longed for the border to disappear behind us so that she could sit and hold my hand. She wanted to simply hold my hand. I remembered our conversation, as the grasses became a memory out of the window.

Eventually I spoke.

"Look. Out there. Isn't it beautiful?"

She looked at me for a long time. Then she glanced out of the window but said nothing at all. She stared and smiled, flicking her eyes backwards and forwards, following the telegraph poles, watching the telephone wires rise and fall. Watching the hedgerows and the trees. Not counting the trees, but nearly counting them. Like I did on that coach through Bergen many months before. Her eyes began to ache, and she looked further and further back into the passing scene at the spiders and flies and ants and snakes and mice and rats and voles and badgers and rabbits and hares that lived there.

She looked at the fields that passed, all purple-green and blue, salmon-green, bottle-red, and bottle-blue, clear, fire-yellow, orange, red and fire-green.

"Look at the fields. Look at their patchy colours," I said.

And she smiled at me, and for the second time in just a few hours she had told me that she thought maybe she loved me.

I felt a tear for Edie slip from my eye and I turned my head so that I was now staring out of the train window again. Up close. Again the image fogged. And again I wrote her name on the glass.

My memory of her was so strong. My heart a forest fire.

There were a lot of people crowded near to me now, each trying to make some space in the buffet car. I didn't want to have to explain myself to any of them and my tears continued to fall.

But then there was a tap on my shoulder.

"Excuse me," I heard a girl's voice say. "Is this seat taken?"

FIFTEEN

It's funny how things turn out. Without intending events to occur, or even trying to influence them in any way, they can so often fall in your favour, or they can stack up strongly against you. The Fates. Clotho made this shirt, and Lachesis placed it on my back. But it was Atropos who refused to alter my destiny. She was certain to ensure that what was written for me would inevitably come to pass.

The die was cast. The scene set. No choices left to make.

Edie was there for me all along, and I had loved her for that. Somewhere in my heart I knew that she would remain a constant in my life regardless of all else, and I was resolved then that either with or without her, she would always be with me. I did indeed take some kind of comfort in that. But what did it all mean, and to whom did it really matter? How would this newly declared, platonic love measure up against any other kind? Only time could tell. Time, and the Fates.

At that very moment I understood.

I understood fully. My actions, my behaviour – it didn't matter. Because, ultimately, when love is so powerful, then the manner in which you recognise it, and the form it eventually takes, ultimately doesn't matter at all. If love lasts for one second, or for two lifetimes, it is and always will be the strongest and most profound emotion that humans can experience.

It is universal. It is unpredictable. It is indestructible.

Is it love that separates us from other species? Yes. It is. Are love and the Fates entwined? They probably are. In this case, yes they certainly were.

I embraced then their will, these three daughters of Zeus that laughed in my face and pointed their bony fingers in my direction, opening and closing their wordless mouths like fish in a bowl, their pale silent faces hollow and ghoulish.

They had done for me and had cursed me to a life of success. The anonymity of failure was not going to be a place where I could hide away and fester throughout my days. I would need to lick my wounds in public. I would need to share my sorrow in words, and I would have to write about what I had done. I, from that moment on, understood that I was strong and weak in equal measure.

I could go to Boaz, and I could convince him to leave Edie alone. I could try to convince him that I would make good the wrong we had done to him. I was going to be able to stand up tall and straight and face this devil of a man. The Fates had decided that that alone was my true destiny.

I felt a breathtaking optimism come flooding over me as I turned to the girl who asked if the seat was taken, the sun playing on her face and in her hair.

"No, it's not," I replied, "You can take it."

I smiled at her and then nonchalantly turned my attention back to the world flashing past my window. I wondered if she would want to speak to me. Would she want to get to know me?

I pulled my backpack in a little more tightly and I glanced at her as she took a book from her bag and opened it mid-way through. Something by someone I had heard of.

She had a coffee in her hand, and steam rose from the paper cup in gossamer trails, weightless and ephemeral. She smiled in my direction once. Just once. Her eyes glittered like the surface of the Mediterranean Sea. They flickered past mine, and made the briefest of contact, before she was quickly transfixed by the book that she was cradling.

She seemed to have manners and was well-composed. She seemed to be correct in her actions. I liked that in a person. Considerate, not slovenly. Concerned by nothing. Confident. Positive and irresistible things. A good-looking girl. Her poise was statuesque, her grace understated. Supine. She held herself straight in her seat, deceptively strong, framed like a ballerina.

Minutes passed before I looked at her again. She was reading and I didn't exist at those moments. More minutes passed. I did nothing, and the minutes eventually turned into an hour before the countryside melted away and several large buildings crept into view. Clouds rolled down from the hills and came tumbling towards us, carrying the rain, and the air grew cooler as the afternoon began to dissolve.

The train slowed a little and she got up from her seat and went to collect her things. The low sun shone like the gold in her eyes as she peered through the window at which I was seated, her eyes grey, marbled by copper. I recognised that the train would soon be stopping, and it seemed as if she were about to leave it. I felt a kind of panic then. Why did I?

We were approaching Beaune, and I could see the town

from a distance as it rose a little around the bend in the tracks. I knew then that Paris was becoming ever more real. By the late afternoon I would be arriving at the Gare de Lyon. I had to make a single connection and would board just one more train after this one. I would be in Amsterdam by the evening.

The girl took her bag from the overhead rack and turned to smile in my direction.

"It looks like it might rain," I said to her. She smiled.

"Yes," she said demurely.

I thought then of my dream. It came at me from nowhere. Beaune felt like a place I had been to once upon a time, even before I had arrived there.

I felt the hair on my arms slowly rise and a shiver slid between my shoulders. Alert now, I was taking everything in. I could sense Edie then and, in that moment, she seemed more real to me than if she had been standing right before me.

This girl who had been sitting alongside me, standing now with her back to me, waiting for the train to stop, seemed familiar too. But I had never seen her before. Not once before now. Not ever. I looked at the black coat she had draped across her arm. The book in her hand. Her blouse, feminine, pastel coloured, pressed and tidy. Her hair long, curled. Blonde. Nothing about her spoke of the girl in my dream.

This was not the place.

This was not the girl.

No matter how much I could have pleaded with the Fates at that moment, they were not going to alter the course of things. They were not going adjust the events of my life that they, collectively, had cast for me. *You're on your own*, I muttered to myself, in my head, and as I said it, this girl turned to me and smiled once more.

"I hope I don't get too wet," she said, looking at the window that now had trails of water running down it and smiling, nonetheless. I said nothing. I was a complete idiot in that moment.

The train came to a halt directly alongside the platform sign that told me we had arrived in Beaune. I saw the sign. Yellow lettering. Blue background. I was aware then that I was breathing hard and sitting up straight, watching the faces that left the train and watching the faces that came aboard. I was surveying the faces on the platform, and there were not so many, but the girl of my dreams was not among them. The buildings were not pulling me in. The feeling wasn't right.

It was not the busy station of my dream. I listened for church bells. I was looking for water. Rain, yes. But a church, a fountain. None of it!

Nothing appeared.

So close. So close.

Away from the train now, the girl who had been sitting opposite me walked past my window. She didn't look once in my direction, her eyes fixed on the platform beneath her feet, her movements intent on avoiding the rain that was beginning to fall more heavily.

This was not my girl.

This was not my dream.

*

Puddles were forming on the station platform as the train pulled away and my journey resumed. I soon put on my headphones again and played some soft music. Ambient stuff. Mature and thoughtful notes from a reverb soaked piano drifted laconically through and across one another. As a boy, Harold Budd used to sit and listen to the tones made by the wind as it was sliced into pieces by telegraph cables out in the deserts of California. The resonance of the cables made music that Harold could naturally decipher. Music that he sought to replicate throughout his entire life. I was able to relate strongly to that at that moment, watching as I was the incessant rise and fall of pylons and their interconnecting cables as the TGV picked up speed once again.

Soon we would hit Auxerre, and from there Paris was little more than an hour away. I settled back and thought about what was coming my way as I looked dreamily up the hill around the foot of which the train was now beginning to fly. At the top of the crest stood a church. Or maybe a castle, or an old fort, from this distance it was hard to tell. Silhouetted against the deadening sky, the building stood defiant in the face of time. It was very old. How much had it seen? Over how many years had it stood watch? And how insignificant was I in the face of such a building? Or even the men who built it. They had achieved something that remained standing after hundreds of years. What could I possibly hope to do by comparison? I had my whole life ahead of me when I was younger. So many plans, and so many dreams. So much emotion bubbling away, forcing itself up and out through all of my emotional and erratic actions. Life was suffocating me back then and I had already embarked on the process of killing myself, only I didn't know it. But it was happening.

A million bugs and insects flashed past me in the space of ten seconds. I didn't see a single one of them. It made me feel very, very small indeed.

The sun was beginning to dip below the horizon by the time the train left Gare d'Auxerre-Saint-Gervais. Paris was close now.

All thought was directed at Edie. Where did she go? Where was she now? Was she behind me? Back in Barcelona with Yannis? The thought was too painful. Everything about Barcelona was becoming too painful. The memory of us together in the tapas bar, laughing and drinking beers, my hand on her leg. Her hand on mine.

Me smiling at her as she spoke with Elena, and Edie, not looking at me and then noticing I was staring at her. I could see her silently ask the question, 'What?' before looking back to Elena and then back at me again. She smiled and gave me her full attention. I winked at her, and she stuck out her tongue and wrinkled her nose.

Yannis talking to me, Elena talking to Edie, but both of us looking at one another. Marco watching us as we smiled at one another, and Marco smiling at me in turn, nodding his head with an expression on his face something like adulation, or so I assumed.

I thought about the game that Edie and I had played crossing the wide road at the top of La Rambla, waiting for ten seconds after the little green man had appeared on the crossing before setting foot on the road and then racing one another across to the other side. I can see Edie finishing a little behind me and grabbing at my arm as she falls laughing by my side, the traffic sounding its collective horn to show us its disapproval. Us catching our breath and laughing. Breathing hard. Panting.

Again, the strong image I have of Edie laying by the pool in the Algarve, carrying two cocktails back from the bar, a peach-coloured towel wrapped around her narrow hips. Peach, with orange and red stripes.

A crimson heat.

She sways a little in my mind, and water runs down her slender, freckled legs. I swim across the pool and look at the insects as they struggle to free themselves from the large puddles of water that have gathered there. Edie passes me my cocktail and I close my eyes to the sunlight, and I see her in my mind then, silhouetted orange, against a dark red background.

I can hear her laughter. I can smell her skin. I can taste her perfume.

I think about our time in Oporto, and about Antonio in that studio, and about Edie in that shoe shop and Rosa, her boss there. I think about me in that dystopian petrol station, clacking at the tills that seemed to echo through the nights, taking money and clipping it away.

I remember the moment she saw Franck and thought about the fear we had felt. I figured that was the moment our decline began, and then I realised clearly that our decline began on the day we stole Boaz's drugs. On the day, in fact, that Edie had the idea to do that. For, after all, it was Edie's idea. Not mine.

So perhaps I shouldn't be so hard on myself.

I felt then how hard I threw her small figurine against the wall at our apartment beside the car park entrance in Barcelona, and I can hear her softly sobbing and telling her long-dead grandmother that she loved her still, and that she missed her.

That she missed all of her family.

And I realised that yes, I should be bloody hard on myself. I wanted to go back in time and to glue it all together again. All of it. I wanted to fix it all up, the pieces of our life. Bring them together. Make something new. Make it strong.

If Yannis had taken her from me, it was only what I deserved.

Where was Edie? I needed to know that she was safe. I needed to know that I could do something positive to protect her now and that I owed this to her. I told myself that I owed her my life.

If I couldn't hold her again, I needed to know that someone else could, and that someone else, someone kinder, could give her the love she deserved. That someone else could help her make a life for her that she could be proud to call her own. It was never going to be me. And that made me sad. I was going to do something for Edie. Give her freedom back to her. Go and see Boaz. Take the blame. My purpose was renewed.

Paris came upon me like only Paris can, imposing and definite. Warm, in an oddly maternal way. Both welcoming and aloof at the same time.

The buildings all around the Gare de Lyon looked down proudly all around me. Cafés, beauty parlours, travel agents, kebab shops; all of them beneath the most ornate, wrought iron balconies. The kind of architectural finishing found all across France, and Spain too.

Nervously I stepped onto the bus that was going to shuttle me through the city from the Gare du Lyon to the Gare de Nord. I had to make my connection within thirty minutes. I doubted it would be possible, but it was.

And then I remembered the last time that I was in Paris. It

was with Edie to meet the motorcyclist who ran our stash to Lisbon and looking back on it at that time I could see what an unreal moment that was. It felt like a long time before, but it was in fact little more than a year. If she was nervous, she didn't show it, but that was true of Edie in so many ways.

We had waited outside a burger shop in a suburb near St Denis, just up from the Parc de la Legion d'Honneur. It was not the most comfortable place, and we didn't like hanging out there for too long. That day it was cold, and I remember how damp the roads were. There was a team of motorcycle couriers buzzing like wasps up and down the shallow ramp outside the burger place, and they all seemed to be looking for us.

Finally, our guy turned up and we handed him the drugs we had stolen from Boaz. He never took his helmet off, I realise now. Who was he? Could it have been Iker? Was he the one who had been feeding information of our whereabouts back to Amsterdam?

Two kilos. It was easy for this biker to conceal. It was never an enormous theft in terms of size. The money was good though. While it lasted.

I'm pretty sure Boaz could have replaced it all fairly quickly and just moved on, that is if it hadn't been for the fact that it was Edie who had crossed him. Boaz, and Dieter of course, whatever he might have told me, had a soft spot for Edie. I pictured her then, smiling with her sparkling eyes peeping out from under her hair, black as a raven's tail. I could see in my mind's eye her low-hanging silver earring as it shone in the rain and how it reflected the luminescence of any number of neon lit bars. We were always in bars. All of us. We were all always drinking, or smoking pot. It had been a singularly destructive way to live, and it was now that we were finally paying the price for it.

Not all of us.

But Edie and me? For sure.

The bus drifted languidly along, parallel to the Seine and past the Pompidou Centre where it turned right and continued north into the Tenth Arrondissement, finally pulling into the Gare du Nord after less than ten minutes. Bang on schedule but still I had to hurry to make my connection.

I found the platform sooner than I expected and the blood-red train looked primed and ready for action. I went back out on to the concourse to get myself a coffee that I could take on board and I stood at the far end of this vast space and looked back down at the iron trellis work that held the magnificent ceiling up so high, propping up the very sky above our heads. These grand old railway stations as impressive as cathedrals, conceived to install awe in any who stood inside.

Pigeons nested high up in the eaves and their droppings were slowly corroding the paintwork that gave the station it's gothic feel but still, to my eye it didn't look tarnished. The height of the ceiling is what gave the place such an imposing character.

I looked then at all the people around me and I thought about what they would all be doing this evening. Some would be at home in the embrace of those they loved and who loved them in return. I would not be among them.

Others might be drunk in the company of strangers. In a club, or maybe at a party given by somebody they didn't know. I would not want to be among them.

The day was already tipping beyond the mid-point of the

afternoon. I would be in Amsterdam just before darkness arrived to reclaim the light for itself. I thought then about how days were born, and died, in darkness. I wondered if that had any negative effect on us. In the same way that many people start their days by being shocked out of sleep by an alarm, I wondered if the fact that darkness heralded both end points of our time, as we measured it, had any kind of psychological influence on the way we behaved. Perhaps we were nocturnal by nature after all.

There were a lot of people all around me now. I looked up at the station clock, it was three-fifteen, so I hurried back to platform six and boarded my connecting train. There were barely a handful of minutes before it was due to depart. I took my seat, against another window. Where else? I stowed my backpack in the overhead rack of the seat in front of me and I nervously sipped my coffee. The train soon began its gentle tipping from side to side, as it hesitantly heaved itself away before beginning to pick up pace.

I settled in for the final part of my journey and for an odd reason, I remember thinking then about the girl I'd seen laying tables outside the corner restaurant in Nice, the girl who the waiter told me was going to be travelling to Paris today.

Had she been on the same train as me the whole journey from Nice? Or had she got on a later train? I didn't know, but it was funny I considered, that I hadn't thought of her again after he told me that she was travelling my way, and that she may have been sitting just a few metres from me was a strange thought. There was something about her. If she had been on the same train as me, then I would have certainly seen her. But I hadn't, and it didn't matter to me now.

She, too, was a part of my past.

Of that I could surely be certain.

*

I then began to focus hard on what was ahead of me. It was starting to feel all too real. Should I go to Boaz right away, or should I try to find Dieter first? I felt that I knew pretty much where he would be. If I didn't find him right away, I was sure that he'd be able to find me.

Despite the danger I was without doubt going to be in, I suddenly felt good at the idea of trying to rekindle some old scenes by having a beer in Emmelot once again. I remembered sitting there the year before, after I had first arrived in Amsterdam, reading, and drinking beer, watching the world go by. Watching my new life as it unfolded around me. But that was all gone now. That was over. And I was now alone.

It had all been for nothing in the end. No dream. No lost girl. Or was there something else? Something I couldn't see, or that I hadn't seen yet? What was it all about? Why had I given up everything I had in search of this adventure? I figured that at the very least I had had fun and ultimately, I said to myself, that in itself was an achievement.

So I watched Paris slip behind me as the train on which I was travelling once again plunged deep into the heart of a verdant, felt-green countryside. It would soon be four o'clock and I would be arriving in Amsterdam in just a couple of hours. I would need to find digs, that would be my first concern. Should I go back to Balance in the hostel? Or back to the boat I stayed on when I first arrived? To see the woman with the angular fringe. Haircut! That was her name. I remembered it then and wondered how I could have forgotten.

Like salmon returning upstream to die. Was that what I was doing?

The train was flying now and the towns and stations that it passed through were a blur, nothing more than a blend of colours, ill-defined and unspectacular, disappearing too quickly to understand. Another of life's metaphors. Every community that each town contained was passing me by in a single instant. A woman I could love, and who could forgive me my weaknesses. A woman who could see the best in me when I needed to feel wanted. She could be in among that flash that just went by. Or that flash. Or that one. This is how impermanent our lives have become.

We have the ability to see so much more of life in the modern age, but almost because of that, we lack the time to see it properly. We lack the time to experience things, to experience life itself. So much choice has highlighted our inability to process it all and if we, in our lifetimes, learned to control time to the degree that we could see the entire planet in a single day, or the entire universe in a single week, it would only highlight our inability to experience it all so much more. It would destroy us.

Perhaps it is destroying us.

We cannot do it all. We cannot see it all. It would kill us if we could.

I decided then that I would slow down in my new life. If Boaz granted me one. I would take my time and I would focus on fewer things. Always my mind has been a butterfly, or a bee, hopping from one flower to the next. Focus. That was going to be my new approach.

But first I was going to face up to what I had done to Edie.

And to how badly behaved I had become.

In the distance I watched the sun start to lower on the horizon. This day was drawing to a close. But what I didn't know for sure was how it would end.

As the train flew past Tournai, I picked up my things and walked down to the buffet car. I wanted a beer, and I couldn't wait any longer. I was doing well, and I owed myself one. In truth, my nerves were kicking me hard now that I had crossed into Belgium.

Was I doing the right thing? There had to be no doubt in my mind about this. Yes. This was the right thing. I told myself this a hundred, no, a thousand times.

In the buffet car, a guy was leaning against the little bar that ran along one part of the far corner. I stood behind him waiting my turn. Towards the end of the car people were smoking and it was uncomfortable to breathe. My eyes were stinging and the tar in the air was staining the walls virtually right before my eyes, but I kind of quite liked it all the same. It made me feel real. Real, in a way that I couldn't clearly define.

I watched as the guy in front of me took his beer and went and stood with the smokers at the back of the carriage. I ordered mine, a Stella Artois, and I went and stood back there with them and lit a cigarette. He nodded at me. A greeting of sorts.

"How's it going?" I asked him in London English. It was only one of a few times that I had spoken in the last few days, not since I had yelled at Edie, and then sobbed pitifully to Yannis.

"Yes, not bad," he said in a thick Dutch accent. "Are you going to Amsterdam?" he asked me then.

I nodded and took a sip of my beer.

"Yes," I said and added, "Going back there. I've been away for a little while."

He seemed interested in my story.

"You live there?" he asked.

"I did," I nodded. "I have friends there." And then I corrected myself, "I *had* friends there. I'm going back to see if they're still my friends."

He smiled at that, raising first his eyes, and then his glass.

"Yes, I know what you mean," he chuckled. "Is that why you left? Because of your friends?"

My turn to chuckle. He seemed to be accurate.

"You could say that." I smiled, and went on, "I needed to put distance between us all."

"We could all use that from time to time," he replied.

I liked this guy. He was easy to talk to. Sometimes strangers are the easiest people to communicate with. I don't know why, but then, at that moment it felt like the most obvious thing in the world to talk to this man.

He had a kind face. He was little older than me, tall and sharp with dark, thick hair. He seemed learned, in some way intelligent. A practical intelligence perhaps. He had a professional air about him, and I could imagine that he was a doctor or a psychologist. I could imagine that he listened for a living. I didn't once consider that he might be a police officer.

I told him my story, from the very start. I didn't mean to, but he seemed like he might be able to advise me. I didn't tell him about the drugs, of course not, but I did allude to 'something terrible', and he stuck out his lower lip and shrugged a little, shaking his chin from side to side and indicating that I didn't need to tell him any details. He winced when I told him about how I had struck out at Edie, and he even backed away a little at that point.

I don't know why I felt compelled to tell him everything. Maybe it was a catharsis of some kind, maybe I was trying to purge myself, or to get my story straight before I presented it to Boaz. This was probably a dress rehearsal for the event that was drawing closer all the time.

Much, much closer.

When I finished my beer, I went to the car to get he and I another, and in fact his glass was still half full when I gave him a second bottle.

"Cheers," he said lifting it slightly and tipping it in my direction a little. There was silence between us then. Finally, I broke it by apologising.

"Sorry," I said softly.

"It's okay," he said. "I was just thinking about what you were telling me." I waited. And he continued, "I think you're doing the right thing."

I was encouraged then, and he said, "I think that you have to go and face these guys. If you really love this girl, as you say you do. I mean if you really love her, then you have to go."

"I do," I told him.

And I meant it.

I was relieved at his opinion. I don't know why that should be, but I was.

"Do you think they'll understand?" I asked him, desperate for good news.

"No, of course they won't! Are you mad?"

He laughed. I laughed too. Perhaps a little too hard in fact. A nervous laugh. I was on the verge of becoming hysterical with concern.

"I think they'll want to destroy you," he said. "That's for sure. But I do also think that if they listen to you, then you have a chance and all the while we have chances in life, then we have life itself, no?"

Words I have rarely ever forgotten. I clinked my beer bottle against his and smiled.

"Thank you," I said.

"Good luck," he replied.

I walked back down the train to find another seat by another window, and I sat, and I looked.

And I watched.

And I watched.

The train was now in Holland.

We rocked our way at a more leisurely pace. Belgium, and Holland, were much more built-up than the pastoral idyll of France that I had been witness to over the proceeding eight or nine hours and now here I was, barely half an hour from the centre of the nation's capital city.

Amsterdam.

I could feel it.

Something was building.

Something was coming.

Finally, the train slowed and turned on a steep bend gliding into Amsterdam Lelylaan station. I didn't notice it pass a church, but I did hear the bells ring out for seven o'clock. I also didn't notice the train as it passed across the Heemstedestraat bridge, and over a wide canal, but I did see the fountain and I did see the shopping plaza in which it was sitting, although I didn't take full notice of any of it right away.

The world outside was serene and calm. The afternoon was fading into evening, and all around the buildings were turning on their lights and, although still bright, the sun was beginning then to descend. Still strong, the sun in the amber sky was shifting to a tangerine colour. A golden light.

The train was stopping now.

Soon it would be stopped completely.

I looked into my lap as the door hissed, and the hydraulics pulled them apart. Several people got off. Several more got on. I felt very odd at that moment, and it was as if a big cushion had been put over my head. My ears lost any sense of high frequency, like I had been rolled up in a blanket.

The first thing I noticed was a woman at the far end of the carriage. She had just got on the train. She was completely bald, and she was cradling, in her forearm, a small dog. I couldn't believe my eyes. I was almost paralysed with shock. I simply stared at her. Uncomprehending. I'm pretty sure that, yes, I was open mouthed. There was no doubting it, this woman featured in my dream. It was the same woman. Identical. Red hoops in her ears.

The next thing I registered, or rather I sensed, was a flash of blue from the other side of the window at which I was sitting. The time between me seeing this bald woman and sensing the flash of blue was less than a second, but for me the world was standing still.

I saw then the girl on the platform as she raised her blue asthma medication to her lips. This was the blue. All along. This was the blue!

An asthma inhaler!

Behind her the lighting along the platform was artificial. Harsh. It was illuminating all of the platform and the signs so that they stood out distinctly, and all of them, every single one, had yellow lettering on a blue, dark blue background.

It was my dream!

I felt dizzy. Faintly nauseous. Here it was. I had dreamed this scene for the majority of my life. This had haunted me for so many years.

Could it now be so real? How was it possible?

The girl shook her head as she inhaled on her medication. She gave a second slight shake of her head and then she gently put her fingertips to her throat and looked upwards, her red hair falling across the green canvas jacket that she wore. A jacket that had a small star on the lapel. A jacket that I recognised long before I looked at the girl that was wearing it.

She looked at the sky again and breathed it crisply in, and I knew her instantly, despite the redness of her hair. But she hadn't seen me yet.

Edie!

I froze.

She was wearing the clothes we had bought in Barcelona. She was here, in Holland, just a handful of stops from Amsterdam Central and now I understood why she had taken the wig and jacket when she left. She must have planned to come here all along! To disguise herself so that she might have some kind of chance back in her old hometown.

The train doors closed with a resounding thump. There was an announcement I didn't hear.

She saw me then and her face opened up for the entire world to read. I saw her properly. Right then. Deeply. With wordless affection. It all happened in a single moment. But it's so clear to me now. It is etched in my mind forever.

The train started to pull out. Edie ran toward the window at which I was sitting and began to bang on it, trying to embrace me through the glass.

"David!" I heard a muffled cry mixed with real tears. "David! What are you doing here?"

I could hear her through the window, but not well enough and so I leapt up and opened the small ventilator window at the top of the main one, caring nothing for the people around me. I climbed up on to the seat, totally oblivious to everything, and I squeezed my face against the opening and called to her as the train pulled away very slowly. She was running now alongside the train. Trying to keep up with me.

She cried, "I love you!" and I said the same thing back to her.

And it was true.

I loved her more than anything in my life. More than anything.

"I'll come back!" I called. "Wait for me. I'll get off at the next stop and come back."

I don't think she could have heard the last part of what I said because the train was moving quickly now, and Edie was left behind looking helpless and alone, her arms hanging limply at her sides. She disappeared into the distance like that, growing smaller and smaller until I couldn't see her anymore.

But I had to get back to her. I had to!

I was in a state of shock. The people around me said nothing. I was crying now, frantically pushing the button to make the train stop but it was doing nothing. These people could surely sense my anguish. The bald woman with her dog just looked at me disdainfully, as if she had never known love in her entire life, as if she had never been moved or motivated by a single emotion.

"How long to the next stop?" I pleaded with some of the other passengers who chose not to understand me.

One guy eventually said, "A few minutes. Not long."

I was relieved and felt a small stab of hope. I still had a chance to get back to her. How could this have happened? What was she doing in Amsterdam? Had she had the same thought as me? Was she going to see Boaz too? I needed to get back to her. I was standing by the door hopping from foot to foot, desperate to get back to Lelylaan station.

I realised I didn't have my backpack and so I ran back down the carriage to retrieve it from the overhead rack, pushing people out of my way. I ran back to the door. The train hadn't even entered the station and I was trying to get off.

When eventually it did stop, I leapt down and pushed away from me those who were trying to get aboard. I ran down one flight of steps and up another just, as luck would have it, a train going back the other way pulled up at the platform at which I was standing.

As soon as I was on this train, I began to mutter to myself for it to pull away and I began willing it to move. It seemed like an eternity, but finally the thing began a leisurely, all too long journey back down the line and within five more minutes arrived back at Lelylaan station.

I looked across to the opposite platform. Edie was nowhere to be seen. Maybe she had gone outside?

I looked along the track in both directions, and then ran down the stairs to the road outside. I couldn't see her. I began to cry. Months of pain was flooding from me now. Everything was too much now. All of it.

"Edie!" I shouted it now. I didn't care about my own safety. I simply didn't care. I was beyond that. This was an outpouring of guilt. I cried harder. And harder still. And I have cried every day since.

"Edie!" I sobbed. "I love you. Come back!"

But she didn't come. I waited. It was all I could do. I waited an hour, but she never came to me. It grew dark and I sat on a step outside the station. I waited for two more hours and still she didn't come. I smoked an entire pack of cigarettes. I cried. And I waited. But Edie never came back to me.

She never came to me again.

It was over. She was gone. And for many years, I never knew what became of Edith Hoffman after that.

I missed her then.

And I miss her still.

EPILOGUE

The story that I wanted to tell ... this is where it ends. There is more to say, but for now it can keep. What is important has passed.

The day after I saw Edie at the train station, I went to Amsterdam and very quickly met up with Dieter. It wasn't difficult to find him, I just had to be seen in Emmelot and a call went out that I was in town. I guess I should have been honoured that it was Dieter himself that turned up to see me, and not Franck or any of the others. I think, in truth, Dieter must have been expecting me because he appeared to know a lot about what had been going on, or at least he had the air of a man that appeared to know a lot.

He then told me that Boaz had gone back to Yugoslavia. I'm not entirely sure how truthful that was. He said that it was over six months now that he, Dieter, had been running the company, and he straight away warned me to get out of Holland as quickly as possible. He said that his bosses would be unforgiving if they found out that he'd been sitting with someone who'd stolen two keys of coke from them, and that he had then let that person get away unharmed.

He told me that, sure, Franck was supposed to have brought us back. But he also said that it was Edie that Boaz was most furious with. He'd taken it personally, he said. Boaz liked her style. He had plans for her to be working more closely with him. *But she was always too much of a maverick.* That's what he said.

I thought back to when Edie told me she had met up with Maartje in Oporto. She had said the opposite. She told me then that it was me that Boaz was after. Dieter was now telling me that it was the other way round and that Boaz had Edie in his crosshairs all along. The truth, as ever throughout my whole time in Amsterdam, was always difficult to decipher.

Of course, Boaz had wanted us both to pay for what we'd done, but it was Edie's disloyalty that angered him the most. He took it personally. I considered then that, yes, she was a maverick. But more than that, she was an enigma. To all of us it would now seem.

The endless subterfuge was hard to live with. Hard to read. Dieter said that after Boaz went away, and he had started running things, he straight away felt that it was a waste of resource to have Franck and sometimes Maartje or Jurgen away from the business for long periods at a time. He said that, after all, the theft happened on Boaz's watch and he, Dieter, wasn't responsible for it, he was not to blame. He told his bosses that he would never have sanctioned such a trip as the one Edie and I undertook, and that Boaz was dangerous. He said that Boaz was a fool and that everyone in the family would be better off without him being around. I didn't hear Dieter say anything of the sort while Boaz was in charge.

When Dieter spoke about his bosses, I knew he was referring

to the van Eycks. This was alarming. I knew what they were capable of or, at least I had heard about it. It was probably ninety percent myth but even so, I wasn't keen on testing the remaining ten percent.

But for all of this, Dieter flatly refused to tell me what became of Edie. He said he didn't know. I knew that he did, of course.

"Where is she, Dieter?" I pleaded with him over beers that day. "Why didn't she come back to me at the station yesterday? Where did she go? What have you done to her?"

"I don't know. Please don't ask me," was his evasive reply. He said it three or four times.

I continued to ask him the same question, in a variety of different ways.

"Please tell me, mate," I tried to appeal to his comradeship, "for old time's sake."

He had hardened considerably since we'd last properly spoken.

"I'm in love with that girl," I said, "I need to know where she is."

"You're in love with her!" he scoffed loudly. "Then why did you live in that shit hole in Barcelona with her? Why did you take her to that place and fill her up with all those pills and powders? That doesn't sound like love to me. You don't love her! How could you? And do that? You only think you do!"

I considered briefly if he was right, and then later I thought about it far more deeply. Maybe I was blinded by my own failings. Maybe my sorrow and self-pity had morphed into some kind of false love, a phantom love brought about by some deep-rooted unhappiness, which had probably started when I was a kid. Maybe on the day that I threw the blue ball into the road, an action that inadvertently killed a girl. My guilt. Forever.

Who knows?

I considered all of this, and I even started to marvel at how right Dieter could have been, how insightful he probably was. I knew in my heart, deep down in my own soul, what it was that was driving me to find her. It was my infatuation with her. Obsession. An illness. I couldn't stop. One day, she would come to me. I was convinced of it. Convinced.

"My advice to you," he told me then, "would be to get the fuck out of this town before I change my mind and have you taken out by the airport."

He had a steel in his eye when he said it.

"You can remember what that might mean can't you?"

Dieter had changed, there was no doubt about it. He was now the man calling the shots in that business. I begged him several times to tell me where Edie was, but he simply wouldn't say and eventually, after two or three days of blindly looking around town for her, exactly like I had in Nice, I had to leave.

I went to a bar one night where I sat nursing a single beer for hours. Reading books was out of the question. I was permanently on edge. Sleep was hard to come by, and I was possibly traumatised by the whole adventure. Edie was gone. I had to face it. Then, as I left the bar, late, I was followed back to the boat where I was staying. I know there was no intent to hurt me, but it was someone sending me a message. Of that I was convinced. I sensed that it was only a matter of time until something bad happened and decided that, yes, I had to go.

But first, one more evening with Dieter. In spite of everything, we got along and there was a small friendship between us still.

"Consider yourself fortunate that I like you, David," Dieter said to me. "You've had, what, twenty thousand guilders from Boaz? Man, it sounds like a lot, and it is a lot. Of course, it is. But to us it's no great disaster. We can move that in a couple of days. Easy. And if we go out across Holland, which we can do from time to time, then we can move twice that in a day. So, I'm in a position to mark it up as Boaz's mistake. It might even have done me a favour, eh."

He said this with a telling light in his eye, and a half-smile on his lips.

"After all, I might have been waiting for a chance to blame him for something and get him removed."

When he said this, I understood things a little bit more, and another part of the puzzle slid into place.

"You mean ...?" and I didn't say any more. I didn't have to.

He'd set it all up.

Get Boaz removed.

For all I knew, he and Edie were in it from the start.

I'd been used.

"I don't mean anything, David," he smiled then. "But I wonder where Edie got that idea from in the first place? To steal that coke?"

He looked at me then with a broad grin.

An all-knowing look on his face.

I took it all in. Said nothing.

"Look," he said plaintively, his hands spread out before him, palms up as if he was performing a magic trick. His elbows resting on his knees, as he said, "Think it through. I want Boaz to be gone. What would ensure he finally toppled over? What would make people who trusted him most angry? He'd been making mistakes for months. Years even, and yet still he was in a position of control. Why? Well, that's what I kept asking myself. Why? The bosses must have had good confidence in him and all the while he was earning for them, they could overlook certain failings. So long as the money kept pouring in. So long as the balance sheet looked good. That was when I thought it might work out in my favour if someone stole something of theirs."

I remained silent, as a picture began to emerge.

Dieter continued, "So I figured I could easily set up a transaction with some good friends of mine in Germany, and then ask Edie to 'steal' it from Boaz."

He leaned back in his chair, a smirk of self-satisfaction spreading like spilt milk across his face.

"So, what do you think of that, David?"

I took my time before answering, and then I said, "It's clever, I guess," and added, "it seems to have worked out for you."

He folded his hands across his tight belly.

"It did," he said. "Nicely."

"So where is Edie now?" I asked him again, hoping that he could continue with keeping counsel in me.

"I saw her at Lelylaan station," I said, "coming into Amsterdam, and she saw me. I told her I was coming back and when I got there, not even fifteen minutes later, she was gone. I don't understand why. Or where she went. Why didn't she wait for me?"

"Maybe we don't want you to meet with her, David," he said cruelly and with a sharp degree of assertiveness now. "Maybe that chapter in both of your lives is over?"

Dieter made it clear that he had used us all along. And that he would continue to do so.

"She's okay," he said then. "She'll be fine. Don't forget that from the start Edie was fully on board with this whole scam. She and I were always, shall we say, friendly."

His smirk then made me suddenly angry about my naivete, and in that moment I think I had reached my fill of the whole lot of them.

Edie included.

"You two were not supposed to get so close," he said. "I told her that a little bit would be okay, but she had to fall in love with you didn't she. I have to tell you, none of us ever saw that coming! Edie! In love! Ha! No chance. Not ever."

He continued, "Do you think Franck is so useless that he'd not pick you up the very moment he saw you in that bar in Barcelona? Or Edie in that ridiculous shoe shop in Portugal!" He was laughing now. "What she was doing in there we don't know! We thought that was hilarious I can tell you!"

I felt hollow at the crassness of this remark. Edie was trying hard to make a go of it. A straight life. What did she call it? *Something out in the light*. She made that sacrifice for me. I let her down. She tried hard to make to it work out for us and I threw it all back in her face.

Dieter went on, "You had a good run with her, David, but it was you that fucked things up with her. Not us. You're the one who lost your shit in a big way down in Barcelona. It was spectacular!"

I nodded sadly. He continued, "So just lick your wounds and

go now. Go back to London and start a new life. Be a teacher or something. You'd be good at that. God alone knows you're a shit drug dealer!"

I asked him, "Can't you let me see her once more? Can't you do it for Edie if not for me? Don't you owe us anything in all of this Dieter? We put our sanity on the line so you could advance your career!"

"Me? Owe you! Are you kidding me? You, my friend, owe me roughly twenty thousand. Think about it before I change my mind. You're not seeing Edie. You have to get out of town and don't come back."

"But Edie and I deserve a life together!" I persisted. "Surely you can see that we had become close. Doesn't that mean anything at all to you? Can't you do that for us? It seems to me that you're the one holding all the cards here, Dieter. You're the one calling every shot."

He was beaming again, "Keep going," he said, smugly, "I like what I'm hearing. It sounds to me like respect."

"Dieter," I tried again and again to appeal to his human side. I knew he had one. Or he used to.

"Please mate, can't you set it up for me to see her, just one more time? Please, I'm begging you. Once only!"

"Don't beg, David," he replied. "It's not nice to see."

"Well that's how desperate I am."

He cut me off then. "Stop!" he barked and suddenly reminded me of Boaz in so many ways. "Enough! It's over between you, okay."

I became frustrated at his inflexibility, but it was clear that he was not going to give an inch.

"David, I'll say it again," he spoke patiently and slowly now. "You had a chance with Edie. You were not supposed to have had a chance. She was supposed to have come back to us right after Boaz ..." and he paused to choose his word carefully, "... disappeared. But when she didn't, I wanted to get Maartje down there to persuade her to come back, but she was having none of it. She wanted to be with you, man," he said. "Don't you understand? You had that girl right where you wanted her, and we let you have that! So you've had your chance and you fucked it up. She even stitched Maartje and Franck up to buy time and to get you to safety. I mean, yeah, I was cross about it, but I knew she'd come back one day. A dog always goes to its master, eh. A bitch especially."

I bristled with anger then. I went to shout, but something about his calm demeanour took the impetus away. I was cornered. I would not be winning against this guy. Not now. Not at any time. I couldn't win. There was no point in trying.

"She doesn't want to see you. No woman would, not after what you did to her. You're going to destroy each other if you get together. There's too much history there now. Take my advice and go. You've got two days to leave Amsterdam. Two days, and if I ever see you again after that ..." He left the sentence suspended in the air between us before he concluded, "Now stop following me, David. Your time in this town is over. Go back to London. Go back to your family and don't ever bother me again. The less you two see of each other, the better it is for all of us. She owes me, big time. Don't forget it. I think you need to move on. We're done with you. Just go away and accept everything. Take whatever you want from the whole experience. Who knows, maybe one day you can write a book about it. If you do, then it's a good job I've never given you my real name, hey."

He laughed. Hollow. Cavernous. Sinister.

*

I am in a pram. Excited. Low down. The pram is at the foot of an alleyway as it opens out on to a main road that runs out of the eastern end of the town. There's an expanse of water. A swimming pool. And a fountain. There is a cathedral. Or a church. There are many people. They are all moving. They are carrying many bags. Shopping bags. The bags are dropped all around. My vision blurs and the crowd shimmers, as if reflected on the surface of a lake.

There's a van. A small white van. I smell petrol. There's a vast red pond spreading out in an arc under the wheels of the parm. I hear bells. Large bells. Deeply sonorous. I hear children and then hysteria as they start to run. A woman carries a small dog. Hooped, red earrings. A lead. Heavy breasted. Duplicate. Tweed hats and jackets. Red stitching. Sepia tweed. Soldiers. Many, many soldiers.

And there's something blue that bounces five or six times before finally it stops by the side of the road. I see myself as a child, a sticky mess of white chocolate squeezing between my fingers on an overheated day. I see nobody else. I see myself endlessly. My image repeated. Infinite. A cloud looms and the entire scene grows dark.

Then I see her as she climbs out from beneath the van and walks towards me, but still the soldiers are trying to lift the van and no one else has seen her. There is an intense pale-yellow light that surrounds her as she glides lightly to the pram. She reaches out and touches my face and she is smiling a smile filled with love. She looks behind her just once as if to tell whoever is waiting that she'll just be a few moments. She turns to me, and she looks at me and she kisses my head, and she says, "I'll look after you, David. For all of your life I'll be there for you."

My heart skips a beat as she turns to leave me. Beautiful, beautiful girl. Where were you? Auburn-haired, green jacket. Army jacket? Soldiers? French? She turns to face me, she smiles and blows me a kiss and then languidly drifts silently up into the sky above me, high above the wreckage of her final moments and out beyond the heavy grey clouds, where the sky is always blue, and where the sun always shines ...

... and slowly, I awake.

*

After all the adventures, after all the time that I had been away, after everything that had happened in my life in the previous eighteen months or so, one of the most difficult things to do was to go back to the way things were before. In fact, I'll be honest, I already knew on day one that it was going to be impossible for me to readjust completely. Mum had moved back to the estate where we first grew up after my brother had been convicted, and even though I always preferred living over that way, I also knew that staying back at my mum's was only ever going to be temporary. I just had to work out what I was going to do next.

For all the time that we had been apart, and for the distinct lack of communication on my part, Mum accepted me back effortlessly, and I have to say, made me feel welcome right away. I think she'd missed having some company around. After all, my brother had been inside for over a year at that point, and Mum told me later, he showed some signs of sorting himself out finally. I think by then the novelty of Mum having her own space was wearing a bit thin, so she was glad to have me around, I guess. But we both knew that it was not going to be a permanent thing ever again, and that finally, with my trip around Europe, I'd grown enough to strike out on my own.

So suddenly there I was. I simply turned up unannounced one afternoon and walked right into the kitchen where Mum was sitting smoking a cigarette and nursing a cup of tea.

"Hi, Mum," I said as nonchalantly as I could. "Guess who's home?" I laughed and gave her a hug which I think she barely registered. Of course, she took it all in her stride.

"Oh, hi David, there's tea in the pot if you want one." And then she said, "Did you have a nice time?"

That was about all she ever asked me about my trip. Honestly, it was barely mentioned again.

So I tried to settle back in. To be a good son. To find a job and all that, and, indeed, I did get some work in the library in the town centre which I liked but it was never going to be a living, and so I looked to see Christmas through and in the new year I had already resolved to either go somewhere else and try my luck again or stay around and try to pin down a proper job.

Or maybe even go back to Amsterdam, although I knew that this would not be a good idea.

It was troubling me that my dream seemed to have returned,

and it was even more concerning, I thought, that it was now changing, morphing into something new. Gone was the girl on the platform, replaced instead by the macabre image of a dead woman ascending to heaven and a blue ball bouncing across the road in front of me.

I knew, of course, that this must have been my subconscious mind replaying a traumatic event that undoubtedly would have marked me deeply when I was a small child but still, elements of it chimed with the dream that I had been having for so many years, a dream that had propelled me into Holland and on the adventure of a lifetime, looking for a woman in the future when all along I should have been looking for a woman in the past.

I saw it now. The women and the dogs, the soldiers, the body of water, a swimming pool. The kids, the shoppers. Something blue.

All along I must have been trying to say sorry, or something, to Lindsey Thomas. I must have been somehow trying to contact her in the great beyond, if such a place existed, which I seriously doubt. But still this new dream was disturbing me as it grew steadily more and more graphic as the nights evolved. In a way, I felt that I had a closure of some kind on the original dream, with the girl who I now assumed to have been Edie.

But what if this girl was Lindsey all along? What if this girl never was a manifestation of a perfect love? What if my subconscious knew nothing at all of Edie? Or anyone else for that matter, and was all along trying to bring me towards another person? A dead person.

I asked my mum about that day back in August nineteen-seventy when a dark, deep cloud descended over my tiny life. A cloud I could never see, and from which it seemed I would never escape.

Mum didn't say much.

"Oh, you know, it wasn't easy, David," she muttered. "A lot of the mums on the estate gave me a bloody hard time because of all that."

"But you were my son. You are my son," she corrected herself. "You didn't do that on purpose. A lot of people didn't see it like that though. As if you'd kill a girl you loved?"

"Did I?" I asked.

"Did you what?"

"Did I love her, do you think?"

"Oh, yes, I'd say so," Mum replied. "Obviously not in a deep, emotional way, but every time she and her friend came to get you, you would bounce up and down in your high-chair or wherever you were sitting, with the most adorable smile on your face, obviously excited to see her for sure. You know, in your baby way of course. She adored you. Loved taking you for walks."

And then after a brief silence, Mum said, "Do you know how many nights I tortured myself about that van? If it had been just another foot and a half up on the pavement it'd have taken all three of you out."

I thought about that for a moment, and about how that would have affected this woman in front of me now. My own mother.

"What happened to the driver?" I eventually asked.

"I can't remember now," she said. "It was an accident. He wasn't pissed or anything. No alcohol. Simply lost control of the van on that bend by the swimming pool. Always been a bloody dangerous place. He definitely went inside for it. A few years. It was a long time ago and the law wasn't as hard as it is now. Kill a girl now and you'll go in for ever probably."

"And what about the girl that was with her? Her friend? You told me years ago that she went to France. Is that right?"

"Oh, I don't know," Mum said. "Did I say that? Maybe it's what I heard. What was her name? The girl?"

But Mum answered her own question then.

"Sara!" she said. "That was it. Did she marry a French guy? I'm sure she married a French guy. A twin on a farm or something like that. I don't really know now. She was a teacher for a while, that was the last I heard but goodness me, all of that was more than twenty years ago now. If you want any more, you'll have to go and ask old Dotty Thomas herself. I think she stayed in touch with her."

"Mrs Thomas is still alive?" I exclaimed.

"Easy," Mum said. "She's only a year or two older than me, you cheeky sod!" And she smiled.

"Sorry, Mum," I laughed lightly. "But she always seemed a lot older than everyone else on the estate."

"Yes, I know what you mean," she said. "But that's what grief will do to you, I guess. Grief that hard. I missed out on that torture by just a few inches. That's all. It could so easily have been you," she said again before standing and pouring another cup of tea. "It's still hot," she said. "Do you want one?"

After we'd finished our tea, Mum said, "Anyhow, come and have a look at this," and she led me out to the garden shed where she'd set up an easel and some paints and was making these enormous, vibrant landscape paintings. I was impressed, and she seemed very proud of her work, as she was right to do.

I loved her. My mum.

Unconventional, and uncompromising. In equal part.

She seemed to have finally found some peace at last.

A few days later I walked the handful of roads back up to the estate where we used to live, looking for Mrs Thomas. I wanted to get some closure on a few things, although really I doubted she would want to talk to me after all these years.

I'm certain that after all this time she would have become tired of the company of ghosts, but even so I wanted to know about the driver, and about Sara as well. What happened to her. Presumably she's still out there. Still alive. Maybe it wasn't Lindsey in my dreams. Maybe it's Sara that holds all the keys. Maybe Sara is the one that's been in my dreams for all of these years.

It was strange to be on the estate again after ten years or so. It was strange to smell all the big bins again, and to see the paint-peeled climbing frames on the green around which the houses were gathered, the green on which we played as kids, the green where we scared ourselves shitless with ghost stories, that always involved Lindsey coming back to play with us. I wondered now how true that possibly was.

But could I really ask Mrs Thomas all of these things?

As soon as I arrived, I was surprised that I remembered where she lived. The exact house. Memory is a fascinating thing. I walked straight up to her door which was the same crimson red, thin framed door that I remembered, with an enormous pane of frosted glass, easy for anyone to kick in if they wanted to burgle the place. The letterbox was mounted vertically, and it sprang back aggressively if you tried to push it inwards.

I paused before I rattled the small door knocker above it. I had agreed with myself that I would knock once only. If she didn't answer, then it was never meant to be, and I would walk away for ever. One knock. That was all I was going to give it. So I made sure that the one knock was going to be loud, and sharp. Confident. Even though I was feeling far from that myself.

And so I knocked. And I waited a few moments.

No movement. Nothing.

Although I have a feeling now, looking back, that there was a shadow down the hallway. I'm not sure.

She's not at home, I said to myself. *OK. So that's that then.*

And even though I had resolved to knock only once, I broke my own rule and knocked a second time.

I waited. But nothing. No answer. I decided then that I didn't need closure after all, and that I wouldn't get it anyway. Some things go on forever and can never end. For some things, 'closure' doesn't exist.

I waited some more and then turned and walked down Mrs Thomas's pathway, looking then at the small homes that we used to play among as kids. And I remembered being a child and I remembered the summers, and the butterflies in the tall grass on the green and the autumnal bonfires with potatoes baking in foil and us kids playing hide and seek in the dark evenings of winter.

I remembered the grown-ups drinking in the tavern by the road and I remembered Christmas then, and the music that filled our evenings and I remembered my family and my dad and all the fun we used to have when times were good.

I turned my back on it all then and I walked away from my

childhood forever. I was moving on now. I had a life to live after all.

*

Six months later and I'm watching spring settle across London, like a freshly laundered sheet drifting slowly across a king-sized bed. Delicate and clean and fragrant.

All along the Thames embankment, trees are starting to blossom. Apple white and cherry pink the buds are reaching up to kiss the sky and scent the air that the Londoners are breathing down there on the south bank by the river. I'm in a favourite place, among the books that festoon the tables beneath Waterloo Bridge. Every day, from now until the winter, book sellers will come and lay out hundreds upon hundreds of fiction paperbacks, first edition hardbacks, encyclopaedias, books on history, politics, books on art, books on books. I go there and drink a coffee. Browse. Watch a movie with friends or sometimes alone.

On that day, six months after returning from Amsterdam, I was alone, with coffee and cigarettes and all those books. I'd buy one and sit reading for the entire day. To me, this was bliss.

And so I am watching the boats drift by and I'm looking across at the Houses of Parliament and the iconic tower that houses that most famous of bells, Big Ben. I'm looking up at Hungerford Bridge, with its red painted walkway that stretches from here to the north bank of the river. I watch the trains as they move in and out of Charing Cross station. Oh, how many times have I done this in my life? How often have I sat in the shade of the bridge and smiled at the sound of the bell as it shed its peals across the Thames at Westminster?

And still, I think of Edie. I think of Dieter's words. Did I really love her? Or did I confuse my sorrow with love? Did I feel such deep self-pity for the way in which I had treated her, that I convinced myself that it was true love? I don't know.

How does love manifest itself anyway? Who was I to analyse the hell out of all of my emotions every time? Could I not just succumb to them whenever they took hold of me? Why did I need to keep thinking all of the time? About everything. Relentlessly. Why could I not rest? Not ever?

I thought of that time when I saw her on the platform. I was so shocked. She was exactly like the girl in my dreams. I understand now that I was always looking for something that was right in front of me. *You were there all the time*! How could I have been so blind?

I remembered then that she was wearing black jeans and a red neck scarf on the day that we met outside the movie themed cafe close to the Grasshopper on the Damrak. I remember that she seemed unhappy. Hostile, perhaps. Haunted, almost. It was clear she didn't like Dieter or me. And that she didn't want to be there with us. I remember Maartje from that day.

And Dieter said he liked Edie then. But did he really? I'm not sure about Dieter. Not since the boys in the family house told me about him when I lived with them briefly out on the edge of the city. But did Edie know him better than all of us? Did they plan this all along?

Do you miss me, Edie? Do you even think about me?

I remembered us in Timo's apartment, as I looked up then at

the underside of Waterloo Bridge. I closed my eyes as I thought about how she went to the bathroom right before we left that place. I thought then about that dealer who sold coke in Ibiza, or was it Majorca? I forget now. I thought about the kids hanging around outside the kebab shop when we left Timo's place. I chuckled to myself about the fear I had that we were going to be jumped. If they only knew what we were carrying, then I'm sure they would have jumped us!

I finished my coffee and took a stroll among the books. I left my cup on the table and a waiter came to retrieve it, making a space that was immediately taken. I lit a cigarette and wandered along the embankment, stopping to lean on the handrail that separated me from the river.

The tide was low, and I could see the little bit of sand that people laughingly called a beach. I thought then of the Mediterranean, and of how much Edie would have liked it in Nice. I'm not sure now that she was ever there. I think maybe she told Elena she was going there. I'm not sure about a lot of things. *Were you ever really the person you claimed to be?* For all I know, she might have been in a relationship with Dieter for many years. It's all too much for me. *I guess, in hindsight, you often were too much for me.*

I wandered back to the books and stood the other side of the bridge looking up at the trains again, incessantly slipping in and out of Charing Cross station.

I looked then at the river.

I could hear some children laughing as their teacher walked them along the bank of the Thames on this beautiful sunny day. Screeching and yelling, it made me smile. I looked back at the stalls of books and walked towards one that had yellow lettering on a blue background. Behind it there were jets of water from a fountain that were shooting up from the plaza and sending sprays of water high into the air. The kids were running in and out of them and laughing now. Shrieking. Having fun. Off to one side there were a hundred shoppers carrying bags, all coming back from a busy morning in the West End. Big Ben began to let us all know it was three o'clock. The chime echoing across the river.

We didn't say goodbye, did we, Edie.

I don't remember saying goodbye.

I turned my back to the bridge, looked down at my shoes, and walked back to the book stalls. The cloudless sky that day was a beautiful clear blue. Liquid almost. Azure. Very much like the colour of the Mediterranean Sea. She would have loved it, I thought again. And I smiled a half smile. One filled with sadness.

"Goodbye, Edie," I whispered to myself. "I love you. But goodbye."

I stood at a stall, and a book caught my eye. A beautiful pale blue cover. Like the sky, I thought. I reached out to pick it up. And as I did so, I accidentally brushed the fingers of a girl who had reached for it at the same time as me.

"I'm sorry," I said. "After you."

She smiled at me, and I thought she was quite beautiful. And she said, in a thick French accent, "No, you go."

I looked at her directly. And I smiled and felt bold enough to reach out and shake her hand gently. Her fingers were thin. Graceful and languid. Her eyes, grey. Flecked with amber and gold.

"Hi, I'm David," I said.

"Imogen," she replied.

"It's nice to meet you, Imogen," I said.